Praise for Jane Yol

"The Hans Christian Andersen of Americ
—*Newsweek*

"The Aesop of the twentieth century."
—*The New York Times*

"Jane Yolen is a gem in the diadem of science fiction and fantasy."
—*Analog*

Praise for *The Emerald Circus*

"This excellent collection reimagines folktales, fairy tales, and sometimes historical people in new and surprising light. It is a brilliant example of short-form storytelling by one of the treasures of the science-fiction community."
—Brandon Sanderson, author of *Mistborn*

"Jane Yolen facets her glittering stories with the craft of a master jeweller. Everything she writes, including *The Emerald Circus,* is original and timeless, deliciously creepy and disturbingly lovely."
—Elizabeth Wein, author of *Code Name Verity*

"Jane Yolen's *The Emerald Circus* is full of marvels. She turns toads into witches, Sir Lancelot into a 600-year-old monk, Dorothy into a tightrope walker, and Emily Dickinson into a spacefarer. From Snow Queen to spaceship, *The Emerald Circus* is a delight."
—Patricia A. McKillip, author of *The Riddle-Master of Hed*

"In this masterful collection, Jane Yolen draws upon myth, fairy tales, history, poetry, and children's classics from Alice to Oz to fashion new tales from the bones of the old. There is simply no

better storyteller working in the fantasy field today. She's a national treasure."
—Terri Windling, author of *The Wood Wife* and *The Essential Bordertown*

"Jane Yolen is a consummate storyteller, weaving old and new threads to create tales rich in wisdom and depth. *The Emerald Circus* is an utter delight."
—Juliet Marillier, award-winning author of the Sevenwaters series

"Talk about imaginary gardens with real toads in them! In this wide-ranging short story collection, Jane Yolen's scholarship and creative genius combine to bestow upon the reader fantastic new intimacy with venerable tales and persons."
—Nancy Springer, author of *The White Hart* and *I Am Mordred*

"What a joy it is to watch Jane Yolen burrow into the hearts of familiar stories and dwell in possibilities we'd never imagined. It's all done with Yolen's trademark wisdom, a healthy dollop of subversion, and a twinkle in the eye. A delight!"
—Susan Fletcher, author of *Dragon's Milk* and *Shadow Spinner*

"An impressive overview of the author's breadth and career, this collection will appeal to the author's existing devotees—or to anyone who has ever thought that 'happily ever after' left too many questions."
—*Kirkus*

"Jane Yolen's collection *The Emerald Circus* is pure delight for anyone who craves inspired retellings of classics from literature, or re-imaginings of the lives of real literary figures. 5/5 stars."
—*YA Books Central*

Also by Jane Yolen

Novels

The Wizard of Washington Square (1969)
Hobo Toad and the Motorcycle Gang (1970)
The Bird of Time (1971)
The Magic Three of Solatia (1974)
The Transfigured Hart (1975)
The Mermaid's Three Wisdoms (1978)
The Acorn Quest (1981)
Dragon's Blood (1982)
Heart's Blood (1984)
The Stone Silenus (1984)
Cards of Grief (1985)
A Sending of Dragons (1987)
The Devil's Arithmetic (1988)
Sister Light, Sister Dark (1989)
White Jenna (1989)
The Dragon's Boy (1990)
Wizard's Hall (1991)
Briar Rose (1992)
Good Griselle (1994)
The Wild Hunt (1995)
The Sea Man (1997)
Here There Be Ghosts (1998)
The One-Armed Queen (1998)
The Wizard's Map (1999)
The Pictish Child (1999)
Boots and the Seven Leaguers (2000)
The Bagpiper's Ghost (2002)
Sword of the Rightful King (2003)
The Young Merlin Trilogy: Passager, Hobby, and Merlin (2004)
Pay the Piper: A Rock 'n' Roll Fairy Tale (with Adam Stemple, 2005)
Troll Bridge: A Rock 'n' Roll Fairy Tale (with Adam Stemple, 2006)
Dragon's Heart (2009)
Except the Queen (with Midori Snyder, 2010)
Snow in Summer (2011)
Curse of the Thirteenth Fey (2012)
B. U. G. (Big Ugly Guy) (with Adam Stemple, 2013)
The Last Changeling (with Adam Stemple, 2014)
Centaur Rising (2014)
A Plague of Unicorns (2014)
Trash Mountain (2015)
The Seelie King's War (with Adam Stemple, 2016)

Young Heroes series

Odysseus in the Serpent Maze (with Robert J. Harris, 2001)
Hippolyta and the Curse of the Amazon (with Robert J. Harris, 2002)
Atalanta and the Arcadian Beast (with Robert J. Harris, 2003)
Jason and the Gorgon's Blood (with Robert J. Harris, 2004)

Collections

The Girl Who Cried Flowers and Other Tales (1974)
The Moon Ribbon (1976)
The Hundredth Dove and Other Tales (1977)
Dream Weaver (1979)
Neptune Rising: Songs and Tales of the Undersea People (1982)
Tales of Wonder (1983)
The Whitethorn Wood and Other Magicks (1984)
Dragonfield and Other Stories (1985)
Favorite Folktales of the World (1986)
Merlin's Booke (1986)
The Faery Flag (1989)
Storyteller (1992)
Here There Be Dragons (1993)
Here There Be Unicorns (1994)
Here There Be Witches (1995)
Among Angels (with Nancy Willard, 1995)
Here There Be Angels (1996)
Here There Be Ghosts (1998)
Twelve Impossible Things Before Breakfast (1997)
Sister Emily's Lightship and Other Stories (2000)
Not One Damsel in Distress (2000)
Mightier Than the Sword (2003)
Once Upon A Time (She Said) (2005)
The Last Selchie Child (2012)
Grumbles from the Forest: Fairy-Tales Voices with a Twist (with Rebecca Kai Dotlich, 2013)

Graphic Novels

Foiled (2010)
The Last Dragon (2011)
Curses Foiled Again (2013)
Stone Man Mysteries (with Adam Stemple):
Stone Cold (2016)
Sanctuary (2017)

THE EMERALD CIRCUS
JANE YOLEN

tachyon | san francisco

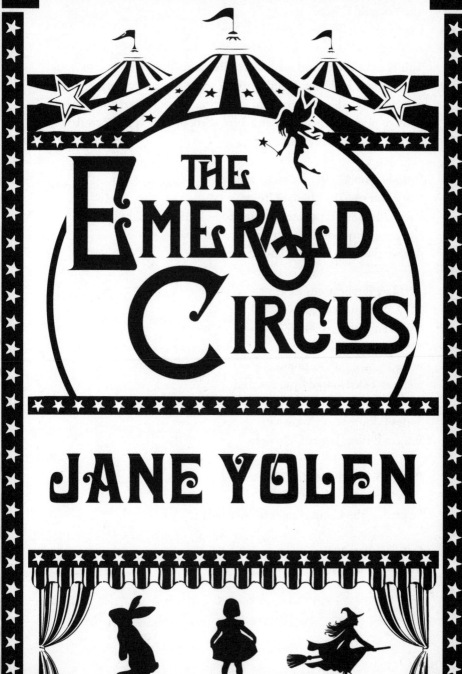

THE EMERALD CIRCUS

JANE YOLEN

Introduction © 2017 by Holly Black
Story notes © 2017 by Jane Yolen
Pages 284-286 constitute an extension of this copyright page
Cover and interior design by Elizabeth Story
Author photo © 2015 by Jason Stemple

Tachyon Publications LLC
1459 18th Street #139
San Francisco, CA 94107
415.285.5615
www.tachyonpublications.com
tachyon@tachyonpublications.com

Series Editor: Jacob Weisman
Project Editor: James DeMaiolo

ISBN 13: 978-1-61696-273-9

Printed in the United States by Worzalla

First Edition: 2017
9 8 7 6 5 4 3 2 1

CONTENTS

Story Notes and Poems

For Adam and Betsy
—their kind of stories,
with love

INTRODUCTION
HOLLY BLACK

I first heard Jane speak at World Fantasy in Minneapolis. My debut novel was about to come out, and I was in awe of this new world where writers I admired sat together on panels, casually spouting wisdom. I listened raptly and said absolutely nothing.

Of course, I had met her many years before, in the pages of her books. I'd started with *Sister Light, Sister Dark*, pressed into my hand by a friend who said it was her favorite book. From there, I found my way to her brutal and beautiful fairy tale retelling, *Briar Rose*, and then on to the Young Merlin books, *Wizard's Hall* and *Devil's Arithmetic*.

It was only a few years after World Fantasy that somehow we were introduced and she was urging me to buy a house in western Massachusetts.

"You'll be house-poor for a while," she told me, unfailingly generous and practical at the same time, like a character from one of her stories. "But you won't starve. We'll bring you soup if it comes to that."

I did buy that house, and since then, she and her huge, hilarious, creative family have come over every New Year's Eve, in costumes to fit the theme of the party. This past year, for Fairy Tale New Year's, they came as redcaps and menaced all the other guests.

Jane is a unique figure. She's been called the Hans Christian Andersen of children's literature, but her contributions to adult fiction are equally notable. She's won Nebulas and a World Fantasy Award as well as a Rhysling. She's been a past president of the Science Fiction and Fantasy Writers of America, the second woman to attain the position. For me, personally, as a writer of fantasy with a body of work published for kids and teens, she's a model for how to navigate the complexities of belonging to two different communities simultaneously. Would that I could do it with the grace and surety she brings to everything she does.

The Emerald Circus is full of all the things I like best about her writing.

From a feminist retelling of Peter Pan in "Lost Girls"; to the surreal, poignant "Blown Away," which recasts Dorothy from *The Wonderful Wizard of Oz* as a circus performer; to the short, raw "Belle Bloody Merciless Dame," in which an encounter with an elf goes far too well; to an imagining of Emily Dickinson seeing the stars in "Sister Emily's Lightship"—Jane gets all the details right. The depth and breadth of her knowledge shine. But more than that, she writes about people generously, gifting her characters with small moments that carry great weight.

This wondrous and wonderful collection will stay with you long after the last page is turned.

> —Holly Black, bestselling author of the Modern Faerie Tale series and the Spiderwick Chronicles (with Tony DiTerlizzi)

ANDERSEN'S WITCH

The boy lay in his too-small settle bed, his feet dangling over the end. Papa had promised and promised a new bed for months now. "Because of your stork legs," as Papa called them. But the green wood brought out of the forest by Grandfather still lay outside the front door, curing on the ground.

"Rotting, you mean," Mama said. She talked like that when she'd had a lot of schnapps, but once she'd been kind and loving. The boy wanted to remember her that way, but she made it very hard to do.

In his long-enough bed, Papa coughed all day and night, his shoemaker's lasts gathering dust and cobwebs on the other side of the one-room house. For weeks he'd been too ill to fix the boy's bed, or work on shoes, or do much of anything at all.

Luckily for the family, Mama had managed to take in more washing this month. Odense, Denmark's second largest city, was growing rapidly, nearly five thousand people at the last census.

"If I could do *all* their laundry, we would be wealthy," Mama said. "And then we could have an elegant house, in a fashionable street. Not this pig hole." Then she added, "And perhaps get invited to the prince's castle dinner."

Papa had roused between coughs. "Get your head out of the clouds, woman. It gives the boy ideas above his station. Don't count chickens before they hatch." He took a breath. "You live in fairy tales. We have to live in the real world."

She turned away from the onslaught of his words, but Papa was not deterred. "Woman, we will live and die on Munkemolle Street. I am, by the devil's wish, a craftsman, though I wanted to be a teacher. And you are a washerwoman, which is all you are capable of doing. And all the laundry in the world will not buy us an elegant house. If you had such a house, someone else would do the laundry and then how would we eat?" But the speech had exhausted him and he fell back against the pillow.

The boy thought this made a certain amount of sense. But perhaps his stepsister, Karen Marie, could just get more money from her gentlemen friends, enough to keep the family for a while. Of course, he knew better than to say this out loud. Karen Marie was not well thought of by Papa or Grandmother. Or even Mama.

"At least for now I can still put food on the table," grumbled Mama, sitting at that very table, another glass of schnapps in front of her. "You lie abed with nothing more than a winter catarrh, while the leather waits in the corner over there, and no shoes are resoled. Men—you are all such babies. If you don't get up soon, husband, I shall be forced to call the Greyfriars to come and take you into the hospital. At least it will be one less mouth to feed."

Papa's lips thinned, and he gave his wife a look that should have frozen her to the spot. But Mama looked away.

When he got no response from her, Papa threw the covers back and sat up—still coughing—his nightshirt well above his bony knees. "At least help me to the pot."

"Help yourself, old man." Though she was years older than her husband, the words stung.

The boy turned his face to the wall, understanding that any old affection between them had soured with the hardships of life on Munkemolle Street, the way children too often chastened out of love turn stubborn. He felt a sudden restlessness in his soul. But he did not weep. It was too cold in the little one-room house for weeping.

And what about my bed? he whined, but only to himself. They all hated it when he whined, or complained aloud about his stomach cramps or about the constant bullying at school. It was bad enough that Mama and Papa seemed to hate each other. The boy knew he could not bear it if they hated him as well. No, it was best to simply fade away while they argued. Closing his eyes, he practiced fading, just like a swamp plant, which is what he sometimes called himself. Feet in the water, the same color as his surroundings. *You cannot see me. I am not here.*

Before he knew it, he'd managed to fade so completely that his parents' argument became a mere mumble that couldn't be heard above the wuthering winter wind or the waves constantly warring against the shore. In fact, he faded himself right into sleep and didn't hear when they went to bed still arguing, that argument ending, as always, in frantic, deep kisses.

Later, with everyone safely snoring, the boy sat up, then stood on the settle so he could stare out of the little window above it. The sky was without stars, for a low cloud cover, like a well-made bed, kept everything neat and tidy. There were few lights in the town except far, far away at Prince Christian Frederick's castle. It was lit up till it sparkled as if the stone walls themselves had been carved out of ice.

The perfect time for prayers, the boy thought, and he climbed off the settle bed, slipping on his wooden shoes for warmth. Sinking down on his knees, he began to pray—not to God, who Mama said had done little enough for the family, but to the Ice Maiden. Mama had told him all about the Ice Maiden, with her white hair and snowy skin and eyes the faded blue of the sky in winter. Mama might not be able to read like Papa, but she knew all about these things.

"The Ice Maiden can grant wishes," Mama had said just that morning. "Three of them." She'd held up three fingers. "But be careful what you wish for. If she thinks the wishes are foolish, she can also carry you away to her cold ice palace, where there are only polar bears and seals."

"Is it colder than here in Odense?" the boy had asked.

"Much colder," Mama answered. "So cold, your nose turns black with the bite of the frost and tears freeze upon your cheeks till they are hard as jewels."

The boy liked seals. And polar bears. Though he wasn't so sure about the cold. Odense was cold enough in the winter for him. He couldn't imagine colder. But how the Ice Maiden could get him to her palace was a puzzle. Would they walk? Or fly? Perhaps she had a sledge pulled by reindeer. He liked reindeer.

"Is she a witch, then?" The boy was wary of witches, knowing that they promised to feed you but shoved you in an oven instead.

"Ice maidens are not witches," Mama said. "It's a very different thing." Then she smiled and patted him on the head. He could smell the schnapps on her breath. She was always happier after her glass of schnapps. "But they do expect payment. Just like witches do."

"I have no money," the boy said. Though not usually so sensible, he did have some sense, especially where money was concerned. Or the lack of it.

"She has all the money she needs already," his mother answered. "After all, she has a castle."

"But don't castles need a lot of money to maintain them? For the chairs and the jewels and the big beds?" the boy asked. "And the wars?"

"The icicles are her jewels, she has all the chairs and beds she needs, and she makes no wars." His mother's smile was broad. The schnapps were making her very happy.

"Then how shall I pay her?" The boy had really needed to know this.

But Mama had gone from his side, back to the schnapps bottle waiting on the table even though it was not yet lunch and Papa said drinking was for nighttime and for fools.

The boy knew he couldn't ask Papa about the Ice Maiden. After all, Papa didn't believe in Mama's stories, not about the Ice Maiden or the trolls or the mermaids or any of the other fairy creatures she talked about. Often Papa read books aloud to him, books with hard words in them and no pictures.

The boy couldn't ask Grandfather, either, for Grandfather was off again, into the snowy woods, to sing and dance under the trees and wear beech leaves in his hair till the policeman brought him back: "Keep old Crazy Anders at home, please."

His half sister, Karen Marie, would be no help, either, for she was away with her gentlemen callers.

And while Grandmother often took care of him, she didn't like to talk about what she called wicked things, which meant— as far as the boy could ascertain—anything even slightly interesting or amusing.

And surely, the boy thought, *there is something wicked about the Ice Maiden if she takes people away.* Which was something witches did as well. So he was still confused on that point.

But the Ice Maiden granted wishes. Both the boy and his mother believed that. And if there was one thing the boy knew the family needed, it was for wishes to come true. Which is why—even without knowing what payment would be exacted— he got down on his knees and prayed. He was five years old. Perhaps old enough to know better.

"Ice Maiden," he called, hoping she would come to him. Three wishes was all he would get. This was so in every story he'd ever heard. He unlaced his fingers from their prayer grip and counted the three. A new, bigger bed, to begin with. And for Papa to feel better and be able to make more money. And then the other thing. The most important thing. The thing he could hardly admit to wanting, even to himself. Three wishes. What payment was to be exacted, he would discuss with the Ice Maiden only if she first promised to grant him all three.

Slipping back into the settle bed and pulling the covers up to his nose, the boy waited to warm up, but instead he only got colder. He glanced up at the little window and finally saw a single star in the sky. At first the star was quite distant, which was proper for a star.

"Star bright," he whispered, and watched as it suddenly fell precipitously in a downward arc. The longer he looked at the star, the closer it seemed to get, until it came right through his window and settled, icy and shimmering, by his bedside.

"Oh," he said. He hadn't any other words for it. Pulling his long legs in, knees to chin, and shivering in the cold, he stared at the star as it slowly resolved into the figure of a tall, beautiful woman with long white hair and eyes the color of a winter sky. Oddly, he could see her clearly through the darkness of the room.

"Are you . . . are you the Ice Maiden?" the boy asked.

She smiled, though the smile did not reach her eyes. "Of course, Hans. Didn't you just ask me to come?"

He nodded and pulled the covers closer, all the while wondering how she knew his name. But, of course, a witch would know.

"Are you afraid of me?" That strange smile again.

He shrugged. What good would it do to be afraid now? Heroes were not afraid. They were . . . heroes. He would be a hero.

"You knew enough to call me." She ran a hand through her hair, and little sparkles of cold fire winked on and off, like stars.

"Mama told me."

"Mamas always do."

Hans was so cold now, he could no longer feel his toes, his fingers, his ears. Even his teeth were cold. It was as if he were already in the Ice Maiden's palace, his nose turning black and the tears freezing like ice jewels on his cheeks. He wished he had some matches to strike to help him keep warm, but they were on the other side of room by the fireplace and he was afraid to get off his bed, because that would mean he'd have to go past the Ice Maiden, go too close to her. Not perhaps how a hero would think, but he was really only a little boy.

"I will grant your wishes, but you will have to tell them to me aloud." She folded her hands together, lacing the fingers, as if she herself were praying.

"Why?" asked Hans.

"Because," she said, just as all grown-ups do when they are waiting for you to do what they say or give a proper answer.

Hans was never good at giving proper answers. He always had different answers in his head, odd answers, answers that his teachers and his parents and his grandmother and even his crazy grandfather seemed to think were wrong. But they weren't *wrong* answers, they were just *his* answers. He wondered suddenly what the Ice Maiden would do if he gave *her* a wrong answer. And, thinking this, he found he couldn't open his mouth at all.

"I'm waiting," the Ice Maiden said. And then again, "I'm waiting, Hans. I do not like to wait."

Hans took a deep breath. He could feel the cold air rush down into his throat, down into his chest, almost stopping his heart. And then he said all in a rush, "I want a new bed long enough for my stork legs, I want Papa to get well enough to make lots of money, and I want to be a *digter*, a poet, and make even more money for the family." There, it was done. Three wishes spoken aloud.

The Snow Queen's hands unlaced and she sketched a little sign in the air before her. As if etched in ice, a picture appeared. It was of a tall, thin, ungainly man, with a big nose and squinty eyes. His clothes looked quite fine. Hans had never seen a tailcoat up close before, or such a high hat. The man seemed to be writing in a notebook.

"This could be you," the Ice Maiden said.

"He is not very handsome," said Hans, wondering if that was the payment due.

"A *digter* needs to *write* beautifully," the Ice Maiden said, "not *be* beautiful."

Hans nodded. It was true. He looked again at the icy picture. The man did not look happy, just hard at work. "Is he sad?"

"Did you wish for happiness?"

Hans shook his head.

Suddenly he worried that he'd have to have much more schooling to become a *digter*, and he hated school, where everybody bullied him, even the masters. It occurred to him that being a *digter* might not be a good a way of earning a living, not even as good as being a shoemaker like Papa or a washerwoman like Mama.

"You worry about the payment," the Ice Maiden said as, with a single movement of her hand, she erased the picture in the air.

How did she know what was in his mind? A witch! He was sure of it now. Afraid to speak further, afraid to get more cold air down inside him, he became silent. He started to fade. But mostly he was afraid that this was just a dream and so there would be no wishes fulfilled.

"Of course there will be a payment. I do not give wishes for nothing." The Ice Maiden's voice was suddenly as cranky as Mama's. "But you do not have to make the payment until much, much later. We will discuss it when you are earning your way, the greatest poet and storyteller Denmark will ever have."

"The greatest in *Denmark*?" Hans breathed. All of a sudden it was like breathing fire and smoke, not ice. He began to cough a deep chesty cough, sounding like Papa. Then without giving it further thought, he burst out with, "Why not the greatest in the *world*?"

To his astonishment, the Ice Maiden laughed, short, sharp sounds, like glass breaking.

"That's okay, then," he said, relieved. Everything would be all right. Wishes would be granted. He would be the hero. Like a fairy tale. Happily ever after. "I will pay. Gladly."

"Lie back down, then, little swamp plant," the Ice Maiden told him, and as he did so she placed her ice-cold hand over the blanket covering his chest.

Hans felt something like a little sliver of ice pierce his heart, and he fell into a sleep that was so deep, his mama found him in the morning and thought he had died in the night. After all, in Odense, such a thing was not unheard of. She was sobbing uncontrollably.

He sat up. "Mama, Mama, why are you crying?"

His mother looked at him. "I thought you were gone, little one, and so who would take care of me in my old age?"

If he thought that an odd thing to say, he didn't mention it. He was only five years old, after all. Instead he said, "I have gone nowhere, Mama. I am right here in Odense. I will take care of you." All thoughts of becoming a *digter* disappeared, and he was only a little boy with his weeping mama, whom he would care for, and that was enough.

It would be another fifty years, when Hans was writing his memoirs, before he remembered clearly what had happened that night with the Ice Maiden, but already the payments had begun. Yes, he'd gotten a new bed within a fortnight, long enough for his stork legs, made for him as soon as Papa was no longer ill. But then Papa chose to go off into the army because he could make more money fighting a war than fixing shoes. He came home from Holstein a broken man and was dead before Hans was eleven. His mother took religiously to the bottle and, no longer having her husband to abuse, turned her flaying tongue on Hans.

To escape this hard life, Hans would walk about with his eyes closed so as not to see all the sadness around him. But of course he could still hear it. So he took himself more and more often to Monk Mill, watching the great splash of water over the mill wheel, happy that it drowned out the sound of everything else. Except . . . except he could still hear stories in his head, and so he lived more and more in them. In his mind's eye he could see the lovely curling turrets of the Empire of China, which he was certain lay beneath the millrace. He believed it was an empire whose prince would someday take Hans to his palace.

And so Hans's childhood passed by in a farrago of dreams, though eventually he understood that Odense could not offer him the Ice Maiden's last promise, not even with the magic of the mill wheel. Just as Papa had to do the actual building of the bigger bed, just as Papa had given his life to make more money for the family, now it was Hans's turn to grab up the final wish with both hands. After all, Odense was too small a place for a boy who'd been promised that he would become Denmark's most famous *digter*.

So he ran off to Copenhagen with his mother's drunken blessing, to do the actual work of writing his books.

Years went by, lonely, hard, amazing years. Everyone from his old life was dead—father, mother, grandparents, half sister. But as the Ice Maiden had promised, Hans prospered.

Did he remember the childhood bargain? Hardly. It was only a fairy story he'd told himself as a child when everyone around him was failing. He knew how hard he'd worked to write, how hard it was to do readings at town halls and great houses. Hard work—not a child's wishes—had made him a great man.

However, sixty-five years after his bargain with the Ice Maiden, lying on his deathbed at a friend's house just outside Copenhagen, Hans sat up after a fright-filled dream. It had been about the ice witch, whom he hadn't thought of in half a century or more. His hands and face were ice cold with fear of the dream, though the cancer in his liver seemed white hot. He was sweating and shivering at the same time.

Surely a price will be demanded, he thought feverishly. *Witches promise you sweets and then shove you in the oven.*

"Sir, shall I call the doctor back again?" asked the manservant his friends had loaned him.

"A doctor for the *digter*?" He laughed at his own play on words. Even in a fevered state, he could not stop himself from making word jokes.

"Sir," the servant said, his face stern. His entire body radiated concern far beyond what Hans's friends were paying him.

"No, no. No doctor. Just help me change out of these wet clothes." Hans did not feel shame in asking. After all, that's what a manservant was for.

When the man came back with a dry nightshirt, Hans shook his head. "No, no, not the nightshirt. I am afraid I have not been clear. I have to dress in my formal clothes. I am expecting a most important visitor."

The manservant looked momentarily confused. "There is nothing written in the diary, sir, about a visitor." In fact, Mrs. Melchior, the mistress of the house where old Hans lay dying, had given the servant specific instructions: *No visitors. Wake me if there is a change. Do not be afraid to send for the doctor. And for the Lord's sake, do not stint on the pain medication.*

"Nevertheless, my visitor is coming today," Hans told him.

"Do you want a dose of morphia, sir, to ease the pain?"

Hans shook his head. "I need to be sharp for *this* visitor. Pain keeps me sharp."

"Pain keeps you . . . in pain," the serving man said.

"Please . . . do as I say."

Once dressed, even down to his leather shoes—shoes that Papa never would have had the skill to produce—Hans dismissed the man. "Wait in the kitchen till I ring," he said.

"But sir—"

"Do it."

The servant went out, for he had to follow orders.

But as soon as the man left and the red-hot flare in his belly subsided once again, Hans remembered the story of his promise to the Ice Maiden as if it were one of his own tales. He spoke the tale aloud, as if telling it in the royal court, as he had often done in Denmark and in Germany. The tale of an old *digter* and his bargain with a powerful witch.

And when he got to the end, he whispered, "Aha, so it is only my death that is the payment. A good bargain after all."

But the story did not sit well in his mouth. Death as a payment for a good life lived was not enough of an ending. Everyone dies: the good people and the bad people, the good storytellers and the bad ones. And people who were not storytellers, well, they died, too. Hans knew that his story demanded a different ending. Something stronger. It needed to be revised. Hadn't his own little mermaid found a way into heaven after her awful bargain with another kind of witch?

He forced himself to tell the story again, this time his voice as slight and light as a child's. He didn't push the story where he willed it, but let it go to its natural end. *Inevitable but surprising,* he reminded himself.

"Ha!" he said when he'd finished. Now all would be right. He settled back to wait for his visitor.

The warm summer's day closed around him. He let go of his vanity and opened the top button of his shirt, loosened the collar.

She would have to take him as she found him. He closed his eyes and, like the swamp plant of old, began to fade.

A sound like wings called him back to himself. He opened his eyes to a shift in the room, like a curtain blowing. Something white and shimmering floated into his sight, cold and distant as any star.

"Hello, Ice Maiden," he said. "You look a great deal older." It really wasn't the way to address a woman of a certain age, but Hans was beyond such niceties now.

"So do you, Hans," she answered, shaking her hair till it was like falling snow. "A *great* deal older. As you can see, I am no longer an Ice Maiden but the Snow Queen, thanks to you. My castle, though, is still the same—seals and polar bears."

"Ah," said Hans, "I remember. And the cold."

"Yes, of course," said the Snow Queen, "always the cold. Are you ready to come away with me now?"

He smiled, maybe more of a grimace, for a sharp pain caught him right before he spoke again. He let it pass through, then said, "Oh, I doubt you'll want me for your palace, you old witch, for I have beaten you at your game."

"No one beats me," the Snow Queen said, smiling, though still the smile did not reach her eyes. "And *no one* calls me a witch." There was a strange tic beating beneath the skin of her right cheek.

"Well, *I* have," said Hans. "It all has to do with storying."

"Storying?" She came a step closer, her breath pluming out before her. He could smell the coldness of it.

"As I was lying here," Hans said, "thinking over my long life—for that is something humans do, you know, when we reach the end—I realized that I have stood alone almost continually since I was a child of five. However kindly people behaved toward me, I still remained cut off from them. And this, I believe, was the bargain we made."

"Ah," she said, but nothing more.

"You told me when I made my wishes that I would understand the payment much, much later. It does not come any later than this."

She nodded, saying nothing, for indeed, what need was there for her to speak? Hans had told the truth.

"You gave me poetry and stories, even a story about you," Hans said, sitting up in the bed despite the pain of the cancer. He ground his fist against his belly to quiet the ache.

She gazed at him without pity, even though she understood how much the talking cost him.

"You knew my soul longed for true recognition as a thirsty man for water, and had so even as a child."

This time when she smiled, it radiated from her eyes. They were greedy eyes, hungry eyes, a witch's eyes.

He leaned toward her despite the pain. "But I realized today that you kept as payment any love that I would have ever gotten. Not from a woman, not from a man. So I never had a single grown person in the entire world who loved me just for myself." Hans shifted his position, trying to find somewhere comfortable, but his body would not obey him. Finally he stopped trying and, with that, the pain seemed for a moment to cease. "I never married, never had a home of my own, always lived in someone else's house." He made a small gesture with his head, indicating the very room they were in. "I am even going to die in someone else's house."

"A fair trade," the Snow Queen said, her voice satisfied. "I have made the same barter with poets and writers and musicians and—"

"Ah, yes, you do not think yourself a witch, but did it ever occur to you that you are a fairy godmother?"

"Never!" she cried, and he realized he had scored a point. Something like a smile passed across his plain face and made him seem almost handsome.

He took a moment more, covering the intense pain with

another smile, before saying, "Your mistake was thinking there is only one kind of love." The pain in his gut was sharp again, and he had to stop, take a shallow breath, before going on. But the years of storytelling helped him here, and he made the moment of silence work for him.

"I make no mistakes." Now the Snow Queen stood very still, arms folded, like a woman who knew how to wait. He had met very few of them in his long life.

Then the pain ebbed a bit, like a receding tide on an Odense beach, and he told her the rest. "You see, my dear ice witch, I have had the love of *children* from all over the world because of my stories. A child's love is the perfect love, for it is given with a whole heart. That love will outlast me a hundredfold. And it will outlast you as well."

"Never," the Snow Queen said, but her voice was way too high, and her face contorted in anger. The tic he'd noticed earlier was beating again under her right eye, but this time it was more pronounced.

"Oh, I am sure of it," said Hans. "The children will know you from my story, and in that story you lose to little Gerda because of her perfect child's love for Kay. And here, in this room, you lose again." He held out his hands, but not to her. She began to tremble, then collapse, and at the last dissipated into water vapor.

Hans no longer saw her. His gaze was focused past the vapor and beyond, his hands held out to the other figures gathering in the room, a group of small children from all over the world, wearing crowns of roses.

One of them, whose crown was made of just the briars and thorns, tiptoed over to Hans's bedside. Now holding the dying man's hands, he said, "We are here to bring you home, Papa Hans, but first you must tell us a story."

"With all my heart," Hans said. "It is about a beautiful witch who was outwitted by an ugly old *digter*."

So saying, he sat up straight on the bed as if he were as young as they, and told them that one final story about his life as a fairy tale. When he finished, the children all clapped their hands and laughed delightedly, and his old worn-out body fell back against the waiting pillow, no longer in pain. But his spirit, set loose of the body's gravity, rose to go hand in hand with the children through the stone walls of Mrs. Melchior's great house, into the soft Danish air, and home.

LOST GIRLS

"It isn't fair!" Darla complained to her mom for the third time during their bedtime reading. She meant it wasn't fair that Wendy only did the housework in Neverland and that Peter Pan and the boys got to fight Captain Hook.

"Well, I can't change it," Mom said in her even, lawyer voice. "That's just the way it is in the book. Your argument is with Mr. Barrie, the author, and he's long dead. Should I go on?"

"Yes. No. I don't know," Darla said, coming down on both sides of the question, as she often did.

Mom shrugged and closed the book, and *that* was the end of the night's reading.

Darla watched impassively as her mom got up and left the room, snapping off the bedside lamp as she went. When she closed the door there was just a rim of light from the hall showing around three sides of the door, making it look like something out of a science fiction movie. Darla pulled the covers up over her nose. Her breath made the space feel like a little oven.

"Not fair at all," Darla said to the dark, and she didn't just mean the book. She wasn't the least bit sleepy.

But the house made its comfortable night-settling noises around her: the breathy whispers of the hot air through the vents, the ticking of the grandfather clock in the hall, the sound of the maple branch *scritch-scratching* against the clapboard siding. They were a familiar lullaby, comforting and soothing. Darla didn't mean to go to sleep, but she did.

Either that or she stepped out of her bed and walked through the closed door into Neverland.

Take your pick.

It didn't feel at all like a dream to Darla. The details were too exact. And she could *smell things*. She'd never smelled anything in a dream before. So Darla had no reason to believe that what happened to her next was anything but real.

One minute she had gotten up out of bed, heading for the bathroom, and the very next she was sliding down the trunk of a very large, smooth tree. The trunk was unlike any of the maples in her yard, being a kind of yellowish color. It felt almost slippery under her hands and smelled like bananas gone slightly bad. Her nightgown made a sound like *whooosh* as she slid along.

When she landed on the ground, she tripped over a large root and stubbed her toe.

"Ow!" she said.

"Shhh!" cautioned someone near her.

She looked up and saw two boys in matching ragged cutoffs and T-shirts staring at her. "Shhh! yourselves," she said, wondering at the same time who they were.

But it hadn't been those boys who spoke. A third boy, behind her, tapped her on the shoulder and whispered, "If you aren't quiet, *He* will find us."

She turned, ready to ask who *He* was. But the boy, dressed in green tights and a green shirt and a rather silly green hat, and smelling like fresh lavender, held a finger up to his lips. They were perfect lips, like a movie star's. Darla knew him at once.

"Peter," she whispered. "Peter Pan."

He swept the hat off and gave her a deep bow. "Wendy," he countered.

"Well, Darla, actually," she said.

"Wendy Darla," he said. "Give us a thimble."

She and her mom had read that part in the book already, where Peter got kiss and thimble mixed up, and she guessed what it was he really meant, but she wasn't about to kiss him. She was much too young to be kissing boys. Especially boys she'd just met. And he had to be more a man than a boy, anyway, no matter how young he looked. The copy of *Peter Pan* she and her mother had been reading had belonged to her grandmother originally. Besides, Darla wasn't sure she liked Peter. Of course, she wasn't sure she *didn't* like him. It was a bit confusing. Darla hated things being confusing, like her parents' divorce and her dad's new young wife and their twins who were—and who weren't exactly—her brothers.

"I don't have a thimble," she said, pretending not to understand.

"I have," he said, smiling with persuasive boyish charm. "Can I give it to you?"

But she looked down at her feet in order not to answer, which was how she mostly responded to her dad these days, and that was that. At least for the moment. She didn't want to think any further ahead, and neither, it seemed, did Peter.

He shrugged and took her hand, dragging her down a path that smelled of moldy old leaves. Darla was too surprised to protest. And besides, Peter was lots stronger than she was. The two boys followed. When they got to a large dark brown tree whose odor reminded Darla of her grandmother's wardrobe, musty and ancient, Peter stopped. He let go of her hand and jumped up on one of the twisted roots that were looped over and around one another like woody snakes. Darla was suddenly reminded of her school principal when he towered above the students at assembly. He was a tall man but the dais he stood on made him seem even taller. When you sat in the front row, you could look up his nose. She could look up Peter's nose now. Like her principal, he didn't look so grand that way. Or so threatening.

"Here's where we live," Peter said, his hand in a large sweeping motion. Throwing his head back, he crowed like a rooster; he no longer seemed afraid of making noise. Then he said, "You'll like it."

"Maybe I will. Maybe I won't," Darla answered, talking to her feet again.

Peter's perfect mouth made a small pout as if that weren't the response he'd been expecting. Then he jumped down into a dark space between the roots. The other boys followed him. Not to be left behind, in case that rooster crow really had called something awful to them, Darla went after the boys into the dark place. She found what they had actually gone through was a door that was still slightly ajar.

The door opened onto a long, even darker passage that wound into the very center of the tree; the passage smelled damp, like bathing suits left still wet in a closet. Peter and the boys seemed to know the way without any need of light. But Darla was constantly afraid of stumbling and she was glad when someone reached out and held her hand.

Then one last turn and there was suddenly plenty of light from hundreds of little candles set in holders that were screwed right into the living heart of the wood. By the candlelight she saw it was Peter who had hold of her hand.

"Welcome to Neverland," Peter said, as if this were supposed to be a big surprise.

Darla took her hand away from his. "It's smaller than I thought it would be," she said. This time she looked right at him.

Peter's perfect mouth turned down again. "It's big enough for us," he said. Then as if a sudden thought had struck him, he smiled. "But too small for *Him*." He put his back to Darla and shouted, "Let's have a party. We've got us a new Wendy."

Suddenly, from all coners of the room, boys came tumbling and stumbling and dancing, and pushing one another to get a look at her. They were shockingly noisy and all smelled like unwashed socks. One of them made fart noises with his mouth. She wondered if any of them had taken a bath recently. They were worse—Darla thought—than her Stemple cousins, who were so awful their parents never took them anywhere anymore, not out to a restaurant or the movies or anyplace at all.

"Stop it!" she said.

The boys stopped at once.

"I told you," Peter said. "She's a regular Wendy, all right. She's even given me a thimble."

Darla's jaw dropped at the lie. *How could he?*

She started to say "I did not!" but the boys were already cheering so loudly her protestations went unheard.

"Tink," Peter called, and one of the candles detached itself from the heartwood to flutter around his head, "tell the Wendys we want a Welcome Feast."

The Wendys? Darla bit her lip. *What did Peter mean by that?*

The little light flickered on and off. *A kind of code,* Darla thought. She assumed it was the fairy Tinker Bell, but she couldn't really make out what this Tink looked like except for that flickering, fluttering presence. But as if understanding Peter's request, the flicker took off toward a black corner and, shedding but a little light, flew right into the dark.

"Good old Tink," Peter said, and he smiled at Darla with such practice, dimples appeared simultaneously on both sides of his mouth.

"What kind of food . . ." Darla began.

"Everything parents won't let you have," Peter answered. "Sticky buns and tipsy cake and Butterfingers and brownies and . . ."

The boys gathered around them, chanting the names as if they were the lyrics to some kind of song, adding, ". . . apple tarts and gingerbread and chocolate mousse and trifle and . . ."

"And stomachaches and sugar highs," Darla said stubbornly. "My dad's a nutritionist. I'm only allowed healthy food."

Peter turned his practiced dimpled smile on her again. "Forget your father. You're in Neverland now, and no one need ever go back home from here."

At that Darla burst into tears, half in frustration and half in fear. She actually liked her dad, as well as loved him, despite the fact that he'd left her for his new wife, and despite the fact of the twins, who were actually adorable as long as she didn't have to live with them. The thought that she'd been caught in Neverland with no way to return was so awful, she couldn't help crying.

Peter shrugged and turned to the boys. "*Girls!*" he said with real disgust.

"All Wendys!" they shouted back at him.

Darla wiped her eyes, and spoke right to Peter. "My name is *not* Wendy," she said clearly. "It's Darla."

Peter looked at her, and there was nothing nice or laughing or young about his eyes. They were dark and cold and very very old.

Darla shivered.

"*Here* you're a Wendy," he said.

And with that, the dark place where Tink had disappeared grew increasingly light, as a door opened and fifteen girls carrying trays piled high with cakes, cookies, biscuits, buns, and other kinds of goodies marched single file into the hall. They were led by a tall, slender, pretty girl with brown hair that fell straight to her shoulders.

The room suddenly smelled overpoweringly of that sickly sweetness of children's birthday parties at school, when their mothers brought in sloppy cupcakes greasy with icing. Darla shuddered.

"Welcome Feast!" shouted the boy who was closest to the door. He made a deep bow.

"Welcome Feast!" they all shouted, laughing and gathering around a great center table.

Only Darla seemed to notice that not one of the Wendys was smiling.

The Feast went on for ages, because each of the boys had to stand up and give a little speech. Of course, most of them only said, "Welcome, Wendy!" and "Glad to meet you!" before sitting down again. A few elaborated a little bit more. But Peter more than made up for it with a long, rambling talk about duty and dessert and how no one loved them out in the World Above as much as he did here in Neverland, and how the cakes proved that.

The boys cheered and clapped at each of Peter's pronouncements, and threw buns and scones across the table at one another as a kind of punctuation. Tink circled Peter's head continuously like a crown of stars, though she never really settled.

But the girls, standing behind the boys like banquet waitresses, did not applaud. Rather they shifted from foot to foot, looking alternately apprehensive and bored. One, no more than four years old, kept yawning behind a chubby hand.

After a polite bite of an apple tart, which she couldn't swallow but spit into her napkin, Darla didn't even try to pretend. The little pie had been much too sweet, not tart at all. And even though Peter kept urging her between the welcomes to eat something, she just couldn't. That small rebellion seemed to annoy him enormously and he stood up once again, this time on the tabletop, to rant on about how some people lacked gratitude, and how difficult it was to provide for so many, especially with *Him* about.

Peter never actually looked at Darla as he spoke, but she knew—and everyone else knew—that he meant *she* was the ungrateful one. That bothered her some, but not as much as it might have. She even found herself enjoying the fact that he was annoyed, and that realization almost made her smile.

When Peter ended with "No more Feasts for them with Bad Attitudes!" the boys leaped from their benches and overturned the big table, mashing the remaining food into the floor. Then they all disappeared, diving down a variety of bolt-holes, with Tink after them, leaving the girls alone in the big candlelit room.

"Now see what you've done." said the oldest girl, the pretty one with the straight brown hair. Obviously the leader of the Wendys, she wore a simple dark dress—*like a uniform*, Darla thought, *a school uniform that's badly stained*. "It's going to take forever to get that stuff off the floor. Ages and ages. Mops and buckets. And nothing left for us to eat."

The other girls agreed loudly.

"*They* made the mess," Darla said sensibly. "Let *them* clean it up! That's how it's done at my house."

There was a horrified silence. For a long moment none of the girls said a word, but their mouths opened and shut like fish on beaches. Finally the littlest one spoke.

"Peter won't 'ike it."

"Well, I don't '*ike* Peter!" Darla answered quickly. "He's nothing but a long-winded bully."

"But," said the little Wendy, "you gave him a thimble." She actually said "simble."

"No," Darla said. "Peter lied. I didn't."

The girls all seemed dumbstruck by that revelation. Without a word more, they began to clean the room, first righting the table and then laboriously picking up what they could with their fingers before resorting, at last, to the dreaded buckets and mops. Soon the place smelled like any institution after a cleaning, like a school bathroom or a hospital corridor, Lysol-fresh with an overcast of pine.

Shaking her head, Darla just watched them until the littlest Wendy handed her a mop.

Darla flung the mop to the floor. "I won't do it," she said. "It's not fair."

The oldest Wendy came over to her and put her hand on Darla's shoulder. "Who ever told you that life is fair?" she asked. "Certainly not a navvy, nor an upstairs maid, nor a poor man trying to feed his family."

"Nor my da," put in one of the girls. She was pale skinned, sharp nosed, gap toothed, homely to a fault. "He allas said life was a crapshoot and all usn's got was snake-eyes."

"And not my father," said another, a whey-faced, doughy-looking eight-year-old. "He used to always say that the world didn't treat him right."

"What I mean is that it's not fair that *they* get to have the adventures and you get to clean the house," Darla explained carefully.

"Who will clean it if we don't?" Wendy asked. She picked up the mop and handed it back to Darla. "Not *them*. Not ever. So if we want it done, we do it. Fair is not the matter here." She went back to her place in the line of girls mopping the floor.

With a sigh that was less a capitulation and more a show of solidarity with the Wendys, Darla picked up her own mop and followed.

When the room was set to rights again, the Wendys—with Darla following close behind—tromped into the kitchen, a cheerless, windowless room they had obviously tried to make homey. There were little stick dollies stuck in every possible niche and hand-painted birch bark signs on the wall.

SMILE, one sign said, YOU ARE ON CANDIED CAMERA. And another: WENDYS ARE WONDERFUL. A third, in very childish script, read: WENDYS ARE WINERS. Darla wondered idly if that was meant to be WINNERS or WHINERS, but she decided not to ask.

Depressing as the kitchen was, it was redolent with bakery smells that seemed to dissipate the effect of a prison. Darla sighed, remembering her own kitchen at home, with the windows overlooking her mother's herb garden and the rockery where four kinds of heather flowered till the first snows of winter.

The girls all sat down—on the floor, on the table, in little bumpy, woody niches. There were only two chairs in the kitchen, a tatty overstuffed chair whose gold brocaded covering had seen much better days, and a rocker. The rocker was taken by the oldest Wendy; the other chair remained empty.

At last, seeing that no one else was going to claim the stuffed chair, Darla sat down on it, and a collective gasp went up from the girls.

"'At's Peter's chair," the littlest one finally volunteered.

"Well, Peter's not here to sit in it," Darla said. But she did not relax back against the cushion, just in case he should suddenly appear.

"I'm hungry, Wendy," said one of the girls, who had two gold braids down to her waist. "Isn't there *anything* left to eat?" She addressed the girl in the rocker.

"You are always hungry, Magda," Wendy said. But she smiled, and it was a smile of such sweetness, Darla was immediately reminded of her mom, in the days before the divorce and her dad's new wife.

"So you *do* have names, and not just Wendy," Darla said.

They looked at her as if she were stupid.

"Of course we have names," said the girl in the rocker. "I'm the only one *truly* named Wendy. But I've been here from the first. So that's what Peter calls us all. That's Magda," she said, pointing to the girl with the braids. "And that's Lizzy." The youngest girl. "And that's Martha, Pansy, Nina, Nancy, Heidi, Betsy, Maddy, JoAnne, Shula, Annie, Corrie, Barbara . . ." She went around the circle of girls.

Darla interrupted. "Then why doesn't Peter—"

"Because he can't be bothered remembering," said Wendy. "And we can't be bothered reminding him."

"And it's all right," said Magda. "Really. He has so much else to worry about. Like—"

"Him!" They all breathed the word together quietly, as if saying it aloud would summon the horror to them.

"Him? You mean Hook, don't you?" asked Darla. "Captain Hook."

The look they gave her was compounded of anger and alarm. Little Lizzy put her hands over her mouth as if she had said the name herself.

"Well, isn't it?"

"You are an extremely stupid girl," said Wendy. "As well as a dangerous one." Then she smiled again—that luminous smile—at all the other girls, excluding Darla, as if Wendy had not just said something that was both rude and horrible. "Now, darlings, how many of you are as hungry as Magda?"

One by one, the hands went up, Lizzy's first. Only Darla kept her hand down and her eyes down as well.

"Not hungry in the slightest?" Wendy asked, and everyone went silent.

Darla felt forced to look up and saw that Wendy's eyes were staring at her, glittering strangely in the candlelight.

It was too much. Darla shivered, and then, all of a sudden, she wanted to get back at Wendy, who seemed as much of a bully as Peter, only in a softer, sneakier way. *But how to do it?* And then she recalled how her mom said that telling a story in a very quiet voice always made a jury lean forward to concentrate that much more. *Maybe,* Darla thought, *I could try that.*

"I remember . . ." Darla began quietly. ". . . I remember a story my mom read to me about a Greek girl who was stolen away by the king of the underworld. He tricked her into eating six seeds and so she had to remain in the underworld six months of every year because of them."

The girls had all gone quiet and were clearly listening. *It works!* Darla thought.

"Don't be daft," Wendy said, her voice loud with authority.

"But Wendy, I remember that story, too," said the whey-faced girl, Nancy, in a kind of whisper, as if by speaking quietly she could later deny having said anything at all.

"And I," put in Magda, in a similarly whispery voice.

"And the fairies," said Lizzy. She was much too young to worry about loud or soft, so she spoke in her normal tone of voice. "If you eat anything in their hall, my mum allas said . . . you never get to go home again. Not ever. I miss my mum." Quite suddenly she began to cry.

"Now see what you've done," said Wendy, standing and stamping her foot. Darla was shocked. She'd never seen anyone over four years old do such a thing. "They'll all be blubbing now, remembering their folks, even the ones who'd been badly beaten at home or worse. And not a sticky bun left to comfort them with. You—girl—ought to be ashamed!"

"Well, it isn't *my* fault!" said Darla, loudly, but she stood, too. The thought of Wendy towering over her just now made her feel edgy and even a bit afraid. "And my name isn't *girl*. It's Darla!"

They glared at one another.

Just then there was a brilliant whistle. A flash of light circled the kitchen like a demented firefly.

"It's Tink!" Lizzy cried, clapping her hands together. "Oh! Oh! It's the Signal. 'Larm! 'Larm!"

"Come on, you lot," Wendy cried. "Places, all." She turned her back to Darla, grabbed up a soup ladle, and ran out of the room.

Each of the girls picked up one of the kitchen implements and followed. Not to be left behind, Darla pounced on the only thing left, a pair of silver sugar tongs, and pounded out after them.

They didn't go far, just to the main room again. There they stood silent guard over the bolt-holes. After a while—not quite fifteen minutes, Darla guessed—Tink fluttered in with a more melodic *all clear* and the boys slowly slid back down into the room.

Peter was the last to arrive.

"Oh, Peter, we were so worried," Wendy said.

The other girls crowded around. "We were scared silly," Magda added.

"Weepers!" cried Nancy.

"Knees all knocking," added JoAnne.

"Oh, this is really *too* stupid for words!" Darla said. "All we did was stand around with kitchen tools. Was I supposed to brain a pirate with these?" She held out the sugar tongs as she spoke.

The hush that followed her outcry was enormous.

Without another word, Peter disappeared back into the dark. One by one, the Lost Boys followed him. Tink was the last to go, flickering out like a candle in the wind.

"Now," said Magda with a pout, "we won't even get to hear about the fight. And it's the very best part of being a Wendy."

Darla stared at the girls for a long moment. "What you all need," she said grimly, "is a backbone transplant." And when no one responded, she added, "It's clear the Wendys need to go out on strike." Being the daughter of a labor lawyer had its advantages. She knew all about strikes.

"What the Wendys *need*," Wendy responded sternly, "is to give the cupboards a good shaking-out." She patted her hair down and looked daggers at Darla. "But first, cups of tea all round." Turning on her heel, she started back toward the kitchen. Only four girls remained behind.

Little Lizzy crept over to Darla's side. "What's a strike?" she asked.

"Work stoppage," Darla said. "Signs and lines."

Nancy, Martha, and JoAnne, who had also stayed to listen, looked equally puzzled.

"Signs?" Nancy said.

"Lines?" JoAnne said.

"*Hello . . .*" Darla couldn't help the exasperation in her voice. "What year do you all live in? I mean, haven't you ever heard of strikes? Watched CNN? Endured social studies?"

"Nineteen fourteen," said Martha.

"Nineteen thirty-three," said Nancy.

"Nineteen seventy-two," said JoAnne.

"Do you mean to say that none of you are . . ." Darla couldn't think of what to call it, so added lamely, "new?"

Lizzy slipped her hand into Darla's. "You are the onliest new Wendy we've had in years."

"Oh," Darla said. "I guess that explains it." But she wasn't sure.

"Explains what?" they asked. Before Darla could answer, Wendy called from the kitchen doorway, "Are you lot coming? Tea's on." She did not sound as if she were including Darla in the invitation.

Martha scurried to Wendy's side, but Nancy and JoAnne hesitated a moment before joining her. That left only Lizzy with Darla.

"Can I help?" Lizzy asked. "For the signs. And the 'ines? I be a good worker. Even Wendy says so."

"You're my only . . ." Darla said, smiling down at her and giving her little hand a squeeze. "My *on*liest worker. Still, as my mom always says, 'Start with one, you're halfway done.'"

Lizzy repeated the rhyme. "Start with one, you're halfway done. Start with one . . ."

"Just remember it. No need to say it aloud," Darla said.

Lizzy looked up at her, eyes like sky-blue marbles. "But I 'ike the way that poem sounds."

"Then 'ike it quietly. We have a long way to go yet before

we're ready for any chants." Darla went into the kitchen hand in hand with Lizzy, who skipped beside her, mouthing the words silently.

Fourteen Wendys stared at them. Not a one was smiling. Each had a teacup—unmatched, chipped, or cracked—in her hand.

"A long way to go where?" Wendy asked in a chilly voice.

"A long way before you can be free of this yoke of oppression," said Darla. *Yoke of oppression* was a favorite expression of her mother's.

"We are not yoked," Wendy said slowly. "And we are not oppressed."

"What's o-ppressed?" asked Lizzy.

"Made to do what you don't want to do," explained Darla, but she never took her eyes off of Wendy. "Treated harshly. Ruled unjustly. Governed with cruelty." Those were the three definitions she had to memorize for her last social studies exam. She never thought she'd ever actually get to use them in the real world. *If,* she thought suddenly, *this world is real.*

"No one treats us harshly or rules us unjustly. And the only cruel ones in Neverland are the pirates," Wendy explained carefully, as if talking to someone feebleminded or slow.

None of the other Wendys said a word. Most of them stared into their cups, *a little*—Darla thought—*like the way I always stare down at my shoes when Mom or Dad wants to talk about something that hurts.*

Lizzy pulled her hand from Darla's. "I think it harsh that we always have to clean up after the boys." Her voice was tiny but still it carried.

"And unjust," someone put in.

"Who said that?" Wendy demanded, staring around the table. "Who *dares* to say that Peter is unjust?"

Darla pursed her lips, wondering how her mom would

answer such a question. She was about to lean forward to say something when JoAnne stood in a rush.

"I said it. And it is unjust. I came to Neverland to get away from that sort of thing. Well . . . and to get away from my stepfather, too," she said. "I mean, I don't mind cleaning up my own mess. And even someone else's, occasionally. But . . ." She sat down as quickly as she had stood, looking accusingly into her cup, as if the cup had spoken and not she.

"*Well!*" Wendy said, sounding so much like Darla's home ec teacher that Darla had to laugh out loud.

As if the laugh freed them, the girls suddenly stood up one after another, voicing complaints. And as each one rose, little Lizzy clapped her hands and skipped around the table, chanting, "Start with one, you're halfway done! Start with one, you're halfway done!"

Darla didn't say a word more. She didn't have to. She just listened as the first trickle of angry voices became a stream and the stream turned into a flood. The girls spoke of the boys' mess and being underappreciated and wanting a larger share of the food. They spoke about needing to go outside every once in a while. They spoke of longing for new stockings and a bathing room all to themselves, not one shared with the boys, who left rings around the tub and dirty underwear everywhere. They spoke of the long hours and the lack of fresh air, and Barbara said they really could use every other Saturday off, at least. It seemed once they started complaining they couldn't stop.

Darla's mom would have understood what had just happened, but Darla was clearly as stunned as Wendy by the rush of demands. They stared at one another, almost like comrades.

The other girls kept on for long minutes, each one stumbling over the next to be heard, until the room positively rocked with complaints. And then, as suddenly as they had begun, they stopped. Red faced, they all sat down again, except for Lizzy, who still capered around the room, but now did it wordlessly.

Into the sudden silence, Wendy rose. "How *could* you . . ." she began. She leaned over the table, clutching the top, her entire body trembling. "After all Peter has done for you, taking you in when no one else wanted you, when you had been tossed aside by the world, when you'd been crushed and corrupted and canceled. How *could* you?"

Lizzy stopped skipping in front of Darla. "Is it time for signs and 'ines now?" she asked, her marble-blue eyes wide.

Darla couldn't help it. She laughed again. Then she held out her arms to Lizzy, who cuddled right in. "Time indeed," Darla said. She looked up at Wendy. "Like it or not, Miss Management, the Lost Girls are going out on strike."

Wendy sat in her rocker, arms folded, a scowl on her face. She looked like a four-year-old having a temper tantrum. But of course it was something worse than that.

The girls ignored her. They threw themselves into making signs with a kind of manic energy, and in about an hour they had a whole range of them, using the backs of their old signs, pages torn from cookbooks, and flattened flour bags.

WENDYS WON'T WORK, one read. EQUAL PLAY FOR EQUAL WORK, went another. MY NAME'S NOT WENDY! said a third, and FRESH AIR IS ONLY FAIR a fourth. Lizzy's sign was decorated with stick figures carrying what Darla took to be swords, or maybe wands. Lizzy had spelled out—or rather misspelled out—what became the girls' marching words: WE AIN'T LOST, WE'RE JUST MIZ-PLAYST.

It turned out that JoAnne was musical. She made up lyrics to the tune of "Yankee Doodle Dandy" and taught them to the others:

> *We ain't lost, we're just misplaced,*
> *The outside foe we've never faced.*

Give us a chance to fight and win
And we'll be sure to keep Neverland neat as a pin.

The girls argued for a while over that last line, which Betsy said had too many syllables and the wrong sentiment, until Magda suggested, rather timidly, that if they actually wanted a chance to fight the pirates, maybe the boys should take a turn at cleaning the house. "Fair's fair," she added.

That got a cheer. "Fair's fair," they told one another, and Pansy scrawled that sentiment on yet another sign. The cheer caused Wendy to get up grumpily from her chair and leave the kitchen in a snit. She must have called for the boys then, because no sooner had the girls decided on an amended line (which still had too many syllables but felt right otherwise)—

And you can keep Neverland neat as a pin!

—than the boys could be heard coming back noisily into the dining room. They shouted and whistled and banged their fists on the table, calling out for the girls and for food. Tink's high-pitched cry overrode the noise, piercing the air. The girls managed to ignore it all until Peter suddenly appeared in the kitchen doorway.

"What's this I hear?" he said, smiling slightly to show he was more amused than angry. Somehow that only made his face seem both sinister and untrustworthy.

But his appearance in the doorway was electrifying. For a moment not one of the girls could speak. It was as if they had all taken a collective breath and were waiting to see which of them had the courage to breathe out first.

Then Lizzy held up her sign. "We're going on strike," she said brightly.

"And what, little Wendy, is that?" Peter asked, leaning forward and speaking in the kind of voice grown-ups use with children. He pointed at her sign. "Is it . . ." he said slyly, "like a thimble?"

"Silly Peter," said Lizzy, "it's signs and 'ines."

"I see the signs, all right," said Peter. "But what do they mean? WENDYS WON'T WORK. Why, Neverland counts on Wendys working. And I count on it, too. You Wendys are the most important part of what we have made here."

"Oh," said Lizzy, turning to Darla, her face shining with pleasure. "*We're* the mostest important . . ."

Darla sighed heavily. "If you are so important, Lizzy, why can't he remember your name? If you're so important, why do you have all the work and none of the fun?"

"Right!" cried JoAnne suddenly, and immediately burst into her song. It was picked up at once by the other girls. Lizzy, caught up in the music, began to march in time all around the table with her sign. The others, still singing, fell in line behind her. They marched once around the kitchen and then right out into the dining room. Darla was at the rear.

At first the Lost Boys were stunned at the sight of the girls and their signs. Then they, too, got caught up in the song and began to pound their hands on the table in rhythm.

Tink flew around and around Wendy's head, flickering on and off and on angrily, looking for all the world like an electric hair-cutting machine. Peter glared at them all until he suddenly seemed to come to some conclusion. Then he leaped onto the dining room table, threw back his head, and crowed loudly.

At that everyone went dead silent. Even Tink.

Peter let the silence prolong itself until it was almost painful. At last he turned and addressed Darla and, through her, all the girls. "What is it you want?" he asked. "What is it you truly want? Because you'd better be careful what you ask for. In Neverland wishes are granted in very strange ways."

"It's not," Darla said carefully, "what I want. It's what *they* want."

In a tight voice, Wendy cried out, "They never wanted for anything until she came, Peter. They never needed or asked—"

"What we want . . ." JoAnne interrupted, "is to be equals."

Peter wheeled about on the table and stared down at JoAnne, and she, poor thing, turned gray under his gaze. "No one is asking you," he said pointedly.

"We want to be equals!" Lizzy shouted. "To the boys. To Peter!"

The dam burst again, and the girls began shouting and singing and crying and laughing all together.

"Equal . . . equal . . . equal . . ."

Even the boys took it up.

Tink flickered frantically, then took off up one of the bolt-holes, emerging almost immediately down another, her piercing alarm signal so loud that everyone stopped chanting, except for Lizzy, whose little voice only trailed off after a bit.

"So," said Peter, "you want equal share in the fighting? Then here's your chance."

Tink's light was sputtering with excitement and she whistled nonstop.

"Tink says Hook's entire crew is out there, waiting. And, boy! are they angry. You want to fight them? Then go ahead." He crossed his arms over his chest and turned his face away from the girls. "I won't stop you."

No longer gray but now pink with excitement, JoAnne grabbed up a knife from the nearest Lost Boy. "I'm not afraid!" she said. She headed up one of the bolt-holes.

Weaponless, Barbara, Pansy, and Betsy followed right after.

"But that's not what I meant them to do," Darla said. "I mean, weren't we supposed to work out some sort of compromise?"

Peter turned back slowly and looked at Darla, his face stern and unforgiving. "I'm Peter Pan. I don't have to compromise in Neverland." Wendy reached up to help him off the tabletop.

The other girls had already scattered up the holes, and only Lizzy was left. And Darla.

"Are you coming to the fight?" Lizzy asked Darla, holding out her hand.

Darla gulped and nodded. They walked to the bolt-hole hand in hand. Darla wasn't sure what to expect, but they began rising up as if in some sort of air elevator. Behind them one of the boys was whining to Peter, "But what are we going to do without them?"

The last thing Darla heard Peter say was, "Don't worry. There are always more Wendys where they came from."

The air outside was crisp and autumny and smelled of apples. There was a full moon, orange and huge. *Harvest moon,* Darla thought, which was odd since it had been spring in her bedroom.

Ahead she saw the other girls. *And* the pirates. Or at least she saw their silhouettes. It obviously hadn't been much of a fight. The smallest of the girls—Martha, Nina, and Heidi—were already captured and riding atop their captors' shoulders. The others, with the exception of JoAnne, were being carried off fireman-style. JoAnne still had her knife and she was standing off one of the largest of the men; she got in one good swipe before being disarmed, and lifted up.

Darla was just digesting this when Lizzy was pulled from her.

"Up you go, little darlin'," came a deep voice.

Lizzy screamed. "Wendy! Wendy!"

Darla had no time to answer her before she, too, was gathered up in enormous arms and carted off.

In less time than it takes to tell of it, they were through the woods and over a shingle, dumped into boats, and rowed out to the pirate ship. There they were hauled up by ropes and—except for Betsy, who struggled so hard she landed in the water and had to be fished out, wrung out, and then hauled up again—it was a silent and well-practiced operation.

The girls stood in a huddle on the well-lit deck and awaited their fate. Darla was glad no one said anything. She felt awful. She hadn't meant them to come to this. Peter had been right. Wishes in Neverland were dangerous.

"Here come the captains," said one of the pirates. It was the first thing anyone had said since the capture.

He must mean captain, singular, thought Darla. But when she heard footsteps nearing them and dared to look up, there were, indeed, two figures coming forward. One was an old man about her grandfather's age, his white hair in two braids, a three-cornered hat on his head. She looked for the infamous hook but he had two regular hands, though the right one was clutching a pen.

The other captain was . . . a woman.

"Welcome to Hook's ship," the woman said. "I'm Mrs. Hook. Also known as Mother Jane. Also known as Pirate Lil. Also called The Pirate Queen. We've been hoping we could get you away from Peter for a very long time." She shook hands with each of the girls and gave Lizzy a hug.

"I need to get to the doctor, ma'am," said one of the pirates. "That little girl. . . ," he pointed to JoAnne, ". . . gave me quite a slice."

JoAnne blanched and shrank back into herself.

But Captain Hook only laughed. It was a hearty laugh, full of good humor. "Good for her. You're getting careless in your old age, Smee," he said. "Stitches will remind you to stay alert. Peter would have got your throat, and even here on the boat that could take a long while to heal."

"Now," said Mrs. Hook, "it's time for a good meal. Pizza, I think. With plenty of veggies on top. Peppers, mushrooms, carrots, onions. But no anchovies. I have never understood why anyone wants a hairy fish on top of pizza."

"What's pizza?" asked Lizzy.

"Ah . . . something you will love, my dear," answered Mrs.

Hook. "Things never do change in Peter's Neverland, but up here on Hook's ship we move with the times."

"Who will do the dishes after?" asked Betsy cautiously.

The crew rustled behind them.

"I'm on dishes this week," said one, a burly, ugly man with a black eye patch.

"And I," said another. She was as big as the ugly man, but attractive in a rough sort of way.

"There's a duty roster on the wall by the galley," explained Mrs. Hook. "That's ship talk for the kitchen. You'll get used to it. We all take turns. A pirate ship is a very democratic place."

"What's demo-rat-ic?" asked Lizzy.

They all laughed. "You will have a long time to learn," said Mrs. Hook. "Time moves more swiftly here than in the stuffy confines of a Neverland tree. But not so swiftly as out in the world. Now let's have that pizza, a hot bath, and a bedtime story, and then tomorrow we'll try and answer your questions."

The girls cheered, JoAnne loudest of them all.

"I *am* hungry," Lizzy added, as if that were all the answer Mrs. Hook needed.

"But I'm not," Darla said. "And I don't want to stay here. Not in Neverland or on Hook's ship. I want to go home."

Captain Hook came over and put his right hand under her chin. Gently he lifted her face into the light. "Father beat you?" he asked.

"Never," Darla said.

"Mother desert you?" he asked.

"Fat chance," said Darla.

"Starving? Miserable? Alone?"

"No. And no. And *no*."

Hook turned to his wife and shrugged. She shrugged back, then asked, "Ever think that the world was unfair, child?"

"Who hasn't?" asked Darla, and Mrs. Hook smiled.

"Thinking it and meaning it are two very different things,"

Mrs. Hook said at last. "I expect you must have been awfully convincing to have landed at Peter's door. Never mind, have pizza with us, and then you can go. I want to hear the latest from outside, anyway. You never know what we might find useful. Pizza was the last really useful thing we learned from one of the girls we snagged before Peter found her. And that—I can tell you—has been a major success."

"Can't I go home with Darla?" Lizzy asked.

Mrs. Hook knelt down till she and Lizzy were face-to-face. "I am afraid that would make for an awful lot of awkward questions," she said.

Lizzy's blue eyes filled up with tears.

"My mom is a lawyer," Darla put in quickly. "Awkward questions are her specialty."

The pizza was great, with a crust that was thin and delicious. And when Darla awoke to the ticking of the grandfather clock in the hall and the sound of the maple branch *scritch-scratching* against the clapboard siding, the taste of the pizza was still in her mouth. She felt a lump at her feet, raised herself up, and saw Lizzy fast asleep under the covers at the foot of the bed.

"I sure hope Mom is as good as I think she is," Darla whispered. Because there was no going back on this one—fair, unfair, or anywhere in between.

TOUGH ALICE

The pig fell down the rabbit-hole, turning snout over tail and squealing as it went. By the third level it had begun to change. Wonderland was like that, one minute pig, the next pork loin.

It passed Alice on the fourth level, for contrary to the law of physics, she was falling much more slowly than the pig. Being quite hungry, she reached out for it. But no sooner had she set her teeth into its well-done flesh than it changed back into a live pig. Its squeals startled her and she dropped it, which made her use a word her mother had never even heard, much less understood. Wonderland's denizens had done much for Alice's education, not all of it good.

"I promise I'll be a vegetarian if only I land safely," Alice said, crossing her fingers as she fell. At that very moment she hit bottom, landing awkwardly on top of the pig.

"Od-say off-ay!" the pig swore, swatting at her with his hard trotter. Luckily he missed and ran right off toward a copse of trees, calling for his mum.

"The same to you," Alice shouted after him. She didn't know

what he'd said but guessed it was in Pig Latin. "You shouldn't complain, you know. After all, you're still whole!" Then she added softly, "And I can't complain, either. If you'd been a pork loin, I wouldn't have had such a soft landing." She had found over the years of regular visits that it was always best to praise Wonderland aloud for its bounty, however bizarre that bounty might be. You didn't want to have Wonderland mad at you. There were things like . . . the Jabberwock, for instance.

The very moment she thought the word, she heard the beast roar behind her. That was another problem with Wonderland. Think about something, and it appeared. *Or don't think about something*, Alice reminded herself, *and it still might appear.* The Jabberwock was her own personal Wonderland demon. It always arrived sometime during her visit, and someone—her chosen champion—had to fight it, which often signaled an end to her time there.

"Not so soon," Alice wailed in the general direction of the roar. "I haven't had much of a visit yet!" The Jabberwock sounded close, so Alice sighed and raced after the pig into the woods.

The woods had a filter of green and yellow leaves overhead, as lacy as one of her mother's parasols. It really would have been quite lovely if Alice hadn't been in such a hurry. But it was best not to linger anywhere in Wonderland before the Jabberwock was dispatched. Tarrying simply invited disaster.

She passed the Caterpillar's toadstool. It was as big as her uncle Martin, and as tall and pasty white, but it was empty. A sign by the stalk said GONE FISHING. Alice wondered idly if the Caterpillar fished with worms, then shook her head. Worms would be too much like using his own family for bait. Though she had some relatives for whom that might not be a bad idea. Her cousin Albert, for example, who liked to stick frogs down the back of her dress.

Behind her the Jabberwock roared again.

"Bother!" said Alice, and began to zigzag through the trees.

"Haste . . ." came a voice from above her, "makes wastrels."

Alice stopped and looked up. The Cheshire Cat's grin hung like a demented quarter moon between two limbs of an elm tree.

"Haste," continued the grin, "is a terrible thing to waste."

"That's really not quite right . . ." Alice began, but the grin went on without pausing:

"Haste is waste control. Haste is wasted on the young. Haste is . . ."

"You are in a loop," said Alice, and not waiting to hear another roar from the Jabberwock, she ran on. Sunlight pleated down through the trees, wider and wider. Ahead a clearing beckoned. Alice could not help being drawn toward it.

In the center of the clearing a tea party was going on. Hatter to Dormouse to Hare, the conversation was thrown around the long oak table like some erratic ball in a game without rules. The Hatter was saying that teapots made bad pets and the Dormouse that teapots were big pests and the Hare that teapots held big tempests.

Alice knew that if she stopped for tea—chamomile would be nice, with a couple of wholemeal biscuits—the Jabberwock would . . .

ROAR!

. . . would be on her in a Wonderland moment. And she hadn't yet found a champion for the fight. So she raced past the tea table, waving her hand.

The tea-party trio did not even stop arguing long enough to call out her name. Alice knew from long experience that Wonderland friends were hardly the kind to send postcards or to remember your birthday, but she had thought they might at least wave back. After all the times she had poured for them, and brought them cakes from the Duchess's pantry! The last trip to Wonderland, she'd even come down the rabbit-hole with her pockets stuffed full of fruit scones because the Dormouse had never tried them with currants. He had spent the entire party after that making jokes about currant affairs, and the Hare had been laughing the whole time. "Hare-sterically," according to the Hatter. *We'd had a simply wonderful time*, Alice thought. It made her a bit cranky that the three ignored her now, but she didn't stop to yell at them or complain. The Jabberwock's roars were too close for that.

Directly across the clearing was a path. On some of her visits the path was there; on others it was twenty feet to the left or right. She raced toward it, hoping the White Knight would be waiting. He was the best of her champions, no matter that he was a bit old and feeble. At least he was always trying. *Quite trying*, she thought suddenly.

She'd even settle for the Tweedle twins, though they fought one another as much as they fought the Jabberwock. Dee and Dum were their names, but—she thought a bit acidly—perhaps Dumb and Dumber more accurately described them.

And then there was the Beamish Boy. She didn't much like him at all, though he *was* the acknowledged Wonderland Ace. Renowned in song and story for beating the Jabberwock, he was too much of a bully for Alice's tastes. And he always insisted on taking the Jabberwock's head off with him. Even for Wonderland, *that* was a messy business.

Of course, this time, with the beast having gotten such an early start, Alice thought miserably, she might need them all. She had hoped for more time before the monster arrived on the scene. Wonderland was usually so much more fun than a vacation at Bath or Baden-Baden, the one being her mother's favorite holiday spot, the other her grandmother's.

But when she got to the path, it was empty. There was no sign of the White Knight or the Tweedles or even the Beamish Boy, who—now that she thought of it—reminded her awfully of Cousin Albert.

And suddenly the Jabberwock's roars were close enough to shake the trees. Green and gold leaves fell around her like rain.

Alice bit her lip. Wonderland might be only a make-believe

place, a dreamscape, or a dream escape. But even in a made-up land, there were real dangers. She'd been hurt twice just falling down the rabbit-hole: a twisted ankle one time, a scratched knee another. And once she had pricked her finger on a thorn in the talking flower garden hard enough to draw blood. How the roses had laughed at that!

However, the Jabberwock presented a different kind of danger altogether. He was a horrible creature, nightmarish, with enormous shark-toothed jaws, claws like gaffing hooks, and a tail that could swat her like a fly. There was no doubt in her mind that the Jabberwock could actually kill her if he wished, even in this imaginary land. He had killed off two of her champions on other visits—a Jack of Clubs and the Dodo—and had to be dispatched by the Beamish Boy. She'd never seen either of the champions again.

The thought alone frightened her, and that was when she started to cry.

"No crying allowed," said a harsh, familiar voice.

"No crying aloud," said a quieter voice, but one equally familiar.

Alice looked up. The Red and White Queens were standing in front of her, the White Queen offering a handkerchief that was slightly tattered and not at all clean. "Here, blow!"

Alice took the handkerchief and blew, a sound not unlike the Jabberwock's roar, only softer and infinitely less threatening. "Oh," she said, "thank goodness you are here. You two can save me."

"Not us," said the Red Queen.

"Never us," added the White.

"But then why else have you come?" Alice asked. "I am always saved on this path . . . wherever this path is at the time."

"The path is past," said the Red Queen. "We are only present, not truly here." As she spoke the dirt path dissolved, first to pebbles, then to grass.

"And you are your own future," added the White Queen.

Alice suddenly found herself standing in the meadow once again, but this time the Hare, the Hatter, and the Dormouse were sitting in stands set atop the table. Next to them were the Caterpillar, his fishing pole over his shoulder; the Cheshire Cat, grinning madly; the White Knight; the Tweedle Twins; the Beamish Boy, in a bright red beanie; the Duchess and her pig baby; and a host of other Wonderlanders. They were exchanging money right and left.

"My money's on you," the White Queen whispered in Alice's ear. "I think you will take the Jabberwock in the first round."

"Take him where?" asked Alice.

"For a fall," the Red Queen answered. Then, shoving a wad of money at the White Queen, she said, "I'll give you three to one against."

"Done," said the White Queen, and they walked off arm-in-arm toward the spectator stands, trailing bits of paper money on the ground.

"But what can I fight the Jabberwock with?" Alice called after them.

"You are a tough child," the White Queen said over her shoulder. "You figure it out."

With that she and the Red Queen climbed onto the table and into the stands, where they sat in the front row and began cheering, the White Queen for Alice, the Red Queen for the beast.

"But I'm not tough at all," Alice wailed. "I've never fought *anything* before. Not even Albert." She had only told on him, and had watched with satisfaction when her mother and his father punished him. Or at least that had seemed satisfactory at first. But when his three older sisters had all persisted in calling "Tattletale twit, your tongue will split" after her for months, it hadn't felt very satisfactory at all.

"I am only," she wept out loud, "a tattletale, not a knight."

"It's not night now!" shouted the Hatter.

"Day! It's day! A frabjous day!" the Hare sang out.

The Beamish Boy giggled and twirled the propeller on the top of his cap.

Puffing five interlocking rings into the air above the crowd, the Caterpillar waved his arms gaily.

And the Jabberwock, with eyes of flame, burst out of the Tulgey Wood, alternately roaring and burbling. It was a horrendous sound and for a moment Alice could not move at all.

"One, two!" shouted the crowd. "Through and through."

The Jabberwock lifted his tail and slammed it down in rhythm to the chanting. Every time his tail hit the ground, the earth shook. Alice could feel each tremor move up from her feet, through her body, till it seemed as if the top of her head would burst open with the force of the blow. She turned to run.

"She ain't got no vorpal blade," cried the Duchess, waving a fist. "How's she gonna fight without her bloomin' blade?"

At her side, the pig squealed: "Orpal-vay ade-blay."

The Beamish Boy giggled once more.

Right! Alice thought. *I haven't a vorpal blade. Or anything else, for that matter.*

For his part, the Jabberwock seemed delighted that she was weaponless, and he stood up on his hind legs, claws out, to slash a right and then a left in Alice's direction.

All Alice could do was duck and run, duck and run again. The crowd cheered and a great deal more money changed hands. The Red Queen stuffed dollars, pounds, lira, and kroner under her crown as fast as she could manage. On the other hand, the Dormouse looked into his teapot and wept.

"Oh, Alice," came a cry from the stands, "be tough, child. Be strong." It was the White Queen's voice. "You do not need a blade. You just need courage."

Courage, Alice thought, *would come much easier with a blade.* But she didn't say that aloud. Her tongue felt as if it had been glued by fear to the roof of her mouth. And her feet, by the Queen's call, to the ground.

And still the Jabberwock advanced, but slowly, as if he were not eager to finish her off all at once.

He is playing with me, Alice thought, *rather like my cat, Dinah*. It was not a pleasant thought. She had rescued many a mouse from Dinah's claws and very few of them had lived for more than a minute or two after. She tried to run again but couldn't.

Suddenly she'd quite enough of Wonderland.

But Wonderland was not quite done with Alice.

The Jabberwock advanced. His eyes lit up like skyrockets and his tongue flicked in and out.

"Oh, Mother," Alice whispered. "I am sorry for all the times I was naughty. Really I am." She could scarcely catch her breath, and she promised herself that she would try and die nobly, though she really didn't want to die at all. Because if she died in Wonderland, who would explain it to her family?

The Jabberwock moved closer. He slobbered a bit over his pointed teeth. Then he slipped on a pound note, staggered like Uncle Martin after a party, and his big yellow eyes rolled up in his head. "Ouf," he said.

"Ouf?" Alice whispered. "Ouf?"

It had all been so horrible and frightening, and now, suddenly, it was rather silly. She stared at the Jabberwock and for the first time noticed a little tag on the underside of his left leg. MADE IN BRIGHTON, it said.

Why, he's nothing but an overlarge windup toy, she thought. And the very minute she thought that, she began to laugh.

And laugh.

And laugh, until she had to bend over to hold her stomach and tears leaked out of her eyes. She could feel the bubbles of laughter still rising inside, getting up her nose like sparkling soda. She could not stop herself.

"Here, now!" shouted the Beamish Boy, "no laughing! It ain't fair."

The Cheshire Cat lost his own grin. "Fight first, laughter after," he advised. "Or maybe flight first. Or fright first."

The Red Queen sneaked out of the stands and was almost off the table, clutching her crown full of money, when the Dormouse stuck out a foot.

"No going off with that moolah, Queenie," the Dormouse said, taking the crown from her and putting it on top of the teapot.

Still laughing but no longer on the edge of hysteria, Alice looked up at the Jabberwock, who had become frozen in place. Not only was he stiff, but he had turned an odd shade of gray and looked rather like a poorly built garden statue that had been out too long in the wind and rain. She leaned toward him.

"Boo!" she said, grinning.

Little cracks ran across the Jabberwock's face and down the front of his long belly.

"Double boo!" Alice said.

Another crack ran right around the Jabberwock's tail, and it broke off with a sound like a tree branch breaking.

"Triple . . ." Alice began, but stopped when someone put a hand on her arm. She turned. It was the White Queen.

"You have won, my dear," the White Queen said, placing the Red Queen's crown—minus all the money—on Alice's head. "A true queen is merciful."

Alice nodded, then thought a moment. "But where was the courage in that? All I did was laugh."

"Laughter in the face of certain death? It is the very definition of the Hero," said the White Queen. "The Jabberwock knew it and therefore could no longer move against you. You would have known it yourself much sooner, had that beastly Albert not been such a tattletale."

"But I was the tattletale," Alice said, hardly daring to breathe.

"Who do you think told Albert's sisters?" asked the White Queen. She patted a few errant strands of hair in place and simultaneously tucked several stray dollars back under her crown.

Alice digested this information for a minute, but something about the conversation was still bothering her. Then she had it. "How do *you* know about Albert?" she asked.

"I'm late!" the White Queen cried suddenly, and dashed off down the road, looking from behind like a large white rabbit.

Alice should have been surprised, but nothing ever really surprised her anymore in Wonderland.

Except . . .

except . . .

herself.

Courage, she thought.

Laughter, she thought.

Maybe I'll try them both out on Albert.

And so thinking, she felt herself suddenly rising, first slowly, then faster and faster still, up the rabbit-hole, all the way back home.

BLOWN AWAY

1.

That little Dorothy Gale was the sorriest child I ever saw. She wore her hair in two braids that—however tight in the morning her aunt had made them—seemed to crawl out of their tidy fittings by noon. She had the goshdarnedest big gap between her upper front teeth and a snub nose that seemed too small for her face. And she was always squinting as if she had trouble seeing things clearly, or as if she was trying hard not to cry.

Well, I suppose she had a lot to cry about, though didn't we all in those days. Both her parents had got themselves killed in a train crash coming home from a weekend in Kansas City. Not unexpected. They'd tried balloon ascension the year before and it went down into the Kansas River which—luckily—wasn't flooding.

They weren't exactly *on* the train; it was their car got stuck— one of the first in our part of Kansas—and it had run out of gas, because Martin Gale had been too tightfisted to buy a full tank in Manhattan. And of course his luck being what it was, they ran out just as they were at a crossing where the streamliner, the *Southern Belle*, usually passed around noon.

They were the only ones who died, because it wasn't the *Belle* at all, thank the Lord, just a freight hauler. But the two of them were dead before an ambulance could even get to them.

That meant little Dorothy, not quite eight, was sent to her aunt and uncle's farm to live out here in the Middle of Nowhere Kansas. It was a small holding with some pigs, horses, a few cows. And the chickens. Always the chickens, who were in Em's special care.

The house itself was quite small, just one room really, there having always been just the two of them—Henry and Em—so in Henry's mind there'd never been a need to build bigger. No kids, though Em had wanted them of course, but by that time she was long past bearing and worn down to a crabbed, stooped, gray middle-aged woman.

Henry was Dorothy's blood uncle, being her father's only brother, though ten years his senior. He might as well have been fifty years older, if you judged by his looks. He was just as tightfisted, and not particularly welcoming to the little girl, either, since now the one room seemed crowded, what with Henry and Em's bed at one end, and little Dorothy's at the other, over by the stove.

At least Em, long-suffering as she was, tried to give the child a bit of her heart, which—after all those years of living with Henry on that old gray farm in the middle of the gray prairie—was as dried up as an old pea. She tried, but she wasn't much good at it. It was a bit like trying to water a budding flower in the middle of a dry Kansas summer with a watering can poked through with holes.

Course the Gale brothers weren't the only misers in those years. I could name a whole bunch more right in our little town, and need six extra hands to count them on, especially my mother-in-law, that old witch, who didn't even have the decency to die till she was well into her eighties, having burned through a good portion of the money that should have come to my wife and me. That money would have changed our story, I'll tell you that.

I'd trained as a carpenter once, loved working with wood, but things being so difficult those days, I never got to make much and I sold less. Instead, I spent my best years hiring out to one tightfisted farmer after another. About the time Dorothy Gale came to stay with Henry and Em, I was working there, bad luck to me.

Henry had enough money saved at that time to hire three farmhands. Though he paid a pittance it was better than nothing. And a pitiful lot we were: me, Stan, who was a big joking presence even when there was nothing to joke about, and Rand, Stan's younger brother, who was as scared of life as he was of death, having been in a near-drowning as a boy and never gotten over it. Imagine finding somewhere in dry Kansas to drown in that wasn't the Kansas River!

None of us had kids, and we felt so awful for little Dorothy, we did what we could to cheer her up.

Rand found her a puppy, the runt of an unwanted litter, that Old Man Baum who owns the farm down the road was about to drown. Rand had an immediate fellow-feeling for that dog, as you would guess. Old Man Baum had already sold the other pups in the litter, but no one wanted this stunted rat of a dog—black, with long hair, berry-black eyes, a real yapper. Even so, young Dorothy took to it the moment she laid eyes on it.

"You done a goodly deed this day," Stan said, after Rand handed her the dog. "Even a Godly one." Stan had recently been saved in a tent meeting and couldn't stop talking about it. Joking about it, too. Called it his *tent*ative change of life. And that he had a *tent*dency towards God. We just learned to ignore him.

Stan gave Dorothy a cracked bowl he'd found thrown out on the road, only about good enough to use for a dog's dinner. Just as well, as she couldn't actually feed the ratty thing from one of Em's best china now, could she? Not that Em fed anybody with that china. It was saved for some special event that never came.

I gave Dorothy a leather rope I'd braided myself, plus a collar cut down from a bridle I'd found in my mother-in-law's barn. And no, I didn't ask permission. She'd have said no anyway.

Dorothy's eyes got big. "For me? Really? For me?" It was about the longest speech I'd heard from her up to that time.

We were afraid she was going to try and kiss us or something right then and there, and so we shuffled out the door to get back to our chores. But when I turned around to see how she was making out, she had her little pug nose on the dog's nose, as if they'd been stuck together by glue.

After that, there wasn't a moment those two weren't in one another's pockets. She named the dog Toto, though where she came up with that, we were never to know. I thought for sure it would be something like Silky or Blackie or Fido. But Dorothy, she was always a queer kind of kid, as you will see.

2.

There were two cyclones, not one as has been reported. Old Man Baum liked to tidy things up, you know. Dogs, twisters, you name it. He tidied. Made for a clean house, but his stories . . . well, take it from me, they weren't to be believed.

Of course we always get cyclones around here. It's kind of an alley for them where we get mugged on a regular basis. But mostly we just hunker down in our dark little underground rooms that are dug into the unforgiving soil. Some folks like to call that kind of hole a cellar. More like a tomb for the hopeful living.

Usually the wind goes zigzagging past a farmhouse, picking up cows and plows, flinging them a county or two away, which does neither cow nor plow any good at all. But sometimes it flattens a whole house and everything in it, which is why we hide ourselves away.

That first twister young Dorothy was part of was one that had the Gale farm in its sight from the very first.

I was the only hand about that day, Stan and Rand were off at a cousin's funeral. Sorry man shot himself on account of losing his farm and land to the bank. He was never meant to be a farmer and was bad at it, and worse at keeping accounts, so no one was surprised.

There I was out in the back acres, hoeing along—*furrowing* I sometimes called it—and suddenly I felt the air pressure change. I heard a low wail of wind, and when I looked north, I could see the long prairie grass bowing in waves all the way to the horizon where the shape of a gray funnel cloud could be seen heading our way.

I dropped the hoe and ran for the house, yelling for Henry and Em and Dorothy to hightail it to the cyclone cellar. It was going to be a tight squeeze, even without Stan and Rand, but the one good thing about twisters is that they don't hang around very long. Just a minute or two, though the damage may last a lifetime.

Inside the Gale farmhouse, like many of the houses hereabouts, was a trapdoor with a ladder leading down into the cellar-hole. By the time I got inside, Em was already lifting the trapdoor up and climbing in. Henry was looking frantically out the window.

"Where's Dorothy?" he cried, his long beard waggling as he spoke.

Em called up, "Probably chasing that dang dog."

Henry grunted, said something like, "You never should have let her keep that blasted animal. It'll be the death of us all." He not only looked like a prophet out of the Good Book, he often sounded like one.

"Well," Em called back, "what was I to do, that poor child so brokenhearted and all?"

While Henry searched for an answer, I turned and ran out the door, and around the side of the house, where I saw Dorothy laying on her belly and trying to coax the frightened Toto out from under the porch.

"He'll be safe enough there," I said, and because I never lie, she believed me. I held out my hand. "But unless you can crawl down there with him, and me after you, we'd better get into the cellar."

She was reluctant to leave the dog, but she trusted me, took my hand, and we raced back inside and climbed down into the hole with hardly a moment or an inch to spare.

Well, you never can tell with a twister. They are as mean, as ornery, and as unpredictable as an unhappy woman. This one only nudged the house off its cinderblocks. We could feel the hump and bump as the house slid onto the ground. But then the wind scooped in under the porch, and dragged the poor dog out of there. We could hear it yelping, a sound that got farther and farther away the longer we listened till it was overpowered by the runaway train sounds a twister makes.

The Lord only knows how long the storm played with the little yapper, tossing him up and down, spinning him around, before finally flinging him into a coal bin some five counties away.

Henry posted a twenty-dollar reward for anyone who found the dog, which was nineteen dollars more than the animal was worth and five dollars more than Em said he should post. The woman who owned the coal bin sent a note but she declined the reward, which was both Christian and silly of her, one and the same.

The twister had watered Toto well and the coal bin woman had combed out his long silky hair. He was a good deal prettier than he'd been in some time. But he was also dead as could be, and no amount of weeping and snuffling and flinging guilt around that little farmhouse for days, like a baseball going around the bases in a game of pepper, was going to bring him back.

Rand had taken a course in taxidermy when he was still in high school, so he volunteered to skin, stuff, and mount little Toto for Dorothy. I was the only one who thought that a bad idea.

"More than likely scare the bejeebies out of her," I said. But to show I was a good sort, I made a little cart out of an old piece of oak I had lying about, too small for a table or anything other than a serving tray, which the wife didn't need. I sanded it down and shaped it a bit, and put on some wheels from a soapbox car I'd scavenged a while back. Then Rand mounted the dog on that.

Now, Rand hadn't done any taxidermy in years so the dog didn't look very alive. The glass eyes were ones he took from a moth-eaten goose he'd mounted on his first try at taxidermy in high school. But Dorothy took to that stuffed dog like she'd taken to the live one, and pulled it after her everywhere she went, using the plaited leash I'd made for Toto when he first came to the farm.

You squinted your eyes some, it looked like the dog was following her around. And now it didn't need much maintaining. That pleased Dorothy as much as it pleased Henry and Em.

So maybe she wasn't the only queer one in the family. After that, I kept my opinions to myself.

3.

We went on like that for three years, and the only thing to change was that Dorothy began to grow up. Grew a little prettier, too, the gap in her teeth closing so it looked more like a path than a main highway.

And then when she was thirteen, after years of near-misses with cyclones, the farmhouse was hit big. Other houses in the county had got flattened in those years, and one little town was just plain wiped off the map. People got parceled out to relatives or they moved to the East Coast, or the West and we never saw them again after that. But for some reason, Henry and Em's place had been spared year after year.

The big hit began just like the last one, except I was cleaning out the pigpen. Rand was working on Henry's plow, which had developed a kind of hiccup between rows, as had his old plow-horse, Frank. Henry and Stan were out checking on fencing and they came roaring back, Henry shouting, "In the cellar! Everyone. It's the biggest twister I've ever seen and it's heading right this way. I'm going to let the horses and cows out into the field."

We piled in one on top of another, Henry coming in last.

About a minute later, Stan noticed that Dorothy wasn't with us. We found out much, much later that she'd gone under her bed to pull out that little dog on wheels. She hadn't played with it for a couple of years. Too grown up, I'd guess. But she wasn't about to have Toto taken from her again.

Well, we kept the trapdoor open for her till the wind hit, howling like a freight train running right through the center of the house. And then Henry reached up and slammed the door down.

That left Dorothy under her bed, the dog on wheels clutched in her arms. Which, under the usual circumstances, might have been just fine.

But there was nothing usual about *this* wind. It was a killer. Should have had its name on a reward poster. It was that bad.

It just lifted up the little house and carried it away. Henry had never gotten it back on the cinderblocks but that didn't seem to matter. Off that house flew, with Dorothy in it. And we never saw the house again.

We sat cowering in the hole, in the dark. Me, I wondered about my wife and her mother and our chickens but there was nothing we could do except sit while that wind fretted and banged and gnawed around the house.

When the noise was finally gone, and Henry lifted the trapdoor, the light nearly blinded us. We were expecting to find ourselves in the house, of course.

"Lord's sake," Em whispered, as if the wind had taken her voice away, too. "There's nothing left." She was too shocked to weep.

But surprising us all, including himself, Henry began to sob, though the only word he got out, over and over and over again, was "Dorothy, Dorothy, Dorothy." Who would have guessed he loved that little child so.

They posted notices all the way to Kansas City, that being the direction the wind had been tracked. And Henry even hired a private detective to search for her. But she was as gone as if she'd never been.

In less than a week, there was a four-room house-raising that all the neighbors attended. One room was set aside for Dorothy. The neighbors brought pies and hot-pots and cider. We men got that new house up and tight in a day, and I did a lot of the inside woodwork, including the bed frames. It felt good to be doing what I loved best for once, being a woodman again.

The newspaper covered the house as it went up, taking some close photographs of the hearth I made, with carvings of the little dog on wheels. I got calls from all around the state for work after that, and my wife and I set a bit of money aside. Not in the banks. We didn't trust the banks any more than Henry did, so we bought land instead. I did really well for almost a year, and then some newspaper reporter wrote that I didn't have a lot of polish, meaning—I think—I couldn't make small talk with the customers. But other people thought it was a judgment on my furniture-making, so the work dried up after that, and I was glad to get my old job back with Henry.

The five of us often sat after the day's chores were done, in front of the hearth. Fire lit, cider in hand, we'd talk about where Dorothy might be now.

Em thought maybe she'd married, because she'd have been sixteen, close to seventeen. "Maybe to a lawyer," she said, "her memory all blowed away by that wind, or she would have sent us an invite. Maybe even to a doctor."

Henry shook his head. "That girl was bound to be a teacher. She read books."

Stan and Rand said, "Bank teller." Stan added, "Bank manager soon enough."

Once in a while, I would wax a bit fanciful. "Balloonist," I said once, "flying through the clouds."

Henry always laughed at my fancies, a slow laugh with little happiness in it. "I think she'd have had enough of flying through the air."

None of us said she was dead. But we all knew that was the most likely.

Em put it this way, "I hope wherever she is, she's treated well. She never did a hurtful thing to anyone."

It was as close to an epitaph as any of us wanted to go, but it was a good one.

4.

I have to say this about the predictable life: it's easier on the body, easier on the soul. We worked the seasons on the Gale farm, we drank cider and talked a bit at the end of the day. Months turned into years.

My mother-in-law went from difficult and cranky to forgetful and cranky. When she became bedridden, my wife took care of her as if she was a colicky infant, the only one we ever had.

I hoed, cleaned pigsties, walked the plow on occasion, anything Henry asked me to do I set my hand to. I rarely thought about working wood unless it was to mend fences. I mean, what was the point?

Then one afternoon, in late autumn, after the chores were all

done, we five were sitting watching the fire. We'd grown silent
with the years and with the predictability of our lives. None of us
seemed to miss the old conversations. If Dorothy was still alive,
she wasn't interesting enough to talk about anymore. Or we'd
run out of *what-ifs*, which is the way stories get started. In the
living room, the only thing contributing to the conversation
was the fire, spitting out snappy one-liners none of us tried to top.

There was a knock on the door. I wondered briefly if someone
had come to tell me my mother-in-law had died, so I stood up
to see. No use letting Em have to come face-to-face with that
particular announcement. She'd been worn down by enough bad
news in her life. I wasn't going to let her be bothered by mine.

As I walked out of the room, for the first time in months the
others all began to speculate. Their ideas followed me into the
hallway. *Police? Twister? Telegram? Doctor's assistant?*

When I opened the door, standing there was a tall, pretty
young woman, her hair in a short bob. Unlike the local farm
girls, she wore careful makeup on her face. It enhanced her odd
beauty. The women in Kansas City, the two or three times I'd
been there, used makeup as a weapon or as a disguise.

She smiled at me with strong, evenly spaced teeth. If she hadn't
been carrying the little dog on wheels, along with a satchel, I
wouldn't have known her.

"Dorothy!" I cried out, my voice carrying back into the living
room where suddenly everything went silent—even the fire.

"Come on in," I said, as if this was an everyday visit, as if it was
my house to invite her into.

She entered, looking around in wonder. "Golly!" is all she said.

It took me a minute to remember that this wasn't the old
farmhouse she recalled. "The neighbors all helped to build it after
. . . after . . ." I hesitated.

"After I was blown away." So she *had* remembered. I wondered
why it'd taken her so long to get in touch. I mean it had been
seven years after all.

Before I could ask, the hallway was as crowded as the cellar-hole had once been. Everyone was touching Dorothy, her hair, her shoulders, her hands, saying her name in soft wonder.

I pulled back, not trusting this part of the story. Could such a glamorous creature really be our Dorothy? And why had she returned, why now?

They drew her into the living room, where the fire had resumed its one-sided conversation, only this time everyone ignored its snap.

"Where have you been, Dorothy?" Rand was the only one innocent enough to just come right out and say it. "All this time?"

Her next words surprised us. "Why, in the Emerald Circus. The performers heard a huge crash near their Missouri campsite, and found me, under a tree, pieces of wood scattered all around. My memory was as shattered as the farmhouse. All my clothes blown away but my shoes. The little people got to me first."

I refused to dignify her story with questions, but no one else had the same reaction.

"Little people?" asked Em.

"Dwarfs, used to be miners in Munich. Though they don't like to be called so," Dorothy said. "Just little people."

"Oh," said Em, "the clowns who run around through the audience. I've seen them. You did, too, Dorothy," she said. "We went to the circus once. Together."

Dorothy got an odd look on her face "I don't remember." It turned out to be something she was to say many times over the next weeks.

If Dorothy was to be believed, her life in the circus, her seven years, were like a dream. Little people. A freak show full of oddities. Wire walkers. A lion who jumped through hoops. Dancing dogs. Bareback riders. Even an elephant.

"And yet," she'd add quickly, "all just people. Like you, like me." Then she laughed softly. "The dogs, the horses, the lions, the elephant—not them of course."

Well, of course circus folk are just people, I thought, *only* not *like us at all.* Though I didn't say it out loud.

Dorothy had become part of the show, dressing in tights and a fitted bodice, silver shoes.

"Tights! Land sakes!" Em said, her hand on her heart as if she was going to faint.

Dorothy even got to wear a blonde wig.

"Think of that!" Henry put in.

Her toenails were painted gold.

"Real gold?" asked Rand.

"Don't be stupid," Stan said, pounding a fist into his brother's shoulder.

At first Dorothy had just walked around the ring, smiling at the folks in the audience, turning and turning like a whirligig. But all the while, when it wasn't show time, she practiced wire-walking with the Italian acrobats, the Antonioni Family, until she was good enough to become part of their act. They even wanted her to marry their son, Little Tony, and carry on the family tradition.

"But I told them I was too young and besides, I wasn't the marrying kind." She smiled at Uncle Henry. "I knew that one day I would remember where I came from and want to go back there." She opened her arms and turned around and around, like she was still performing. "And here I am."

"Here you are," Henry said, grinning.

But I wondered if it was true.

All of it.

Any of it.

Dorothy stayed, taking her turn at the house chores, gathering eggs, making lunches, cooking soups, plucking chickens. The usual. She seemed content.

But then, about a month later, she convinced Stan to get a bunch of strands of strong wire, which she braided together. Then he stretched the wire from one part of the pigsty fence all the way across to the other, nailing it down hard on each end.

We watched as she climbed onto the fence, wearing overalls and a silver shirt. Those little silver dancing slippers on her feet.

The piglets looked up at her squealing, but the sow seemed unconcerned.

I was probably the only one who thought we were going to be picking her out of the pigpen, covered with mud.

She started off cautiously, one small slippered foot after another, testing the tightness of the wire. But after about three steps, she walked as if going along a wide asphalt road. Even stopped in the middle to turn like a whirligig, arms wide open, before lifting one leg high in the air behind her.

"Arabesque," she said, as if that was an explanation.

When she reached the other side of the pen, we all broke into applause.

So the wire-walking at least was true. I told my wife Amelia about it and she insisted on coming over to watch the next time Dorothy did it, which was every Saturday after that. Amelia watched Dorothy on the wire with an intensity she'd never shown for anything else, then turned to me saying it was a homey piece of magic and she wanted to learn it. I put my foot down. Something I rarely ever do. I didn't fancy her falling in the mud. It would have been me having to clean her up. Somehow, at our ages, I didn't like the sound of that.

5.

About three months after that, I was coming back for lunch from where I'd been fixing fences—the prairie wind just devils the wires. I was heading to the cabbage field to give the cabbages a good soaking. Suddenly I noticed a figure standing at the farmhouse door, just fixing to knock. I could only see her from the back, but she looked to be a blonde-haired, shapely woman. In fact her hair wasn't just blonde, but an ashy white-blonde, a color you don't see on a grown woman unless she spends a lot of time at the hairdresser's.

"Pardon me, miss," I called, wondering who it might be, guessing she was there to visit Dorothy.

She turned and I got the shock of my life, because she was sporting a beard. Not just a few face hairs, like some women get in later life. My mother-in-law has them sprouting from her chin and from a mole on her cheek. But a full beard, kind of reddish color, the bottom half of which was tied off with a pink bow.

A bearded lady, by golly, I thought. *Freak show standard.* I'd always figured they were just regular women in makeup. Or a womanish man dressed in female clothes. This one had the bluest eyes I'd ever seen—an eerie color really.

"Are you looking for Dorothy?" I asked, to cover my embarrassment.

"Dottie, yes, is she here? It's where I dropped her off some months ago," the bearded lady said. "She hasn't written since . . ."

"She does that," I said nodding. "We didn't hear from her for seven years."

"Well, it took her all that time to remember," she told me.

I thought that made for a convenient memory, but said nothing.

She held out her hand. "Ozmandia," she said.

"Circus name? Last name? "

She smiled, her teeth pearly above the beard. "Actually, Shirley Osmond, so you're kind of right either way."

The door opened and Em looked out. It took her a moment to put it all together. Then her hand went to her heart. "My word . . ."

"I'm a friend of Dottie's," Ozmandia said, but even as she said it, Dorothy pushed past Em and threw herself into the bearded lady's arms.

"Ozzy!" she cried. "I've missed you so."

"Little bird," the bearded lady said and kissed Dorothy full on the lips, the way a man might do. Then she drew back and looked at Dorothy critically. "You've gained some weight. It might make you too heavy for the wire but it suits you."

"I've been practicing."

"She has," said Em. "And performing."

"Then no potatoes," Ozmandia said. "No bread. No starch."

"What's starch?" Em asked. The only starch she knew was what she ironed with.

"I'll make a list," Ozmandia told her.

She turned to Dorothy. "We're starting again next month. Barnum and Bailey have bought the old man out."

"No more Mr. Wizard?" Dorothy said. "But it's *his* circus."

"He's retiring to Florida," said Ozmandia. "For what they paid him, he can afford it. Him and that elephant."

"Will you stay awhile?" Dorothy said, speaking to her circus friend as if the rest of us hardly mattered. And indeed, probably we didn't.

"Just tonight, Baby Bird," Ozmandia said. "I'm getting around to everyone."

"But I'm special," Dorothy said.

"You always were, falling out of the sky that way." She turned to Em. "I assume, madam, that it is all right for me to stay the one night? I can sleep in Dottie's bed with her. It's an old circus custom."

I bet it is, I thought, but didn't say it aloud.

She stayed two nights, and no one spoke about it until long after. That first evening, being a Saturday, Dorothy did her wire walk over the pigsty. Ozamandia played a flute as Dorothy performed, and though you probably won't believe it, the sow and piglets got up on their hind trotters and danced.

Amelia was there as usual, of course, and she and Ozmandia

became instant pals, both of them enthusing over Dorothy's talents.

When we walked home, I tried to hold Amelia's hand, feeling a sudden tenderness toward her I hadn't felt in years, but she pulled her hand away.

"I can't," she said. "I just can't anymore."

Amelia's mother died that very night, with such a peaceful smile on her face, she hardly looked like the same woman. Only Henry and Em, Stan and Rand, and Dorothy came to the funeral.

Ozmandia sent a message the next month and Dorothy packed up her carpetbag, ready to leave the next morning. Stan was driving her by cart into the city; she was taking a steam engine train from there.

Em watched her go dry-eyed, but Henry was sobbing enough for the two of them. Stan and Rand were openmouthed, breathing hard.

I was there as well, watching Amelia go with her.

"Tom," she'd told me last night, "I have never done anything for myself before. First there was mother, then there was you. I've taken the housekeeping money. I've been saving some for months. Sell Mother's house for me and you keep half. Start that woodworking business for real this time. It's the only thing you've ever really loved. I'll write and tell you where to send my portion when I know."

"Are you going to be a wire-walker?" I asked.

"I'll take tickets, sell popcorn, clean out the lion's cage. I'll do anything they need, wear many hats, many heads. After all," she said, "I'm well practiced in that sort of thing."

And maybe she was, after all.

"Perhaps eventually they'll let me try the wire." She smiled. "Even though I'm probably too old."

"Never too old," I said, remembering her on our wedding day.

"Tom, you never could tell a lie," she said. "Don't start now."

The cart pulled away and rolled down the dusty road, making it look for a minute like little imps were running behind. If you once start thinking that way about the world, it seems to go on and on.

I watched till the cart with my wife in it was out of sight. When I turned back, Henry was still standing there, the little dog on wheels cradled in his arms. I guess Dorothy didn't need it anymore.

I guess Henry did.

A KNOT OF TOADS

"*March 1931: Late on Saturday night,*" the old man had written, "*a toad came into my study and looked at me with goggled eyes, reflecting my candlelight back at me. It seemed utterly unafraid. Although nothing so far seems linked with this appearance, I have had enough formidable visitants to know this for a harbinger.*"

A harbinger of spring, I would have told him, but I arrived too late to tell him anything. I'd been summoned from my Cambridge rooms to his little whitewashed stone house with its red pantile roof overlooking St. Monans harbor. The summons had come from his housekeeper, Mrs. Marr, in a frantic early morning phone call. Hers was from the town's one hotel, to me in the porter's room, which boasted the only telephone at our college.

I was a miserable ten hours getting there. All during the long train ride, though I tried to pray for him, I could not, having given up that sort of thing long before leaving Scotland. Loss of faith, lack of faith—that had been my real reason for going away from home. Taking up a place at Girton College had only been an excuse.

What I had wanted to do this return was to mend our fences before it was too late to mend anything at all. Father and I had broken so many fences—stones, dykes, stiles, and all—that the mending would have taken more than the fortnight's holiday I had planned for later in the summer. But I'd been summoned home early this March because, as Mrs. Marr said, Father had had a bad turn.

"A *verrry* bad turn," was what she'd actually said, before the line had gone dead, her r's rattling like a kettle on the boil. In her understated way, she might have meant anything from a twisted ankle to a major heart attack.

The wire that had followed, delivered by a man with a limp and a harelip, had been from my father's doctor, Ewan Kinnear. "Do not delay," it read. Still, there was no diagnosis.

Even so, I did not delay. We'd had no connection in ten years beside a holiday letter exchange. Me to him, not the other way round. But the old man was my only father. I was his only child.

He was dead by the time I got there, and Mrs. Marr stood at the doorway of the house wringing her hands, her black hair caught up in a net. She had not aged a day since I last saw her.

"So ye've left it too late, Janet," she cried. "And wearing green I see."

I looked down at my best dress, a soft green linen now badly creased with travel.

She shook her head at me, and only then did I remember. In St. Monans they always said, "After green comes grief."

"I didn't know he was that ill. I came as fast as I could."

But Mrs. Marr's face showed her disdain for my excuse. Her eyes narrowed and she didn't put out her hand. She'd always been on Father's side, especially in the matter of my faith. "His old heart's burst in twa." She was of the old school in speech as well as faith.

"His heart was stone, Maggie, and well you know it." A

widow, she'd waited twenty-seven years, since my mother died birthing me, for the old man to notice her. She must be old herself now.

"Stane can still feel pain," she cried.

"What pain?" I asked.

"Of your leaving."

What good would it have done to point out I'd left more than ten years earlier and he'd hardly noticed? He'd had a decade more of calcification, a decade more of pouring over his bloody old books—the Latin texts of apostates and heretics. A decade more of filling notebooks with his crabbed script.

A decade more of ignoring his only child.

My God, I thought, meaning no appeal to a deity but a simple swear, *I am still furious with him. It's no wonder I've never married.* Though I'd had chances. Plenty of them. Well, two that were real enough.

I went into the house, and the smell of candle wax and fish and salt sea were as familiar to me as though I'd never left. But there was another smell, too.

Death.

And something more.

It was fear. But I was not to know that till later.

The study where evidently he'd died, sitting up in his chair, was a dark place, even when the curtains were drawn back, which had not been frequent in my childhood. Father liked the close, wood-paneled room, made closer by the ever-burning fire. I'd been allowed in there only when being punished, standing just inside the doorway, with my hands clasped behind me, to listen to my sins being counted. My sins were homey ones, like shouting in the hallway, walking too loudly by his door, or refusing to learn my verses from the Bible. I was far too innocent a child for more than that.

Even at five and six and seven I'd been an unbeliever. Not having a mother had made me so. How could I worship a God whom both Mrs. Marr and my father assured me had so wanted Mother, He'd called her away? A selfish God, that, who had listened to his own desires and not mine. Such a God was not for me. Not then. Not now.

I had a sudden urge—me, a postgraduate in a prestigious university who should have known better—to clasp my hands behind me and await my punishment.

But, I thought, *the old punisher is dead. And—if he's to be believed—gone to his own punishment.* Though I was certain that the only place he had gone was to the upstairs bedroom where he was laid out, awaiting my instructions as to his burial.

I went into every other room of the house but that bedroom, memory like an old fishing line dragging me on. The smells, the dark moody smells, remained the same, though Mrs. Marr had a good wood fire burning in the grate, not peat, a wee change in this changeless place. But everything else was so much smaller than I remembered, my little bedroom at the back of the house the smallest of them all.

To my surprise, nothing in my bedroom had been removed. My bed, my toys—the little wooden doll with jointed arms and legs I called Annie, my ragged copy of *Rhymes and Tunes for Little Folks*, the boxed chess set just the size for little hands, my cloth bag filled with buttons—the rag rug, the overworked sampler on the wall. All were the same. I was surprised to even find one of my old pinafores and black stockings in the wardrobe. I charged Mrs. Marr with more sentiment than sense. It was a shrine to the child that I'd been, not the young woman who had run off. It had to have been Mrs. Marr's idea. Father would never have countenanced false gods.

Staring out of the low window, I looked off toward the sea.

A fog sat on the horizon, white and patchy. Below it the sea was a deep, solitary blue. Spring comes early to the East Neuk but summer stays away. I guessed that pussy willows had already appeared around the edges of the lochans, snowdrops and aconite decorating the inland gardens.

Once I'd loved to stare out at that sea, escaping the dark brooding house whenever I could, even in a cutting wind, the kind that could raise bruises. Down I'd go to the beach to play amongst the yawls hauled up on the high wooden trestles, ready for tarring. Once I'd dreamed of going off to sea with the fishermen, coming home to the harbor in the late summer light, and seeing the silver scales glinting on the beach. Though of course fishing was not a woman's job. Not then, not now. A woman in a boat was unthinkable even this far into the twentieth century. St. Monans is firmly eighteenth century and likely to remain so forever.

But I'd been sent off to school, away from the father who found me a loud and heretical discomfort. At first it was just a few towns away, to St. Leonard's in St. Andrews, but as I was a boarder—my father's one extravagance—it might as well have been across the country, or the ocean, as far as seeing my father was concerned. And there I'd fallen in love with words in books.

Words—not water, not wind.

In that way I showed myself to be my father's daughter. Only I never said so to him, nor he to me.

Making my way back down the stairs, I overheard several folk in the kitchen. They were speaking of those things St. Monans folk always speak of, no matter their occupations: fish and weather.

"There's been nae herring in the firth this winter," came a light man's voice. "Nane." Dr. Kinnear.

"It's a bitter wind to keep the men at hame, the fish awa," Mrs. Marr agreed.

Weather and the fishing. Always the same.

But a third voice, one I didn't immediately recognize, a rumbling growl of a voice, added, "Does she know?"

"Do I know what?" I asked, coming into the room where the big black-leaded grate threw out enough heat to warm the entire house. "How Father died?"

I stared at the last speaker, a stranger I thought, but somehow familiar. He was tall for a St. Monans man, but dressed as one of the fisherfolk, in dark trousers, a heavy white sweater, thick white sea stockings. And he was sunburnt like them, too, with eyes the exact blue of the April sea, gathered round with laugh lines. A ginger mustache, thick and full, hung down the sides of his mouth like a parenthesis.

"By God, Alec Hughes," I said, startled to have remembered, surprised that I could have forgotten. He grinned.

When we'd been young—very young—Alec and I were inseparable. Never mind that boys and girls never played together in St. Monans. Boys from the Bass, girls from the May, the old folk wisdom went. The Bass Rock, the Isle of May, the original separation of the sexes. Apart at birth and ever after. Yet Alec and I had done everything together: messed about with the boats, played cards, built sand castles, fished with *pelns*—shore crabs about to cast their shells—and stolen jam pieces from his mother's kitchen to eat down by one of the gates in the drystone dykes. We'd even often hied off to the low cliff below the ruins of Andross Castle to look for *croupies*, fossils, though whether we ever found any I couldn't recall. When I'd been sent away to school, he'd stayed on in St. Monans, going to Anstruther's Waid Academy in the next town but one, until he was old enough—I presumed—to join the fishing fleet, like his father before him. His father was a stern and dour soul, a Temperance man who used to preach in the open air.

88

Alec had been the first boy to kiss me, my back against the stone windmill down by the salt pans. And until I'd graduated from St. Leonard's, the only boy to do so, though I'd made up for that since.

"I thought, Jan," he said slowly, "that God was not in your vocabulary."

"Except as a swear," I retorted. "Good to see you, too, Alec."

Mrs. Marr's eyebrows both rose considerably, like fulmars over the green-grey sea of her eyes.

Alec laughed, and it was astonishing how that laugh reminded me of the boy who'd stayed behind. "Yes," he said. "Do you know how your father died?"

"Heart attack, so Mrs. Marr told me."

I stared at the three of them. Mrs. Marr was wringing her hands again, an oddly old-fashioned motion at which she seemed well practiced. Dr. Kinnear polished his eyeglasses with a large white piece of cloth, his flyaway eyebrows proclaiming his advancing age. And Alec—had I remembered how blue his eyes were? Alec nibbled on the right end of his mustache.

"Did I say that?" Mrs. Marr asked. "Bless me, I didna."

And indeed, she hadn't. She'd been more poetic.

"*Burst in twa*, you said." I smiled, trying to apologize for misspeaking. Not a good trait in a scholar.

"Indeed. Indeed." Mrs. Marr's wrangling hands began again. Any minute I supposed she would break out into a psalm. I remembered how her one boast was that she'd learned them all by heart as a child and never forgot a one of them.

"A shock, I would have said," Alec added.

"A fright," the doctor added.

"Really? Is that the medical term?" I asked. "What in St. Monans could my father possibly be frightened of?"

Astonishingly, Mrs. Marr began to wail then, a high, thin keening that went on and on till Alec put his arm around her and marched her over to the stone sink where he splashed her face with cold water and she quieted at once. Then she turned to the blackened kettle squalling on the grate and started to make us all tea.

I turned to the doctor, who had his glasses on now, which made him look like a somewhat surprised barn owl. "What do you really mean, Dr. Kinnear?"

"Have you nae seen him yet?" he asked, his head gesturing towards the back stairs.

"I . . . I couldn't," I admitted. But I said no more. How could I tell this man I hardly knew that my father and I were virtual strangers. No—it was more than that. I was afraid of my father dead as I'd never been alive. Because now he knew for certain whether he was right or I was, about God and Heaven and the rest.

"Come," said Dr. Kinnear in a voice that seemed permanently gentle. He held out a hand and led me back up the stairs and down the hall to my father's room. Then he went in with me and stood by my side as I looked down.

My father was laid out on his bed, the Scottish double my mother had died in, the one he'd slept in every night of his adult life except the day she'd given birth, the day she died.

Like the house, he was much smaller than I remembered. His wild, white hair lay untamed around his head in a kind of corolla. The skin of his face was parchment stretched over bone. That great prow of a nose was, in death, strong enough to guide a ship in. Thankfully his eyes were shut. His hands were crossed on his chest. He was dressed in an old dark suit. I remembered it well.

"He doesn't look afraid," I said. Though he didn't look peaceful either. Just dead.

"Once he'd lost the stiffness, I smoothed his face a bit," the doctor told me. "Smoothed it out. Otherwise Mrs. Marr would no have settled."

"Settled?"

He nodded. "She found him at his desk, stone dead. Ran down the road screaming all the way to the pub. And lucky I was there, having a drink with friends. I came up to see yer father sitting up in his chair, with a face so full of fear, I looked around mysel' to discover the cause of it."

"And did you?"

His blank expression said it all. He simply handed me a pile of five notebooks. "These were on the desk in front of him. Some of the writing is in Latin, which I have but little of. Perhaps ye can read it, being the scholar. Mrs. Marr has said that they should be thrown on the fire, or at least much of them scored out. But I told her that had to be yer decision and Alec agrees."

I took the notebooks, thinking that this was what had stolen my father from me and now was all I had of him. But I said none of that aloud. After glancing over at the old man again, I asked, "May I have a moment with him?" My voice cracked on the final word.

Dr. Kinnear nodded again and left the room.

I went over to the bed and looked down at the silent body. *The old dragon*, I thought, *has no teeth.* Then I heard a sound, something so tiny I scarcely registered it. Turning, I saw a toad by the bedfoot.

I bent down and picked it up. "Nothing for you here, *puddock*," I said, reverting to the old Scots word. Though I'd worked so hard to lose my accent and vocabulary, here in my father's house the old way of speech came flooding back. Shifting the books to one hand, I picked the toad up with the other. Then, I tiptoed out of the door as if my father would have minded the sound of my footsteps.

Once outside, I set the toad gently in the garden, or the remains of the garden, now so sadly neglected, its vines running rampant across what was once an arbor of white roses and red. I watched as it hopped under some large dock leaves and, quite effectively, disappeared.

Later that afternoon my father's body was taken away by three burly men for its chesting, being placed into its coffin and the lid screwed down. Then it would lie in the cold kirk till the funeral the next day.

Once he was gone from the house, I finally felt I could look in his journals. I might have sat comfortably in the study, but I'd never been welcomed there before, so didn't feel it my place now. The kitchen and sitting room were more Mrs. Marr's domain than mine. And if I never had to go back into the old man's bedroom, it would be years too soon for me.

So I lay in my childhood bed, the covers up to my chin, and read by the flickering lamplight. Mrs. Marr, bless her, had brought up a warming pan which she came twice to refill. And she brought up as well a pot of tea and jam pieces and several slabs of good honest cheddar.

"I didna think ye'd want a big supper."

She was right. Food was the last thing on my mind.

After she left the room, I took a silver hip flask from under my pillow where I'd hidden it, and then poured a hefty dram of whisky into the teapot. I would need more than Mrs. Marr's offerings to stay warm this night. Outside the sea moaned as it pushed past the skellies, on its way to the shore. I'd all but forgotten that sound. It made me smile.

I read the last part of the last journal first, where Father talked about the toad, wondering briefly if it was the very same toad I had found at his bedfoot. But it was the bit right after, where he spoke of "formidable visitants," that riveted me. What had he meant? From the tone of it, I didn't think he meant any of our St. Monans neighbors.

The scholar in me asserted itself, and I turned to the first of the journals, marked 1926, some five years earlier. There was one book for each year. I started with that first notebook and read long into the night.

The journals were not easy to decipher, for my father's handwriting was crabbed with age and, I expect, arthritis. The early works were splotchy and, in places, faded. Also he had inserted sketchy pictures and diagrams. Occasionally he'd written whole paragraphs in corrupted Latin, or at least in a dialect unknown to me.

What he seemed engaged upon was a study of a famous trial of local witches in 1590, supervised by King James VI himself. The VI of Scotland, for he was Mary Queen of Scots' own son, and Queen Elizabeth's heir.

The witches, some ninety in all according to my father's notes, had been accused of sailing over the Firth to North Berwick in riddles—sieves, I think he meant—to plot the death of the king by raising a storm when he sailed to Denmark. However, I stumbled so often over my Latin translations, I decided I needed a dictionary. And me a classics scholar.

So halfway through the night, I rose and, taking the lamp, made my way through the cold dark, tiptoeing so as not to wake Mrs. Marr. Nothing was unfamiliar beneath my bare feet. The kitchen stove would not have gone out completely, only filled with gathering coal and kept minimally warm. All those years of my childhood came rushing back. I could have gone into the study without the lamp, I suppose. But to find the book I needed, I'd have to have light.

And lucky indeed I took it, for in its light it I saw—gathered on the floor of my father's study—a group of toads throwing strange shadows up against the bookshelves. I shuddered to think what might have happened had I stepped barefooted amongst them.

But how had they gotten in? And was the toad I'd taken into the garden amongst them? Then I wondered aloud at what such a gathering should be called. I'd heard of a murder of crows, an exaltation of larks. Perhaps toads came in a congregation? For that is what they looked like, a squat congregation, huddled together, nodding their heads, and waiting on the minister in this most unlikely of kirks.

It was too dark even with the lamp, and far too late, for me to round them up. So I sidestepped them and, after much searching, found the Latin dictionary where it sat cracked open on my father's desk. I grabbed it up, avoided the congregation of toads, and went out the door. When I looked back, I could still see the odd shadows dancing along the walls.

I almost ran back to my bed, shutting the door carefully behind me. I didn't want that dark presbytery coming in, as if they could possibly hop up the stairs like the frog in the old tale, demanding to be taken to my little bed.

But the shock of my father's death and the long day of travel, another healthy swallow of my whisky, as well as that bizarre huddle of toads, all seemed to combine to put me into a deep sleep. If I dreamed, I didn't remember any of it. I woke to one of those dawn choruses of my childhood, comprised of blackbirds, song thrushes, gulls, rooks, and jackdaws, all arguing over who should wake me first.

For a moment I couldn't recall where I was. Eyes closed, I listened to the birds, so different from the softer, more lyrical sounds outside my Cambridge windows. But I woke fully in the knowledge that I was back in my childhood home, that my father was dead and to be buried that afternoon if possible, as I had requested of the doctor and Mrs. Marr, and I had only hours to make things tidy in my mind. Then I would be away from St. Monans and its small-mindedness, back to Cambridge where I truly belonged.

I got out of bed, washed, dressed in the simple black dress I always travel with, a black bandeau on my fair hair, and went into the kitchen to make myself some tea.

Mrs. Marr was there before me, sitting on a hardback chair and knitting a navy blue guernsey sweater with its complicated patterning. She set the steel needles down and handed me a full cup, the tea nearly black even with its splash of milk. There was a heaping bowl of porridge, sprinkled generously with salt, plus bread slathered with golden syrup.

"Thank you," I said. It would have done no good to argue that I drank coffee now; nor did I like either oatmeal or treacle, and never ate till noon. Besides, I was suddenly ravenous. "What do you need me to do?" I asked between mouthfuls, stuffing them in the way I'd done as a youngster.

"'Tis all arranged," she said, taking up the needles again. No proper St. Monans woman was ever idle long. "Though sooner than is proper. But all to accommodate ye, he'll be in the kirkyard this afternoon. Lucky for ye it's a Sunday, or we couldna do it. The men are home from fishing." She was clearly not pleased with me. "Ye just need to be there at the service. Not that many will come. He was no generous with his company." By which she meant he had few friends. Nor relatives except me.

"Then I'm going to walk down by the water this morning," I told her. "Unless you have something that needs doing. I want to clear my head."

"Aye, ye would."

Was that condemnation or acceptance? Who could tell? Perhaps she meant I was still the thankless child she remembered. Or that I was like my father. Or that she wanted only to see the back of me, sweeping me from her domain so she could clean and bake without my worrying presence. I thanked her again for the meal, but she wanted me gone. As I had been for the past ten years. And I was as eager to be gone as she was to have me. The funeral was not till mid afternoon.

"There are toads in the study," I said as I started out the door.

"Toads?" She looked startled. Or perhaps frightened.

"*Puddocks.* A congregation of them."

Her head cocked to one side. "Och, ye mean a knot. A knot of toads."

A knot. Of course. I should have remembered. "Shall I put them out?" At least I could do that for her.

She nodded. "Aye."

I found a paper sack and went into the study, but though I looked around for quite some time, I couldn't find the toads anywhere. If I hadn't still had the Latin dictionary in my bedroom, I would have thought my night visit amongst them and my scare from their shadows had been but a dream.

"All gone," I called to Mrs. Marr before slipping out through the front door and heading toward the strand.

Nowhere in St. Monans is far from the sea. I didn't realize how much the sound of it was in my bones until I moved to Cambridge. Or how much I'd missed that sound till I slept the night in my old room.

I found my way to the foot of the church walls where boats lay upturned, looking like beached dolphins. A few of the older men, past their fishing days, sat with their backs against the salted stone, smoking silently, and staring out to the grey slatey waters of the Firth. Nodding to them, I took off along the beach. Overhead gulls squabbled, and far out, near the Bass Rock, I could see gannets diving head-first into the water.

A large boat, some kind of yacht, had just passed the Bass and was sailing west majestically toward a mooring, probably in South Queensferry. I wondered who would be sailing these waters in such a ship.

But then I was interrupted by the wind sighing my name. Or so I thought at first. Then I looked back at the old kirk on the cliff above me. Someone was waving at me in the ancient kirkyard. It was Alec.

He signaled that he was coming down to walk with me, and as I waited, I thought about what a handsome man he'd turned into. *But a fisherman*, I reminded myself, a bit of the old snobbery biting me on the back of the neck. St. Monans, like the other fishing villages of the East Neuk, was made up of three classes—fisherfolk, farmers, and the shopkeepers and tradesmen. My father being a scholar was outside of them all, which meant that as his daughter, I belonged to none of them either.

Still, in this place, where I was once so much a girl of the town—from the May—I felt my heart give a small stutter. I remembered that first kiss, so soft and sweet and innocent, the windmill hard against my back. My last serious relationship had been almost a year ago, and I was more than ready to fall in love again. Even at the foot of my father's grave. But not with a fisherman. Not in St. Monans.

Alec found his way down to the sand and came toward me. "Off to find *croupies*?" he called.

I laughed. "The only fossil I've found recently has been my father," I said, then bit my lower lip at his scowl.

"He was nae a bad man, Jan," he said, catching up to me. "Just undone by his reading."

I turned a glare at him. "Do you think reading an ailment then?"

He put up his hands palms towards me. "Whoa, lass. I'm a big reader myself. But what the old man had been reading lately had clearly unnerved him. He couldna put it into context. Mrs. Marr said as much before you came. These last few months he'd stayed away from the pub, from the kirk, from everyone who'd known him well. No one kenned what he'd been on about."

I wondered what sort of thing Alec would be reading. *The fishing report? The local paper?* Feeling out of sorts, I said sharply, "Well, I was going over his journals last night and what he's been on about are the old North Berwick witches."

Alec's lips pursed. "The ones who plotted to blow King James off the map." It was a statement, not a question.

"The very ones."

"Not a smart thing for the unprepared to tackle."

I wondered if Alec had become as hag-ridden and superstitious as any St. Monans fisherman. Ready to turn home from his boat if he met a woman on the way. Or not daring to say "salmon" or "pig" and instead speaking of "red fish" and "curly tail," or shouting out "Cauld iron!" at any mention of them. All the East Neuk tip-leavings I was glad to be shed of.

He took the measure of my disapproving face, and laughed. "Ye take me for a gowk," he said. "But there are more things in heaven and earth, Janet, than are dreamt of in yer philosophy."

I laughed as Shakespeare tumbled from his lips. Alec could always make me laugh. "Pax," I said.

He reached over, took my hand, gave it a squeeze. "Pax." Then he dropped it again as we walked along the beach, a comfortable silence between us.

The tide had just turned and was heading out. Gulls, like satisfied housewives, sat happily in the receding waves. One lone boat was on the horizon, a small fishing boat, not the yacht I had seen earlier, which must already be coming into its port. The sky was that wonderful spring blue, without a threatening cloud, not even the fluffy Babylonians, as the fishermen called them.

"Shouldn't you be out there?" I said, pointing at the boat as we passed by the smoky fish-curing sheds.

"I rarely get out there anymore," he answered, not looking at me but at the sea. "Too busy until summer. And why old man Sinclair is fishing when the last of the winter herring have been hauled in, I canna fathom."

I turned toward him. "Too busy with what?"

He laughed. "Och, Janet, yer so caught up in yer own preconceptions, ye canna see what's here before yer eyes."

I didn't answer right away, and the moment stretched between us, as the silence had before. Only this was not comfortable. At last I said, "Are you too busy to help me solve the mystery of my father's death?"

"Solve the mystery of his life first," he told me, "and the mystery of his death will inevitably be revealed." Then he touched his cap, nodded at me, and strolled away.

I was left to ponder what he said. Or what he meant. I certainly wasn't going to chase after him. I was too proud to do that. Instead, I went back to the house, changed my shoes, made myself a plate of bread and cheese. There was no wine in the house. Mrs. Marr was as Temperance as Alec's old father had been. But I found some miserable sherry hidden in my father's study. It smelled like turpentine, so I made do with fresh milk, taking the plate and glass up to my bedroom, to read some more of my father's journals until it was time to bury him.

It is not too broad a statement to say that Father was clearly out of his mind. For one, he was obsessed with local witches. For another, he seemed to believe in them. While he spared a few paragraphs for Christian Dote, St. Monans's homegrown witch of the 1640s, and a bit more about the various Anstruther, St. Andrews, and Crail trials—listing the hideous tortures, and executions, of hundreds of poor old women in his journal entries—it was the earlier North Berwick crew who really seemed to capture his imagination. By the third year's journal, I could see that he obviously considered the North Berwick witchery evil real, whereas the others, a century later, he dismissed as deluded or senile old women, as deluded and senile as the men who hunted them.

Here is what he wrote about the Berwick corps: *"They were a scabrous bunch, these ninety greedy women and six men, wanting no more than what they considered their due: a king and his bride dead in the sea, a kingdom in ruins, themselves set up in high places."*

"Oh, Father," I whispered, "what a noble mind is here o'erthrown," for whatever problems I'd had with him—and they were many—I had always admired his intelligence.

He described the ceremonies they indulged in, and they were awful. In the small North Berwick church, fueled on wine and sex, the witches had begun a ritual to call up a wind that would turn over the royal ship and drown King James. First they'd christened a cat with the name of Hecate, while black candles flickered fitfully along the walls of the apse and nave. Then they tortured the poor creature by passing it back and forth across a flaming hearth. Its elf-knotted hair caught fire and burned slowly, and the little beastie screamed in agony. The smell must have been appalling, but he doesn't mention that. I once caught my hair on fire, bending over a stove on a cold night in Cambridge, and it was the smell that was the worst of it. It lingered in my room for days.

Then I thought of my own dear moggie at home, a sweet orange-colored puss who slept each night at my bedfoot. If anyone ever treated her the way the North Berwick witches had that poor cat, I'd be more than ready to kill. And not with any wind, either.

But there was worse yet, and I shuddered as I continued reading. One of the men, so Father reported, had dug up a corpse from the church cemetery, and with a companion had cut off the dead man's hands and feet. Then the witches attached the severed parts to the cat's paws. After this they attached the corpse's sex organs to the cat's. I could only hope the poor creature was dead by this point. After this desecration, they proceeded to a pier at the port of Leith where they flung the wee beastie into the sea.

Father wrote: *"A storm was summarily raised by this foul method, along with the more traditional knotted twine. The storm blackened the skies, with wild gales churning the sea. The howl of the wind could be heard all the way across the Firth to Fife. But the odious crew had made a deadly miscalculation. The squall caught a ship crossing from Kinghorn to Leith and smashed it to pieces all right, but it was not the king's ship. The magic lasted only long enough to kill a few innocent sailors on that first ship, and then blew itself out to sea. As for the king, he proceeded over calmer waters with his bride, arriving safely in Denmark and thence home again to write that great treatise on witchcraft,* Demonology, *and preside over a number of witch trials thereafter."*

I did not read quickly because, as I have said, parts of the journal were in a strange Latin and for those passages I needed the help of the dictionary. I was like a girl at school with lines to translate by morning, frustrated, achingly close to comprehension, but somehow missing the point. In fact, I did not understand them completely until I read them aloud. And then suddenly, as a roiled liquid settles at last, all became clear. The passages were some sort of incantation, or invitation, to the witches and to the evil they so devoutly and hideously served.

I closed the journal and shook my head. Poor Father. He wrote as if the witchcraft were fact, not a coincidence of gales from the southeast that threw up vast quantities of seaweed on the shore, and the haverings of tortured old women. Put a scold's bridle on me, and I would probably admit to intercourse with the devil. Any devil. And describe him and his nether parts as well.

But Father's words, as wild and unbelievable as they were, held me in a kind of thrall. And I would have remained on my bed reading further if Mrs. Marr hadn't knocked on the door and summoned me to his funeral.

She looked me over carefully, but for once I seemed to pass muster, my smart black Cambridge dress suitable for the occasion. She handed me a black hat. "I didna think ye'd have thought to bring one." Her lips drew down into a thin, straight line.

Standing before me, her plain black dress covered at the top by a solemn dark shawl, and on her head an astonishing hat covered with artificial black flowers, she was clearly waiting for me to say something.

"Thank you," I said at last. And it was true, bringing a hat along hadn't occurred to me at all. I took off the bandeau, and set the proffered hat on my head. It was a perfect fit, though it made me look fifteen years older, with its masses of black feathers, or so the mirror told me.

Lips pursed, she nodded at me, then turned, saying over her shoulder, "Young Mary McDougall did for him."

It took me a moment to figure out what she meant. Then I remembered. Though she must be nearer sixty than thirty, Mary McDougall had been both midwife and dresser of the dead when I was a child. So it had been she and not Mrs. Marr who must have washed my father and put him into the clothes he'd be buried in. *So Mrs. Marr missed out on her last great opportunity to touch him*, I thought.

"What do I give her?" I asked to Mrs. Marr's ramrod back.

Without turning around again, she said, "We'll give her all yer father's old clothes. She'll be happy enough with that."

"But surely a fee . . ."

She walked out of the door.

It was clear to me then that nothing had changed since I'd left. It was still the nineteenth century. Or maybe the eighteenth. I longed for the burial to be over and done with, my father's meager possessions sorted, the house sold, and me back on a train heading south.

We walked to the kirk in silence, crossing over the burn which rushed along beneath the little bridge. St. Monans has always been justifiably proud of its ancient kirk and even in this dreary moment I could remark its beauty. Some of its stonework runs back in an unbroken line to the thirteenth century.

And some of its customs, I told myself without real bitterness.

When we entered the kirk proper, I was surprised to see that Mrs. Marr had been wrong. She'd said not many would come, but the church was overfull with visitants.

We walked down to the front. As the major mourners, we commanded the first pew, Mrs. Marr, the de facto wife, and me, the runaway daughter. There was a murmur when we sat down together, not quite of disapproval, but certainly of interest. Gossip in a town like St. Monans is everybody's business.

Behind us, Alec and Dr. Kinnear were already settled in. And three men sat beside them, men whose faces I recognized, friends of my father's, but grown so old. I turned, nodded at them with, I hope, a smile that thanked them for coming. They didn't smile back.

In the other pews were fishermen and shopkeepers and the few teachers I could put a name to. But behind them was a congregation of strangers who leaned forward with an avidity that one sees only in the faces of vultures at their feed. I knew none of them and wondered if they were newcomers to the town. Or if it was just that I hadn't been home in so long, even those families who'd been here forever were strangers to me now.

Father's pine box was set before the altar and I kept my eyes averted, watching instead an ettercap, a spider, slowly spinning her way from one edge of the pulpit to the other. No one in the town would have removed her, for it was considered bad luck. It kept me from sighing, it kept me from weeping.

The minister went on for nearly half an hour, lauding my father's graces, his intelligence, his dedication. If any of us wondered about whom he was talking, we didn't answer back. But when it was over, and six large fishermen, uneasy in their Sunday clothes, stood to shoulder the coffin, I leaped up with them. Putting my hand on the pine top, I whispered, "I forgive you, Father. Do you forgive me?"

There was an audible gasp from the congregation behind me,

though I'd spoken so low, I doubted any of them—not even Alec—could have heard me. I sat down again, shaken and cold.

And then the fishermen took him off to the kirkyard, to a grave so recently and quickly carved out of the cold ground, its edges were jagged. As we stood there, a huge black cloud covered the sun. The tide was dead low and the bones of the sea, those dark grey rock skellies, showed in profusion like the spines of some prehistoric dragons.

As I held on to Mrs. Marr's arm, she suddenly started shaking so hard, I thought she would shake me off.

How she must have loved my father, I thought, and found myself momentarily jealous.

Then the coffin was lowered, and that stopped her shaking. As the first clods were shoveled into the gaping hole, she turned to me and said, "Well, that's it then."

So we walked back to the house where a half dozen people stopped in for a dram or three of whisky—brought in by Alec despite Mrs. Marr's strong disapproval. "There's a deil in every mouthful of whisky," she muttered, setting out the fresh baked shortbread and sultana cakes with a pitcher of lemonade. To mollify her, I drank the lemonade, but I was the only one.

Soon I was taken aside by an old man—Jock was his name—and told that my father had been a great gentleman though late had turned peculiar. Another, bald and wrinkled, drank his whisky down in a single gulp, before declaring loudly that my father had been "one for the books." He managed to make that sound like an affliction. One woman of a certain age, who addressed me as "Mistress," added, apropos of nothing, "He needs a lang-shankit spoon that sups wi' the Deil." Even Alec, sounding like the drone on a bagpipe, said, "Now you can get on with your own living, Jan," as if I hadn't been doing just that all along.

For a wake, it was most peculiar. No humorous anecdotes

about the dearly departed, no toasts to his soul, only half-baked praise and a series of veiled warnings.

Thank goodness no one stayed long. After the last had gone, I insisted on doing the washing up, and this time Mrs. Marr let me. And then she, too, left. Where she went I wasn't to know. One minute she was there, and the next away.

I wondered at that. After all, this was her home, certainly more than mine. I was sure she'd loved my father who, God knows, was not particularly loveable, but she walked out the door clutching her big handbag, without a word more to me; not a goodbye or "I'll not be long," or anything. And suddenly, there I was, all alone in the house for the first time in years. It was an uncomfortable feeling. I am not afraid of ghosts, but that house fairly burst with ill will, dark and brooding. So as soon as I'd tidied away the dishes, I went out, too, though not before slipping the final journal into the pocket of my overcoat and winding a long woolen scarf twice around my neck to ward the chill.

The evening was drawing in slowly, but there was otherwise a soft feel in the air, unusual for the middle of March. The East Neuk is like that—one minute still and the next a flanny wind rising.

I headed east along the coastal path, my guide the stone head of the windmill with its narrow, ruined vanes lording it over the flat land. Perhaps sentiment was leading me there, the memory of that adolescent kiss that Alec had given me, so wonderfully innocent and full of desire at the same time. Perhaps I just wanted a short, pleasant walk to the old salt pans. I don't know why I went that way. It was almost as if I were being called there.

For a moment I turned back and looked at the town behind me, which showed, from this side, how precariously the houses perched on the rocks, like gannets nesting on the Bass.

Then I turned again and took the walk slowly; it was still only ten or fifteen minutes to the windmill from the town. No boats sailed on the Firth today. I could not spot the large yacht so it must have been in its berth. And the air was so clear, I could see the Bass and the May with equal distinction. How often I'd come to this place as a child. I probably could still walk to it barefooted and without stumbling, even in the blackest night. The body has a memory of its own.

Halfway there, a solitary curlew flew up before me, and as I watched it flap away, I thought how the townsfolk would have cringed at the sight, for the bird was thought to bring bad luck, carrying away the spirits of the wicked at nightfall.

"But I've not been wicked," I cried after it, and laughed. *Or at least not wicked for a year, more's the pity.*

At last I came to the windmill with its rough stones rising high above the land. Once it had been used for pumping seawater to extract the salt. Not a particularly easy operation, it took something like thirty-two tons of water to produce one ton of salt. We'd learned all about it in primary school, of course. But the days of the salt pans were a hundred years in the past, and the poor windmill had seen better times.

Even run down, though, it was still a lovely place, with its own memories. Settling back against the mill's stone wall, I nestled down and drew out the last journal from my coat pocket. Then I began to read it from the beginning as the light slowly faded around me.

Now, I am a focused reader, which is to say that once caught up in a book, I can barely swim back up to the surface of any other consciousness. The world dims around me. Time and space compress. Like a Wellsian hero, I am drawn into an elsewhere that becomes absolute and real. So as I read my father's final journal, I was in his head and his madness so completely, I heard nothing around me, not the raucous cry of gulls nor the wash of water onto the stones far below.

So it was with a start that I came to the final page, with its mention of the goggle-eyed toad. Looking up, I found myself in the grey gloaming surrounded by nearly a hundred such toads, all staring at me with their horrid wide eyes, a hideous echo of my father's written words.

I stood up quickly, trying desperately not to squash any of the poor *puddocks*. They leaned forward like children trying to catch the warmth of a fire. Then their shadows lengthened and grew.

Please understand, there was no longer any sun and very little light. There was no moon overhead for the clouds crowded one on to the other, and the sky was completely curtained. So there should not have been any shadows at all. Yet, I state again—their shadows lengthened and grew. Shadows like and unlike the ones I had seen against my father's study walls. They grew into dark-caped creatures, almost as tall as humans yet with those goggly eyes.

I still held my father's journal in my left hand, but my right covered my mouth to keep myself from screaming. My sane mind knew it to be only a trick of the light, of the dark. It was the result of bad dreams and just having put my only living relative into the ground. But the primitive brain urged me to cry out with all my ancestors, "Cauld iron!" and run away in terror.

And still the horrid creatures grew until now they towered over me, pushing me back against the windmill, their shadowy fingers grabbing at both ends of my scarf.

Who are you? What are you? I mouthed, as the breath was forced from me. Then they pulled and pulled the scarf until they'd choked me into unconsciousness.

When I awoke, I was tied to a windmill vane, my hands bound high above me, the ropes too tight and well-knotted for any escape.

"Who are you?" I whispered aloud this time, my voice sounding froglike, raspy, hoarse. "What are you?" Though I feared I knew. "What do you want of me? Why are you here?"

In concert, their voices wailed back. "A wind! A wind!"

And then in horror all that Father had written—about the hands and feet and sex organs of the corpse being cut off and attached to the dead cat—bore down upon me. Were they about to dig poor father's corpse up? Was I to be the offering? Were we to be combined in some sort of desecration too disgusting to be named? I began to shudder within my bonds, both hot and cold. For a moment I couldn't breathe again, as if they were tugging on the scarf once more.

Then suddenly, finding some latent courage, I stood tall and screamed at them, "I'm not dead yet!" Not like my father whom they'd frightened into his grave.

They crowded around me, shadow folk with wide white eyes, laughing. "A wind! A wind!"

I kicked out at the closest one, caught my foot in its black cape, but connected with nothing more solid than air. Still that kick forced them back for a moment.

"Get away from me!" I screamed. But screaming only made my throat ache, for I'd been badly choked just moments earlier. I began to cough and it was as if a nail were being driven through my temples with each spasm.

The shadows crowded forward again, their fingers little breezes running over my face and hair, down my neck, touching my breasts.

I took a deep breath for another scream, another kick. But before I could deliver either, I heard a cry.

"Aroint, witches!"

Suddenly I distinguished the sound of running feet. Straining to see down the dark corridor that was the path to Pittenweem, I leaned against the cords that bound me. It was a voice I did and did not recognize.

The shadow folk turned as one and flowed along the path, hands before them as if they were blindly seeking the interrupter.

"Aroint, I say!"

Now I knew the voice. It was Mrs. Marr, in full cry. But her curse seemed little help and I feared that she, too, would soon be trussed up by my side.

But then, from the east, along the path nearer town, there came another call.

"Janet! Janet!" That voice I recognized at once.

"Alec . . ." I said between coughs.

The shadows turned from Mrs. Marr and flowed back, surrounding Alec, but he held something up in his hand. A bit of a gleam from a crossbar. His fisherman's knife.

The shadows fell away from him in confusion.

"Cauld iron!" he cried at them. "Cauld iron!"

So they turned to go back again towards Mrs. Marr, but she reached into her large handbag and pulled out her knitting needles. Holding them before her in the sign of a cross, she echoed Alec's cry. "Cauld iron." And then she added, her voice rising as she spoke, "Oh let the wickedness of the wicked come to an end; but establish the just: for the righteous God trieth the hearts and reigns."

I recognized it as part of a psalm, one of the many she'd presumably memorized as a child, but I could not have said which.

Then the two of them advanced on the witches, coming from east and west, forcing the awful crew to shrink down, as if melting, into dark *puddocks* once again.

Step by careful step, Alec and Mrs. Marr herded the knot of toads off the path and over the cliff's edge.

Suddenly the clouds parted and a brilliant half moon shone down on us, its glare as strong as the lighthouse on Anster's pier. I watched as the entire knot of toads slid down the embankment, some falling onto the rocks and some into the water below.

Only when the last *puddock* was gone did Alec turn to me. Holding the knife in his teeth, he reached above my head to my bound hands and began to untie the first knot.

A wind started to shake the vanes and for a second I was lifted off my feet as the mill tried to grind, though it had not done so for a century.

"Stop!" Mrs. Marr's voice held a note of desperation.

Alec turned. "Would ye leave her tied, woman? What if those shades come back again? I told ye what the witches had done before. It was all in the journals."

"No, Alec," I cried, hating myself for trusting the old ways, but changed beyond caring. "They're elfknots. Don't untie them. Don't!" I shrank away from his touch.

"Aye," Mrs. Marr said, coming over and laying light fingers on Alec's arm. "The lass is still of St. Monans though she talks like a Sassanach." She laughed. "It's no the drink and the carousing that brings the wind. That's just for fun. Nor the corpse and the cat. That's just for show. My man told me. It's the knots, he says."

"The knot of toads?" Alec asked hoarsely.

The wind was still blowing and it took Alec's hard arms around me to anchor me fast or I would have gone right around, spinning with the vanes.

Mrs. Marr came close till they were eye to eye. "The knots in the rope, lad," she said. "One brings a wind, two bring a gale, and the third . . ." She shook her head. "Ye dinna want to know about the third."

"But—" Alec began.

"Och, but me know buts, my lad. Cut between," Mrs. Marr said. "Just dinna untie them or King George's yacht at South Queensferry will go down in a squall, with the king and queen aboard, and we'll all be to blame."

He nodded and slashed the ropes with his knife, between the knots, freeing my hands. Then he lifted me down. I tried to take it all in: his arms, his breath on my cheek, the smell of him so close. I tried to understand what had happened here in the gloaming. I tried until I started to sob and he began stroking my hair, whispering, "There, lass, it's over. It's over."

"Not until we've had some tea and burned those journals," Mrs. Marr said. "I told ye we should have done it before."

"And I told ye," he retorted, "that they are invaluable to historians."

"Burn them," I croaked, knowing at last that the invitation in Latin they contained was what had called the witches back. Knowing that my speaking the words aloud had brought them to our house again. Knowing that the witches were Father's "visitants" who had, in the end, frightened him to death. "Burn them. No historian worth his salt would touch them."

Alec laughed bitterly. "I would." He set me on my feet and walked away down the path toward town.

"Now ye've done it," Mrs. Marr told me. "Ye never were a lass to watch what ye say. Ye've injured his pride and broken his heart."

"But . . ." We were walking back along the path, her hand on my arm, leading me on. The wind had died and the sky was alert with stars. "But he's not a historian."

"Ye foolish lass, yon lad's nae fisherman, for all he dresses like one. He's a lecturer in history at the university, in St. Andrews," she said. "And the two of ye the glory of this village. Yer father and his father always talking about the pair of ye. Hoping to see ye married one day, when pride didna keep the two of ye apart. Scheming they were."

I could hardly take this in. Drawing my arm from her, I looked to see if she was making a joke. Though in all the years I'd known her, I'd never heard her laugh.

She glared ahead at the darkened path. "Yer father kept yer room the way it was when ye were a child, though I tried to make him see the foolishness of it. He said that someday yer own child would be glad of it."

"My father—"

"But then he went all queer in the head after Alec's father died. I think he believed that by uncovering all he could about the old witches, he might help Alec in his research. To bring ye together. Though what he really fetched was too terrible to contemplate."

"Which do you think came first?" I asked slowly. "Father's summoning the witches, or the shadows sensing an opportunity?"

She gave a bob of her head to show she was thinking, then said at last, "Dinna mess with witches and weather, my man says . . ."

"Your man?" She'd said it before, but I thought she'd meant her dead husband. "Weren't you . . . I mean, I thought you were in love with my father."

She stopped dead in her tracks and turned to me. The half moon lit her face. "Yer father?" She stopped, considered, then began again. "Yer father had a heart only for two women in his life, yer mother and ye, Janet, though he had a hard time showing it.

"And. . . ," she laughed, "he was no a bonnie man."

I thought of him lying in his bed, his great prow of a nose dominating his face. No, he was not a bonnie man.

"Och, lass, I had promised yer mother on her deathbed to take care of him, and how could I go back on such a promise? I didna feel free to marry as long as he remained alive. Now my Pittenweem man and I have set a date, and it will be soon. We've wasted enough time already."

I had been wrong, so wrong, and in so many ways I could hardly comprehend them all. And didn't I understand about wasted time. But at least I could make one thing right again.

"I'll go after Alec, I'll . . ."

Mrs. Marr clapped her hands. "Then run, lass, run like the wind."

And untying the knot around my own pride, I ran.

THE QUIET MONK

Glastonbury Abbey, in the year of Our Lord 1191

He was a tall man, and his shoulders looked broad even under the shapeless disguise of the brown sacking. The hood hid the color of his hair and, when he pushed the hood back, the tonsure was so close cropped, he might have been a blonde or a redhead or gray. It was his eyes that held one's interest most. They were the kind of blue that I had only seen on midsummer skies, with the whites the color of bleached muslin. He was a handsome man, with a strong, thin nose and a mouth that would make all the women in the parish sure to shake their heads with the waste of it. They were a lusty lot, the parish dames, so I had been warned.

I was to be his guide as I was the spriest of the brothers, even with my twisted leg, for I was that much younger than the rest, being newly come to my vocation, one of the few infant oblates who actually joined that convocation of saints. Most left to go into trade, though a few, it must be admitted, joined the army, safe in their hearts for a peaceful death.

Father Joseph said I was not to call the small community "saints," for sainthood must be earned not conferred, but my birth father told me, before he gave me to the abbey, that by living in such close quarters with saintly men I could become one. And that he, by gifting me, would win a place on high. I am not sure if all this was truly accomplished, for my father died of a disease his third wife brought to their marriage bed, a strange wedding portion indeed. And mostly my time in the abbey was taken up not in prayer side by side with saints but on my knees cleaning the abbot's room, the long dark halls, and the *dortoir*. Still, it was better than being back at home in Meade's Hall where I was the butt of every joke, no matter I was the son of the lord. His eighth son, born twisted ankle to thigh, the murderer of his own mother at the hard birthing. At least in Glastonbury Abbey I was needed, if not exactly loved.

So when the tall wanderer knocked on the door late that Sunday night, and I was the watcher at the gate, Brother Sanctus being abed with a shaking fever, I got to see the quiet monk first.

It is wrong, I know, to love another man in that way. It is wrong to worship a fellow human even above God. It is the one great warning dunned into infant oblates from the start. For a boy's heart is a natural altar and many strange deities ask for sacrifice there. But I loved him when first I saw him for the hope I saw imprinted on his face and the mask of sorrow over it.

He did not ask to come in; he demanded it. But he never raised his voice nor spoke other than quietly. That is why we dubbed him the Quiet Monk and rarely used his name. Yet he owned a voice with more authority than even Abbot Giraldus could command, for *he* is a shouter. Until I met the Quiet Monk, I had quaked at the abbot's bluster. Now I know it for what it truly is: fear masquerading as power.

"I seek a quiet corner of your abbey and a word with your abbot after his morning prayers and ablutions," the Quiet Monk said.

I opened the gate, conscious of the squawking lock and the cries of the wood as it moved. Unlike many abbeys, we had no rooms ready for visitors. Indeed we never entertained guests anymore. We could scarce feed ourselves these days. But I did not tell *him* that. I led him to my own room, identical to all the others save the abbot's, which was even meaner, as Abbot Giraldus reminded us daily. The Quiet Monk did not seem to notice, but nodded silently and eased himself onto my thin pallet, falling asleep at once. Only soldiers and monks have such a facility. My father, who once led a cavalry, had it. And I, since coming to the abbey, had it, too. I covered him gently with my one thin blanket and crept from the room.

In the morning, the Quiet Monk talked for a long time with Abbot Giraldus and then with Fathers Joseph and Paul. He joined us in our prayers, and when we sang, his voice leaped over the rest, even over the sopranos of the infant oblates and the lovely tenor of Brother John. He stayed far longer on his knees than any, at the last prostrating himself on the cold stone floor for over an hour. That caused the abbot much distress, which manifested itself in a tantrum aimed at my skills at cleaning. I had to rewash the floor in the abbot's room where the stones were already smooth from his years of penances.

Brother Denneys—for so was the Quiet Monk's name, called he said after the least of boys who shook him out of a dream of apathy—was given leave to stay until a certain task was accomplished. But before the task could be done, permission would have to be gotten from the Pope.

What that task was to be, neither the abbot nor Fathers Joseph or Paul would tell. And if I wanted to know, the only one I might turn to was Brother Denneys himself. Or I could wait until word came from the Holy Father, which word—as we all knew full well—might take days, weeks, even months over the slow roads between Glastonbury and Rome. If word came at all.

Meanwhile, Brother Denneys was a strong back and a stronger hand. And wonder of wonders (a miracle, said Father Joseph, who did not parcel out miracles with any regularity), he also had a deep pocket of gold which he shared with Brother Aermand, who cooked our meagre meals. As long as Brother Denneys remained at the abbey, we all knew we would eat rather better than we had in many a year. Perhaps that is why it took so long for word to come from the Pope. So it was our small convocation of saints became miners, digging gold out of a particular seam. Not all miracles, Father Joseph had once said, proceed from a loving heart. Some, he had mused, come from too little food or too much wine or not enough sleep. And, I added to myself, from too great a longing for gold.

Ours was not a monastery where silence was the rule. We had so little else, talk was our one great privilege, except of course on holy days, which there were rather too many of. As was our custom, we foregathered at meals to share the day's small events: the plants beginning to send through their green hosannahs, the epiphanies of birds' nests, and the prayerful bits of gossip any small community collects. It was rare we talked of our pasts. The past is what had driven most of us to Glastonbury. Even Saint Patrick, that most revered of holy men, it was said came to Glastonbury posting ahead of his long past. Our little wattled church had heard the confessions of good men and bad, saints of passing fairness and sinners of surprising depravity, before it had been destroyed seven years earlier by fire. But the stories that Brother Denneys told us that strange spring were surely the most surprising confessions of all, and I read in the expressions of the abbot and Fathers Joseph and Paul a sudden overwhelming greed that surpassed all understanding.

What Brother Denneys rehearsed for us were the matters that had set him wandering: a king's wife betrayed, a friendship destroyed, a repentance sought, and over the many years a driving need to discover the queen's grave, that he might plead for forgiveness at her crypt. But all this was not new to the father confessors who had listened to lords and ploughmen alike. It was the length of time he had been wandering that surprised us.

Of course we applauded his despair and sanctified his search with a series of oratories sung by our choir. Before the church had burned down, we at Glastonbury had been noted for our voices, one of the three famed perpetual choirs, the others being at Caer Garadawg and at Bangor. I sang the low ground bass, which surprised everyone who saw me, for I am thin and small with a chest many a martyr might envy. But we were rather fewer voices than we might have been seven years previously, the money for the church repair having gone instead to fund the Crusades. Fewer voices—and quite a few skeptics, though the abbot, and Fathers Paul and Joseph, all of whom were in charge of our worldly affairs, were quick to quiet the doubters because of that inexhaustible pocket of gold.

How long had he wandered? Well, he certainly did not look his age. Surely six centuries should have carved deeper runes on his brow and shown the long bones. But in the end, there was not a monk at Glastonbury, including even Brother Thomas, named after that doubting forebear, who remained unconvinced.

Brother Denneys revealed to us that he had once been a knight, the fairest of that fair company of Christendom who had accompanied the mighty King Arthur in his search for the grail.

"I who was Lancelot du Lac," he said, his voice filled with that quiet authority, "am now but a wandering mendicant. I seek the grave of that sweetest lady whom I taught to sin, skin upon skin, tongue into mouth, like fork into meat."

If we shivered deliciously at the moment of the telling, who can blame us, especially those infant oblates just entering their manhood. Even Abbot Giraldus forgot to cross himself, so moved was he by the confession.

But all unaware of the stir he was causing, Brother Denneys continued.

"She loved the king, you know, but not the throne. She loved the man of him, but not the monarch. He did not know how to love a woman. He husbanded a kingdom, you see. It was enough for him. He should have been a saint."

He was silent then, as if in contemplation. We were all silent, as if he had set us a parable that we would take long years unraveling, as scholars do a tale.

A sigh from his mouth, like the wind over an old unused well, recalled us. He did not smile. It was as if there were no smiles left in him, but he nodded and continued.

"What does a kingdom need but to continue? What does a queen need but to bear an heir?" His pause was not to hear the questions answered but to draw deep breath. He went on. "I swear that was all that drove her into my arms, not any great adulterous love for me. Oh, for a century or two I still fancied ours was the world's great love, a love borne on the wings of magic first and then the necromancy of passion alone. I cursed and blamed that witch Morgaine even as I thanked her. I cursed and blamed the stars. But in the end I knew myself a fool, for no man is more foolish than when he is misled by his own base maunderings." He gestured downward with his hand, dismissing the lower half of his body, bit his lip as if in memory, then spoke again.

"When she took herself to Amesbury Convent, I knew the truth but would not admit it. Lacking the hope of a virgin birth, she had chosen me—not God—to fill her womb. In that I failed her even as God had. She could not hold my seed; I could not plant a healthy crop. There was one child that came too soon, a tailed infant with bulging eyes, more *mer* than human. After that there were no more." He shivered.

I shivered.

We all shivered, thinking on that monstrous child.

"When she knew herself a sinner, who had sinned without result, she committed herself to sanctity alone, like the man she worshipped, the husband she adored. I was forgot."

One of the infant oblates chose that moment to sigh out loud, and the abbot threw him a dark look, but Brother Denneys never heard.

"Could I do any less than she?" His voice was so quiet then, we all strained forward in the pews to listen. "Could I strive to forget my sinning self? I had to match her passion for passion, and so I gave my sin to God." He stood and with one swift, practiced movement pulled off his robe and threw himself naked onto the stone floor.

I do not know what others saw, but I was so placed that I could not help but notice. From the back, where he lay full length upon the floor, he was a well-muscled man. But from the front he was as smoothly wrought as a girl. In some frenzy of misplaced penitence in the years past, he had cut his manhood from him, dedicating it—God alone knew where—on an altar of despair.

I covered my face with my hands and wept; wept for his pain and for his hopelessness and wept that I, crooked as I was, could not follow him on his long, lonely road.

We waited for months for word to come from Rome, but either the Holy Father was too busy with the three quarrelsome kings and their Crusades, or the roads between Glastonbury and Rome were closed, as usual, by brigands. At any rate, no message came, and still the Quiet Monk worked at the abbey, paying for the privilege out of his inexhaustible pocket. I spent as much time as I could working by his side, which meant I often did double and triple duty. But just to hear his soft voice rehearsing the tales of his past was enough for me. Dare I say it? I preferred his stories to the ones in the Gospels. They had all the beauty, the magic, the mystery, and one thing more. They had a human passion, a life such as I could never attain.

One night, long after the winter months were safely past and the sun had warmed the abbey gardens enough for our spades to snug down easily between the rows of last year's plantings, Brother Denneys came into my cell. Matins was past for the night and such visits were strictly forbidden.

"My child," he said quietly, "I would talk with you."

"Me?" My voice cracked as it had not this whole year past. "Why me?" I could feel my heart beating out its own canonical hours, but I was not so far from my days as an infant oblate that I could not at the same time keep one ear tuned for footsteps in the hall.

"You, Martin," he said, "because you listen to my stories and follow my every move with the eyes of a hound to his master or a squire his knight."

I looked down at the stone floor unable to protest, for he was right. It was just that I had not known he had noticed my faithfulness.

"Will you do something for me if I ask it?"

"Even if it were to go against God and his saints," I whispered. "Even then."

"Even if it were to go against Abbot Giraldus and his rule?"

"Especially then," I said under my breath, but he heard.

Then he told me what had brought him specifically to Glastonbury, the secret which he had shared with the abbot and Fathers Paul and Joseph, the reason he waited for word from Rome that never came.

"There was a bard, a Welshman, with a voice like a demented dove, who sang of this abbey and its graves. But there are many abbeys and many acres of stones throughout this land. I have seen them all. Or so I thought. But in his rhymes—and in his cups—he spoke of Glastonbury's two pyramids with the grave between. His song had a ring of Merlin's truth in it, which that mage had spoke long before the end of our tale: '*a little green, a private peace, between the standing stones.*'"

I must have shaken my head, for he began to recite a poem with the easy familiarity of the mouth which sometimes remembers what the mind has forgot.

> *A time will come when what is three makes one:*
> *A little green, a private peace, between the standing stones.*
> *A gift of gold shall betray the place at a touch.*
> *Absolution rests upon its mortal couch.*

He spoke with absolute conviction, but the whole spell made less sense to me than the part. I did not answer him.

He sighed. "You do not understand. The grave between those stone pyramids is the one I seek. I am sure of it now. But your abbot is adamant. I cannot have permission to unearth the tomb without a nod from Rome. Yet I must open it, Martin, I must. She is buried within and I must throw myself at her dear dead feet and be absolved." He had me by the shoulders.

"Pyramids?" I was not puzzled by his passion or by his utter conviction that he had to untomb his queen. But as far as I knew there were no pyramids in the abbey's yard.

"There are two tapered plinths," Brother Denneys said. "With carvings on them. A whole roster of saints." He shook my shoulders as if to make me understand.

Then I knew what he meant. Or at least I knew the plinths to which he referred. They looked little like pyramids. They were large standing tablets on which the names of the abbots of the past and other godly men of this place ran down the side like rainfall. It took a great imagining—or a greater need—to read a pair of pyramids there. And something more. I *had* to name it.

"There is no grave there, Brother Denneys. Just a sward, green in the spring and summer, no greener place in all the boneyard. We picnic there once a year to remember God's gifts."

"That is what I hoped. That is how Merlin spoke the spell. *A little green. A private peace.* My lady's place would be that green."

"But there is nothing there!" On this one point I would be adamant.

"You do not know that, my son. And my hopes are greater than your knowledge." There was a strange cast to his eyes that I could just see, for a sliver of moonlight was lighting my cell. "Will you go with me when the moon is full, just two days hence? I cannot dig it alone. Someone must needs stand guardian."

"Against whom?"

"Against the mist maidens, against the spirits of the dead."

"I can only stand against the abbot and those who watch at night." I did not add that I could also take the blame. He was a man who brought out the martyr in me. Perhaps that was what had happened to his queen.

"Will you?"

I looked down the bed at my feet, outlined under the thin blanket in that same moonlight. My right foot was twisted so severely that, even disguised with the blanket, it was grotesque. I looked up at him, perched on my bedside. He was almost smiling at me.

"I will," I said. "God help me, I will."

He embraced me once, rose, and left the room.

How slowly, how quickly those two days flew by. I made myself stay away from his side as if by doing so I could avert all suspicion from our coming deed. I polished the stone floors along the hall until one of the infant oblates, young Christopher of Chedworth, slipped and fell badly enough to have to remain the day under the infirmarer's care. The abbot removed me from my duties and set me to hoeing the herb beds and washing the pots as penance.

And the Quiet Monk did not speak to me again, nor even nod as he passed, having accomplished my complicity. Should we have known that all we did *not* do signaled even more clearly our intent? Should Brother Denneys, who had been a man of battle, have plotted better strategies? I realize now that as a knight he had been a solitary fighter. As a lover, he had been caught out at his amours. Yet even then, even when I most certainly was denying Him, God was looking over us and smoothing the stones in our paths.

Matins was done and I had paid scant attention to the psalms and even less to the antiphons. Instead I watched the moon as it shone through the chapel window, illuminating the glass picture of Lazarus rising from the dead. Twice Brother Thomas had elbowed me into the proper responses and three times Father Joseph had glared down at me from above.

But Brother Denneys never once gave me the sign I awaited, though the moon made a full halo over the lazar's head.

Dejected, I returned to my cell and flung myself onto my knees, a position that was doubly painful to me because of my bad leg, and prayed to the God I had neglected to deliver me from false hopes and wicked promises.

And then I heard the slap of sandals coming down the hall. I did not move from my knees, though the pains shot up my right leg and into my groin, I waited, taking back all the prayers I had sent heavenward just moments before, and was rewarded for my faithlessness by the sight of the Quiet Monk striding into my cell.

He did not have to speak. I pulled myself up without his help, smoothed down the skirts of my cassock so as to hide my crooked leg, and followed him wordlessly down the hall.

It was silent in the dark *dortoir*, except for the noise of Brother Thomas's strong snores and a small *pop-pop-pop* that punctuated the sleep of the infant oblates. I knew that later that night, the novice master would check on the sleeping boys, but he was not astir now. Only the gatekeeper was alert, snug at the front gate and waiting for a knock from Rome that might never come. But we were going out the back door and into the graveyard. No one would hear us there.

Brother Denneys had a great shovel ready by the door. Clearly, he had been busy while I was on my knees. I owed him silence and duty. And my love.

We walked side by side through the cemetery, threading our way past many headstones. He slowed his natural pace to my limping one, though I know he yearned to move ahead rapidly. I thanked him silently and worked hard to keep up.

There were no mist maidens, no white robed ghosts moaning aloud beneath the moon, nor had I expected any. I knew more than most how the mind conjures up monsters. So often jokes had been played upon me as a child, and a night in the boneyard was a favorite in my part of the land. Many a chilly moon I had been left in our castle graveyard, tied up in an open pit or laid flat on a new slab. My father used to laugh at the pranks. He may even have paid the pranksters. After all, he was a great believer in the toughened spirit. But I like to think he was secretly proud that I never complained. I had often been cold and the ache settled permanently in my twisted bones, but I was never abused by ghosts and so did not credit them.

All these memories and more marched across my mind as I followed Brother Denneys to the pyramids that bordered his hopes.

There were no ghosts, but there *were* shadows, and more than once we both leaped away from them, until we came at last to the green, peaceful place where the Quiet Monk believed his lost love lay buried.

"I will dig," he said, "and you will stand there as guard."

He pointed to a spot where I could see the dark outlines of both church and housing, and in that way know quickly if anyone was coming toward us this night. So while he dug, in his quiet, competent manner, I climbed up upon a cold stone dedicated to a certain Brother Silas, and kept the watch.

The only accompaniment to the sound of his spade thudding into the sod was the long, low whinny of a night owl on the hunt and the scream of some small animal that signaled the successful end. After that, there was only the soft *thwack-thwack* of the spade biting deeper and deeper into the dirt of that unproved grave.

He must have dug for hours; I had only the moon to mark the passage of time. But he was well down into the hole with but the crown of his head showing when he cried out.

I ran over to the edge of the pit and stared down.

"What is it?" I asked, staring between the black shadows.

"Some kind of wood," he said.

"A coffin?"

"More like the barrel of a tree," he said. He bent over. "Definitely a tree. Oak, I think."

"Then your bard was wrong," I said. "But then, he was a Welshman."

"It is a Druid burial," he said. "That is what the oak means. Merlin would have fixed it up."

"I thought Merlin died first. Or disappeared. You told me that. In one of your stories."

He shook his head. "It is a Druid trick, no doubt of it. You will see." He started digging again, this time at a much faster pace, the dirt sailing backward and out of the pit, covering my sandals before I moved. A fleck of it hit my eye and made me cry. I was a long while digging it out, a long while weeping.

"That's it, then," came his voice. "And there's more besides."

I looked over into the pit once again. "More?"

"Some sort of stone, with a cross on the bottom side."

"Because she was Christian?" I asked.

He nodded. "The Druids had to give her that. They gave her little else."

The moon was mostly gone, but a thin line of light stretched tight across the horizon. I could hear the first bells from the abbey, which meant Brother Angelus was up and ringing them. If we were not at prayers, they would look for us. If we were not in our cells alone, I knew they would come out here. Abbot Giraldus might have been a blusterer but he was not a stupid man.

"Hurry," I said.

He turned his face up to me and smiled. "All these years waiting," he said. "All these years hoping. All these years of false graves." Then he turned back and, using the shovel as a pry, levered open the oak cask.

Inside were the remains of two people, not one, with the bones intertwined, as if in death they embraced with more passion than in life. One was clearly a man's skeleton, with the long bones of the legs fully half again the length of the other's. There was a helm such as a fighting man might wear lying crookedly near the skull. The other skeleton was marked with fine gold braids of hair, that caught the earliest bit of daylight.

"Guenivere," the Quiet Monk cried out in full voice for the first time, and he bent over the bones, touching the golden hair with a reverent hand.

I felt a hand on my shoulder but did not turn around, for as I watched, the golden skein of hair turned to dust under his fingers, one instant a braid and the next a reminder of time itself.

Brother Denneys threw himself onto the skeletons, weeping hysterically and I—I flung myself down into the pit, though it was a drop of at least six feet. I pulled him off the brittle, broken bones and cradled him against me until his sorrow was spent.

When I looked up, the grave was ringed around with the familiar faces of my brother monks. At the foot of the grave stood the abbot himself, his face as red and as angry as a wound.

Brother Denneys was sent away from Glastonbury, of course. He himself was a willing participant in the exile. For even though the little stone cross had the words HIC IACET ARTHURUS REX QUONDAM REXQUE FUTURUS carved upon it, he said it was not true. That the oak casket was nothing more than a boat from one of the lake villages overturned. That the hair we both saw so clearly in that early morning light was nothing more than grave mold.

"She is somewhere else, not here," he said, dismissing the torn earth with a wave of his hand. "And I must find her."

I followed him out the gate and down the road, keeping pace with him step for step. I follow him still. His hair has gotten grayer over the long years, a strand at a time, but cannot keep up with the script that now runs across my brow. The years as his squire have carved me deeply but his sorrowing face is untouched by time or the hundreds of small miracles he, all unknowing, brings with each opening of a grave: the girl in Westminster whose once blind eyes can now admit light, a Shropshire lad, dumb from birth, with a tongue that can now make rhymes.

And I understand that he will never find this particular grail. He is in his own hell and I but chart its regions, following after him on my two straight legs. A small miracle, true. In the winter, in the deepest snow, the right one pains me, a twisting memory of the old twisted bones. When I cry out in my sleep he does not notice nor does he comfort me. And my ankle still warns of every coming storm. He is never grateful for the news. But I can walk for the most part without pain or limp, and surely every miracle maker needs a witness to his work, an apostle to send letters to the future. That is my burden. It is my duty. It is my everlasting joy.

The Tudor antiquary Bale reported that "In Avallon in 1191, there found they the flesh bothe of Arthur and of hys wyfe Guenever turned all into duste, wythin theyr coffines of strong oke, the boneys only remaynynge. A monke of the same abbeye, standyng and behouldyng the fine broydinges of the womman's hear as yellow as golde there still to remayne, as a man ravyshed, or more than halfe from his wyttes, he leaped into the graffe, xv fote depe, to have caughte them sodenlye. But he fayled of his purpose. For so soon as they were touched they fell all to powder."

By 1193, the monks at Glastonbury had money enough to work again on the rebuilding of their church, for wealthy pilgrims flocked to the relics and King Richard himself presented a sword reputed to be Excalibur to Tancred, the Norman ruler of Sicily, a few short months after the exhumation.

THE BIRD

He had purchased the damnable bird from a friend who was tired of it defecating on everything. Sitting on picture frames or the edges of bookcases, it simply let go. His library, where he gave it permission to fly free, was now painted in its awful defecatory colors, as he complained to his young cousin, Virginia.

"That's the trouble with you," she told him. "You say 'defecate' where the rest of the world says 'shite.'"

Her voice went quieter when she spoke that last word. But then he loved the way she said it, like a sailor on shore leave swearing in front of his mother, the word both strong and apologetic at the same time. *Tone*, he thought, *is all*.

"What did you want the bird for?" She sat primly, ankles crossed, her beautiful heart-shaped face and those astonishing black eyes still bright with curiosity.

She could almost be a bird herself, he thought. *Certainly hardly weighs more than one now.*

"I wanted to teach it to talk," he said. "Ravens can, you know. The whole corvid family can vocalize human sounds—crows, rooks, jackdaws, magpies, ravens. It is said they are the smartest of birds and I am finding it so."

Her head canted to one side, very birdlike. "Isn't that mere imitation?" she asked. "Do you not have to split its tongue?"

What a curious thing to ask, he thought. She always astonished him. Had since she was a toddler, lispingly calling his name. "What *have* you been reading, child?" He called her that because he was a full ten years older than she, though in many ways she was the elder. Certainly the wiser. He was smart, but no one had ever thought him wise. Brilliant, perhaps. He would accept that. Inventive. A *oner* someone once called him. But never, alas, wise.

She smiled. That damnable mysterious, enchanting smile.

"'Tis a myth, you know. Splitting the corvid's tongue. Birds do not speak as we do anyway. It is a different mechanism. A syrinx, not like ours. We have a larynx for vocalization. And they do not use their tongues . . ."

She put her hand up to her mouth, gave a small laugh which turned into a cough that lasted far too long. The cough, damnable and damaging, had gotten worse the last few days but they never spoke about it. Looked away from it. The doctor was banished from the house so they didn't have to think about what it presaged.

She recovered quickly, a matter of her strong will. Smiling, she looked at him through the forest of her lashes. "And what have *you* been reading, dearest husband?"

He sat down next to her and held her hand. She was always comforted by his presence. Her hand was ice but her brow, usually so pale, once again bloomed with fever, bright pink spots against the pallor of her face. It would be a long night.

"Hush now," he said. "I bought the bird to speak when you cannot."

"I can speak," she said, laughing again. "I can *always* speak."

"Always," he repeated the lie as if he, and not the raven, were the imitator.

Then he added, "Well, it shall speak when you can speak never more."

Immediately horrified at the thought . . . that he had articulated *the* thought, the one they had promised one another never to talk about, he rushed forward into something else, a distraction, a switch. He was often having to reroute his thoughts these days so that his heart could keep on beating. And hers. "Now enough, I will let you hold the raven. You will like it. I have named it Mrs. E because it's the color of sin, though I think it is a male bird. Hard to tell except for size."

"La," she said now in full Southern mock, "Mrs. E's sin is jealousy and this is not a green bird."

He responded in kind. "And of course the old hag is jealous—of you." Though the real Mrs. E was hardly that old, not even his age, but he had no interest in her. His mind was ever on Virginia.

She prinked at the compliment and gave a small moue, and he thought that only a Southern girl knew how to do that and still look lovely.

"If it makes a mess of my dress, you shall have to buy me another," she teased.

"I will buy the dress in the morning," he responded, "and take you out for tea in it." Though she had not been outside for weeks now.

But still game, she colluded in the small lie. "I will have Auntie do my hair special for our outing."

He coaxed the bird from a lamp on his desk, with a handful of nuts and raisins. The bird flew down, almost as silent as an owl, settling on his shoulder, a great brooding presence. Soon shells littered the floor around him. But the bird remained steadfastly silent.

"It is very large," Virginia said suddenly. "I am not certain . . ."

"The bird is not heavy," he assured her. "It is only that you have become so light. So made of Light. And it will serve as your muse as it already serves as mine. When it whispers, a story starts. And lines of poetry. You will see."

"I will hear," she corrected, intrigued by the idea, as he had hoped she would be.

The bird opened its beak, stretched its neck oddly, suddenly said, "Lenore." Its voice was a clear imitation of Edgar's, if a bit gruffer.

As Lenore was his pet name for her, Virginia smiled broadly. "You have made good use of your time with Mrs. E."

He placed the raven on her shoulder. The bird's grip on her was strong and he suddenly feared her bones might snap.

"You lied," she told him. "It is very heavy. Like a sin." Her laughter was a waterfall.

"Have we not sinned enough without ravens?" he asked. Another tease.

"I thought we called that love." As ever, she was quicker than he in repartee.

"Always, my dearest heart," he assured her.

She tried to laugh, then began another cough which she quickly suppressed.

The raven seemed uncomfortable on Virginia's small shoulder, which was now heaving with her coughs, but it did not leave. Rather it rode her like a boat on a wave.

There was a sudden flurry of frantic knocks at the front door, and Edgar rose to see who was there. It was an odd time of night for a visitor.

As soon as he left, the bird turned its head and spoke directly into Virginia's ear in a voice that was urgent without being forced. But Edgar, now in the other room, did not hear what it said.

He opened the door, but no one was there. It was then he realized that the frantic knocking had simply been the bird imitating the mailman at the door, not a real announcement at all.

When he turned back, Virginia was shaking as with an ague, and the bird was flying off to the highest photogravure picture on the wall, the one of his mother, where it often perched.

There were tears tracking down Virginia's cheeks, whiter than her face. It took him a moment to realize what they were.

"That pernicious bird has . . ." he shouted. Stopped. Then raged: "I will wring its miserable neck."

"No, no, no," she said, wiping the white tears away with her handkerchief. "It spoke to me. Told me . . ."

He put his hand on her shoulder, pulled her to him, held her, now shaking more than she. He knew what she was going to say, knew it was some dread prophecy, knew that the bird was the harbinger of her death, muse of melancholy, knew that he would write this tale on the longest night of his life, knew it all in one swift and awful revelation.

"No, my darling cousin, my love, my life. Do not tell me what the bird said. That was for your ears alone. Speak of this nevermore."

And she never did, for in the morning—like the bird itself—she was gone, winging off to some further heaven than the one he had tried to make for her by his side, on earth.

BELLE BLOODY MERCILESS DAME

An elf, they say, has no real emotions, cannot love, cannot cry. Do not believe them, that relative of the infinite Anon. Get an elf at the right time, on a Solstice for example, and you will get all the emotions you want.

Only you may not like what you get.

Sam Herriot, for example, ran into one of the elves of the Western Ridings on a Sunday in June. He'd forgotten—if he'd ever actually known—it was the Summer Solstice. He'd had a skinful at the local pub, mostly Tennent's, that Bud wannabe, thin and pale amber, and was making his unsteady way home through the dark alley of Kirk Wynd.

And there was this girl, tall, skinny, actually quite a bit anorexic, Sam thought, leaning against the gray stone wall. Her long ankle-length skirt was rucked up in front and she was scratching her thin thigh lazily with bright red nails, making runnels in her skin that looked like veins, or like track marks. He thought she was some bloody local junkie, you see, out trolling for a john to make enough money for another round of the whatever.

And Sam, being drunk but not that drunk, thought he'd accommodate her, even though he preferred his women plump, two handsful he liked to say, hefting his hands palms upward. He had several unopened safes in his pocket, and enough extra pounds in his wallet because he hadn't had to pay for any of the drinks that night. His Mam didn't expect him home early since it had been his bachelor party. And with Jill gone home to spend the last week before their marriage with her own folks, there was no one to wait up for him. So he thought, *What the hell!* and continued down the alley toward the girl.

She didn't look up. But he was pretty sure she knew he was there; it was the way she got quiet all of a sudden, stopped scratching her leg. A kind of still anticipation.

So he went over to her and said, "Miss?" being polite just in case, and only then did she look up and her eyes were not normal eyes. More like a cat's eyes, with yellow pupils that sat up and down rather than side to side. Only, being drunk, he thought that they were just a junkie's eyes.

She smiled at him, and it was a sudden sweet and ravenous smile, if you can imagine those two things together. He took it for lust, which it was, of a sort. Even had he been sober, he wouldn't have known the difference.

She held out her hand, and he took it, drawing her toward him and she said, "Not here," with a peculiar kind of lilt to her voice. And he asked, "Where?"

Then without quite realizing the how of it, he suddenly found himself sitting on a hillside with her, though the nearest one he knew of was way out of town, about a quarter of a mile, near the Boarside Steadings.

He thought, *I'm really drunk, not remembering walking all this way.* But that didn't stop him from kissing her, putting his tongue up against her teeth until she opened her mouth and sucked him in so quickly, so deeply he nearly passed out. So he drew back for a breath, tasting her saliva like some herbal tea, and watched as she shrugged out of the top of her blouse, some filmy little number, no buttons or anything.

She was naked underneath.

"God!" he said, and he really meant it as a sudden prayer because she was painfully thin. He could actually count her ribs. And she had this odd third nipple, right on the breastbone between the other two. He'd heard that some girls did, but he'd never actually seen anything like it before.

He wondered, suddenly, about Jill and their wedding in a couple of days, and it sobered him a bit, making his own eyes go a bit dead for a moment.

That's when the girl stood up on those long skinny legs and walked over to him, pressing him backward, whispering in some strange, liquid language. Suddenly it all made sense to him. She was a foreigner, not British at all.

"Aren't you cold, lass?" he asked, thinking that maybe he should just cover her up, here on the hillside, and never mind the other stuff at all. Because Jill would kill him if she knew, the girl so skinny and foreign and odd.

But the girl put her hands on his shoulders and pushed him back till he lay on the cold grass staring up at her. It was past midnight and the sky still pearly, this being Scotland where summer days spin across the twenty-four hours with hardly any dark at all. He could see faint stars around her head, and they looked as if they were moving. Then he realized it wasn't stars at all, but something white and fluttering behind her. *Moths*, he thought. *Or gulls*. Only much too big for either.

She lay down on top of him and kissed him again, hard and soft, sighing and weeping. Her hot tears filled his own eyes till he could not see at all. But all the while the wings—not moths, not gulls—wrapped around him. He did not feel the cold.

He woke hours later on the hillside and thought they must have had sex, or had something at any rate, though he couldn't remember any of it, for his trousers were soaked through, back and front. He felt frantically in his pocket. The safes were still there, untouched. His wallet, too. His mouth felt bruised, his head ached from all the beer, and he could feel the heat of a hickey rising on the left side of his neck.

But the girl was gone.

He stood slowly and looked around. Far off was the sea looking, in the morning light, silvery and strange. He was miles from town, not Boarside Steadings at all, and there was no sign of the thin girl, though how she could have disappeared, or when, he did not know. But leaving him here, alone, on the bloody hillside, drained and tired, feeling older than time itself, must have given her some bloody big laugh. Well, he hoped she got sick, hoped she got the clap, hoped she got herself pregnant, little tart. And all he had to show for it was a great white feather, as if from some bloody stupid fairy wing.

And brushing himself off, he started down the cold hillside toward—he hoped—home.

THE JEWEL IN THE TOAD QUEEN'S CROWN

June 1875

"Why, they are *quite* barbaric," the queen said to her prime minister, making small talk since she wasn't actually certain where Zululand was. Somewhere in deepest darkest Africa. Of that much at least she was certain. She would have to get out the atlas. Again. She had several of Albert's old atlases, and the latest American one, a Swinton.

Thinking about the problem with an atlas, and how—unlike the star charts, which never varied—it kept changing with each new discovery on the dark continent, she sniffed into her dainty handkerchief. She was not sniffing at Mr. Disraeli, though, and she was quite careful to make that distinction by glancing up at him and dimpling. It was important that he never know how she really felt about him. Truth to tell, she was unsure herself.

"Barbaric in our eyes, certainly, ma'am," he said, his dark eyes gazing back at her.

She did not trust dark eyes. At least not *that* dark. Give her good British blue any day. Or Albert's blue. But those dark eyes . . . she shuddered. A bit of strangeness in the prime minister's background for all that she'd been assured he was an Anglican.

"What do you mean, Mr. Disraeli?" she asked. She thought she knew, but she wanted to hear him say it. Best to know one's enemies outright. She considered all prime ministers the enemy. After all, they always wanted something from her and only *seemed* to promise something in return. Politics was a nasty business and the crown had to seem to be above it while controlling it at all times.

A tightrope, really.

She thought suddenly of the French tightrope walker at Astley's Amphitheatre who could stand on one foot on a wire suspended high overhead and dangle the other foot into the air. She and Albert had taken the children to see the circus several times, and it had occurred to her then that speaking with a prime minister felt just like that. She was dangling again today with only the smallest of wire between herself and disaster.

Disraeli was master of the circus now, and he frightened her, as had her very first prime minister, Lord Melbourne, who had been careful to try and put her at her ease. It took her a long time to find him amusing.

She thought dismally: *It will take even longer with Disraeli even though this is his second tour of duty.* She barely remembered that first time. It had been only seven years after dear Albert's death and she was still so deep in mourning nothing much registered, not even—she was ashamed to admit—the children.

"To the Zulus," Disraeli answered carefully, "what they do, how they live their lives makes absolute sense, ma'am. They have been at it for centuries the same way. Each moment a perfection. Perhaps to them, *we* are the barbarians!" He smiled slowly at her over the flowered teacup.

I *am no barbarian*, she thought testily. You *might be one.* She sniffed again and this time cared little if he guessed she was sniffing at him. *All Jews are barbarians. Even if they—like Mr. Disraeli—have been baptized.*

There, she had said it! Well, only in her head. And having made the pronouncement, she went on silently. *It is something they are born with. Eastern, oily, brilliant, full of unpronounceable magic, like that Rumplety fellow who spun straw into gold in the story Albert used to tell the children at bedtime.*

Part of her knew that what she was thinking was as much a fairy tale as the Rumplety one. Her mama used to say that Jews had horns, if you felt the tops of their heads. But now she knew that Jews had no such thing as horns, just hair. Albert had taught her that. It was an old story, long discredited, unless you were some sort of peasant. *Which I am certainly not!*

She looked directly at Disraeli, which was another thing dear Albert had taught her. It always disarmed the politicians. No one expected the queen to look directly at a mere jumped-up nobody.

But Disraeli seemed to be paying her no mind, looking instead at his polished nails rather than at her, his ruler, which was rude in the extreme. She recalled suddenly how attentive he had been the first time he was prime minister. What had he said? Something about "We authors . . ." comparing his frothy romantic novels to her much more serious writing. She remembered that she had not been amused then. *Or now.*

She glared at him, willing him to look up. Those silly tangles of curls hung greasily almost to his shoulders. *That arch of nose. Those staring eyes.* She gave a little shudder, then quickly thought better of it and rang the bell for the server.

When the girl arrived, the queen said, "I have caught a chill, please bring me a shawl." Then she leaned back against the chair as if she did, indeed, feel a bit ill.

Disraeli finally looked up briefly, then looked at his nails again and did not ask if there was something he might do for her.

Jews! the queen thought. *No matter how long they have lived in England, converted, learned English, they remain a people apart, unknowable.* She did not trust him. She *dared* not trust him. Even though he was her minister. *Prime. Primo. First.* But she would never say so. She would never let him know, never let *them* know. Instead, she would make everyone think she actually liked him. It was for the best.

He may be prime minister now, she thought fiercely, *but soon he will be gone. All prime ministers disappear in time. Only I go on. Only I am England.* It was an agreeable thought and made her face soften, seeming to become younger.

"Ma'am?" he inquired, just as if he could read her mind.

"More tea, Mr. Disraeli?" She was careful to pronounce all the syllables in his name just as the archbishop—who knew Hebrew as if it were his mother tongue—had taught her.

Just then the girl came back with the shawl, curtsied, gave it to the queen, and left.

Disraeli smiled an alarmingly brilliant smile, his lips too wet. Those wet lips made her shiver. He looked as if he were preparing to eat her up, like some creature out of a tale. *An ogre? A troll? A Tom-tit-tot?* She could not remember.

"Yes, please, ma'am." He was still smiling.

She served the tea. It was a homey gesture she liked to make when sitting with her gentlemen. Her PMs. It was to put them at ease in her presence. If they were comfortable, they were easier to manipulate. Albert didn't teach her that. Long before they'd met she had figured it out, though she was only a girl at the time.

Disraeli sat back in his chair, crossed his grasshopper-like legs, and took a long, deep sip of the Indian tea.

Does she really think, his mind whirling like a Catherine wheel shooting out sparks, *that I do not know about her atlas with all its scribbles along the sides of the pages? Or the pretense at being the housefrau entertaining her "gentlemen callers"? Or what she thinks of my people?* He knew that in the queen's eyes—in all their eyes—he would always be tarred by the Levant.

He thought about an article he'd recently read in *Punch*, that rag, something about a furniture sale which outlandishly mocked Jews: their noses like hawks, their money-hungry ways. He remembered one line of it where the good English Anglican buyer wrote: "Shall I escape without being inveigled into laying out money on a lot of things I don't want?"

He made an effort to become calm, breathing deeply and taking another sip of the tea before letting himself return to the moment.

Is the queen really so unaware of all the house spies who report to me? The gossip below stairs? Her son who will tattle on Mama at the slightest provocation? Does she not recognize that I am the master of the Great Game?

Without willing it, his right hand began stroking his left, an actor's gesture, not a gentleman's. But his mind never stopped its whirl. He remembered that he and the queen had had this very same conversation about the Irish the first time he'd been her minister. And then a similar discussion about the Afghanistan adventure. To her they were *all* barbarians. Only the English were not.

Well, she may have forgotten what we talked about, but not I. It had been his first climb to the top of the greasy pole of the political world, straight into the Irish situation. There was no forgetting that! He had a marvelous memory for all the details.

Leaning back in the chair, he stared at his monarch, moving his lips silently, but no words—no English words—could be heard.

Across the rosewood table the queen slowly melted like butter in a hot skillet. A few more cabbalistic phrases and she reformed into a rather large toad dressed in black silk, with garish rings on either green paw.

"Delicious tea, ma'am," Disraeli said distinctly. "From the Indies, I believe. Assam, I am certain."

The toad, with a single crown jewel in her head, poured him a third cup of tea. "Ribbet!" she said.

Though—Disraeli mused—*that is really what a frog says.*

"Oh, I do agree, ma'am," said Disraeli, "I entirely agree." With a twist of his wrist, he turned her back into Victoria, monarch of Great Britain and Ireland, before anyone might come in and see her. It was not an improvement. However, such small distractions amused him on these necessary visits. He could not say as much for the sour little black-garbed queen.

The queen sat quietly while her lady's maid pulled the silver brush through her hair. Tangles miraculously smoothed out, since she insisted that the maid put oil of lavender on the bristles.

"No one, ma'am, still uses lavender," the woman, Martha, had said the first time she'd had the duty of brushing out the queen's hair.

But Victoria had corrected her immediately. *Best to start as one means to go on,* she had thought. "I have used oil of lavender since I was a child and I am not about to change now. I find the very scent soothing. It is almost magic." She had suffered from the megrims since dear Albert had passed over, and only the lavender worked. Albert would have called that science and explained it to her, but she was quite certain magic was the better explanation.

"What do you think of Mr. Disraeli, ma'am? Have you read his novels?"

"I do not have time to read novels, Martha," the queen scolded, though she had indeed read *Vivian Grey* and found it lamentably lacking and exceedingly vulgar, and the ending positively brutal.

"But you read people so well, it must be like reading a book," Martha said, her plain little face scrunching up as she worked.

"I do indeed read them well," Victoria said.

"And Mr. Disraeli. . . ?"

"He is a puzzle," the queen said, a bit distracted. Normally she would never discuss her prime minister with a servant. But she knew that Martha was discreet.

"Puzzles are meant to be solved, ma'am," Martha ventured.

"Sometimes I think you are less a lady's maid and more a fool, Martha." Victoria turned and smiled. "And by that I mean no offense. I use the word in the old sense, like the fools who entertained the kings of England, with their wit and their wisdom."

"I couldn't be that kind of a fool, ma'am, being a mere woman." Martha swiftly braided the queen's hair and tied it with a band.

"Martha, did you not know that Queen Elizabeth had female fools?"

"No!" Martha's hand flew up to cover her mouth. "The blessed Elizabeth!"

"And her cousin Mary of Scotland as well. In fact she had three."

"That baggage!"

"I am tired. It has been a long day," the queen said. "Leave me."

"You will solve the puzzle of Mr. Disraeli, ma'am," Martha said, helping the little queen to stand and easing her to the bed.

"Indeed I will," Victoria said, nodding her head vigorously. "Indeed I will."

Martha was pleased to see that the band held the braid's end. Some things she could do very well. Even though she was a mere woman. Especially so.

Once home again at Hughenden, Disraeli could finally relax. He got into his writing clothes and headed out into the garden. As he walked the pathways, he nodded at one of the young gardeners, but said not a word. The servants all knew that when he was alone along the garden paths, going in the direction of his writing folly, he was not to be distracted.

No more playing at being the prime minister, he thought, and smiled to himself. *I am to be a writer for a fortnight.* He stopped, turned, looked back at his house for once shining in the last rays of the day's sun.

He cared little that the nearest neighbors had mocked the fanciful pinnacles of his house, calling it witheringly, "The little redbrick palace." It was his comfort and his heart's home. He'd heard that pitiful epithet for the first time from Mary Anne right after he'd transformed the place. Evidently her lady's maid had carried the tale to her and she then to him. She admitted it after he'd found her weeping in her beloved garden, sitting alone on a white bench.

"Silly Peaches," he called her because of her gorgeous skin, even though she was quite a few years older than he. "Silly Peaches, how does it matter what the unwashed masses say of the house? We adore it." He'd sat down beside her and put his arms around her then. "You know I married you for your money, but would do it again in a moment for love." In fact, as they both knew, she'd little money of her own. It had *all* been for love—the courtship, the marriage, the house.

Now that he was prime minister—again—the neighbors were creatively silent about the manor. And darling Mary Anne, dead these three years, couldn't have carried tales to him about the foofaraw even if the neighbors had still been talking.

But, oh—I'd let them natter on if only you were still here beside me, he thought, brushing away an actual tear, which surprised him as he'd begun the gesture without knowing a tear was falling.

Walking along the twisting paths to his little garden house, the place where he wrote his novels, though not his speeches, he forced himself to stop thinking about Mary Anne. He had planned a fortnight to set down the final draft of a climactic chapter of *Endymion* that had been giving him the pip. As long as there was no new disaster in the making that he had to deal with, he would surely get it done. But, as he well knew, the prime minister's vacations were often fraught.

Also, he wanted to read more about a particular sort of Kabbalah that Rabbi Lowe had practiced a century earlier. It was in a book he'd discovered in his father's library many years ago, after the old man had passed away. With all the horror about Mary Anne's death and the fuss about his being raised up again to PM, he'd misplaced the book and only recently rediscovered it.

What he knew about Kabbalah should have been deep enough already. He'd read a great deal about it. He understood the ten Sefirot, the division therein of intellect and emotion. He acknowledged as the Kabbalist did that there were forces that caused change in the natural world as well as corresponding emotional forces that drove people to change both the world and themselves. It was a fascinating idea, and he'd been playing with it for years.

First he had read all about Kabbalah as an exercise in understanding where his ancestors had come from, and perhaps where his personal demons had come from as well, after an anti-Semitic taunt by O'Connell in Parliament to which he'd replied, "Yes, I am a Jew, and when the ancestors of the Right Honourable Gentleman were brutal savages in an unknown island, mine were priests in the Temple of Solomon."

He'd turned again to Kabbalah when Mary Anne had died, hoping to find solace in his reading. He had even built a Kabbalistic maze in the garden where her gravestone rested, thinking that walking it might give him some measure of peace.

Finally, he'd learned a few small Kabbalistic magics, such as the momentary transformation he'd done on the queen over tea. It was for a distraction, really, not that he put great store in magics. He put more in his ability to change England—and thus the world—by improving the conditions of the British people. As he often told his colleagues in the House of Commons, "The Palace is unsafe if the cottage is unhappy."

But it was only when he'd flung himself back into politics, back into the Great Game, that he realized why he'd really studied the old Hebrew magics.

"If I can learn the great miracles, not just the puny little transformations, I can make England rule the world." He whispered the thought aloud, in the sure knowledge that no one was near enough to hear him. "And that will be good for the world, for Britain, and for the queen."

And, so thinking, remembering, justifying, and planning, he finally got to the little folly he'd claimed for his writing. He stopped a minute, turned his back on the building, and surveyed his land. It still surprised him that he had such a holding, having started from so little.

Then he turned, opened the door, and went inside, shutting out the world.

The queen was not amused. The prime minister was late. *Very* late. No prime minister had ever been late to a meeting with the queen. Neither the death of a spouse nor a declaration of war sufficed as an excuse.

She tapped her fingers on the arm of her chair, though resisted the urge to stand up and pace. It was not seemly for a queen to pace. Not seemly at all.

When Disraeli finally arrived, nearly a half hour after he was supposed to be there, in a flourish of grey morning coat and effete hand waves, she was even less amused. She allowed him to see her fury and was even more furious because of that, especially as he did not seem cowed by her anger.

"And where, Mr. Disraeli, have you been?" She pointed imperiously at the clock whose hands were set on nine-twenty-five, in a frown similar to her own. She had already had tea and three small slices of tea cake, two more than were absolutely necessary. Another black mark on his copybook.

"I'm sorry, ma'am. I'm afraid I overslept." His face was pinched as if he hadn't slept at all.

"Afraid . . . you . . . over . . . slept?" Each word was etched in ice. She no longer cared that she was showing how much anger she felt. She was the queen after all. "Have you not a manservant to wake you?" It was unheard of, in his position.

"I was writing late into the night, ma'am," he said by way of explanation, sweat now beading his brow. "In my garden folly. My servants know never to disturb me there. I fell asleep."

"In . . . your . . . garden . . . *folly?*" She could not find the words to set this thing aright between them, watching in horror as he took out a silver-grey handkerchief that matched his coat and wiped his brow.

"I could . . . show you the folly if you like, ma'am. It would be a great honor if you would visit Hughenden." He took an awkward breath. "There is a superb maze I can commend to you. It is a replica of the Great Maze mentioned in the Bible."

The queen could not think where in the Bible a maze was mentioned, and her hand went—all unaccountably—to her mouth, as she used to do as a child when asked a question she should have been able to answer but couldn't. This was, of course, before she had become queen. *Long* before.

"King David's dancing floor," he said, as if he saw her confusion and sought to explain it to her.

She remembered King David dancing, but she thought that was simply done before the ark, not on any kind of dancing floor. There was a dancing floor in one of the Greek myths, she distantly recalled. Then she blushed furiously, suddenly remembering that King David had danced *naked* before the ark. It made her even angrier with Disraeli.

The gall of the man, saying such a thing to a lady. Saying it to the queen! She waved him away with her hand, waited to see him go.

Instead, his own hand described a strange arc in the air. She wondered if he were drawing the maze for her. She wondered why he did not leave. She felt dizzy.

"More tea?" she croaked, at the same moment realizing that he'd had none before. Her hand went a second time to her mouth and she felt sick. If she had been a man, she would have uttered a swear, one of the Scottish ones John Brown had taught her. They were perfect for every occasion.

The only way out of this situation, Disraeli thought, *is to go further in.* He turned the queen into a toad for a second time. He knew he must never do it a third. She might just stick that way. But at least it would buy him a little time. Time to figure out his next move, a move that—should it prove successful—would be for the glory of England and the queen. Would possibly mean an earldom for himself, though such would be worth so much less without Mary Anne alive to be his lady. Still, a peerage was hardly the reason he was doing this thing.

There is danger of course, he thought. *There is always a danger in such grand gestures. And such great magic.*

He'd stayed up all night thinking about all the aspects. He'd even written them down, the reasons for and against. The reasons *for* far outweighed the rest. His plan simply *had* to work.

The toad looked at him oddly, its green hands wrangling together. The jewel in its head was what had given him the original idea, that moment a week ago when he'd first turned the queen into the creature.

He didn't regret doing so then or now. He might, he knew, regret it in the future. But that was part of the chance he had to take, for this was, indeed, the Great Game.

"Ah, Peaches," he whispered, "in the end it's all for love." *Love of queen and country,* he thought, though goodness knows she was a difficult woman to love, black-garbed Victoria, the Widow of Windsor, as the papers called her. *A child and a grandmother at one and the same time. Silly, small in temperament and understanding. Her mind only goes forward or back. Never up and down. Never through the twisting corridors like . . .* like his own mind, he supposed. *She simply isn't interested in . . . well, everything.* His mouth turned down like hers. *Albert, at least, had had a more original mind if a bit . . .* he smiled *. . . well, Germanic.*

He made another quick hand signal, and the queen became human again. Just in time.

"Fresh tea is here, ma'am," he said as the girl came in with the pot on a tray. "Shall I pour or will you?" He put a bit of persuasion in her cup, a simple enough bit of magic, along with the two lumps of sugar. He wasn't certain it would help, but knew it couldn't hurt, something his mother used to say all the time.

The queen was a bit uncomfortable at Hughenden Manor. *All that red brick,* she thought with a shudder. *All those strange gothicisms.* Still, she did nothing but compliment the prime minister. His taste was—the red brick house notwithstanding—actually quite good. Looking back at the house, though, gave her a headache, so she looked ahead at the garden path.

To be fair—she always liked to think of herself as fair—*the ground floor reception rooms with their large plate-glass windows are delightful. And the south-facing terrace, overlooking the grassy* parterre, *has spectacular views over the valley.* She thought it carefully to plant the words firmly in mind for when she spoke of the house later to her family. She wondered where Disraeli had made his money, worried that it might have been in trade. *It can't have been from those books.* She shuddered.

The day was cool but not cold, the skies overcast but not yet raining.

"A lovely afternoon for a walk in the garden, ma'am," Disraeli said.

For once she agreed. Though she was used to her black garments, her stays, it made walking in the summer heat unbearable. Usually, she would be tucked up in her bedroom, a lavender pomander close by, ice chips in a glass of lemonade.

"Lovely indeed." She put her hand on his arm, which allowed him to help her along, he straight-backed and she nodding approvingly at the gardeners and sub-gardeners busy at work but who stood appropriately and bowed as she passed.

Well done, she thought.

The gardens, while not nearly as extensive as her own of course, were nicely plotted, and cared for, the grass perfectly cut and rolled. The flowers—banks of primroses, and a full complement of bedding plants—were in the formal part of the garden surrounding a great stone fountain. She must remember to ask about the fountain later, when Disraeli would certainly introduce her to the head gardener.

There was also a lovely, intimate orchard of apples and pears, only a few of them espaliered, as well as a fine small vinery. None of it was too much. It was, in fact, rather perfect, and the controlled perfection annoyed her slightly. She wanted to find something to scold him for, or to tease him about, and could not.

Disraeli was in full spate about the gardens, the plants, the hedges and sedges, the blooms. But as they headed toward the folly and the maze beyond, he grew unaccountably silent.

I do hope he has no political agenda on his mind, she thought, a bit sniffily. *It would not do to spoil a lovely day out of doors with such talk.* She simply would not allow it.

She was still thinking about this when the sun came out and she began to perspire. It gave her something else to gnaw on.

Now that he'd enticed the queen into the garden, and they were approaching the maze, Disraeli was suddenly full of apprehensions. *What if it is dangerous? Or if not actually dangerous, perhaps wrong? Or if not wrong, perhaps even unsupportable.* He had tested the maze many times over the last few weeks, using first an under-gardener, then his secretary, even his dog. They were all easily tricked into doing his bidding, by a sort of auto-suggestion. Only it wasn't like that German imposter Mesmer a century earlier. There was real magic in the maze. It made the things he wanted to happen, happen.

But, he thought, the worry turning into a stone in his stomach, *this is the* Queen, *not an under-gardener or a secretary.* He felt the pressure of her hand on his arm and turned to give her his most brilliant smile. *She may be resistant to the magic. She may not be so suggestible. She is possibly . . .*

Then he saw a bead of sweat on her brow and chuckled inwardly. *A queen I have twice turned into a toad with a jewel in its head,* he reminded himself. *She is as human as I.* "Ma'am?"

"Are we almost there, Mr. Disraeli?" she asked, like a child in a carriage agonizing about the rest of a long trip.

He wondered if the heat was getting too much for her. *All that black silk. And she is no longer a slender young thing.*

"Just on the other side of that small rise," he said, pointing with his left hand, past the folly that commanded the top of the little hill. "There is a bench at the center of the maze that will make the perfect garden throne. You shall rule my garden, ma'am, and my heart from there."

"Then I shall have to solve the maze quickly," she said, "to get to that throne." She smiled winningly up at him, almost as if they were a courting pair.

"*All* thrones in England belong to you, ma'am," he said. "And in the Empire as well." There, his plan was begun.

He recalled saying to a friend long ago, during his first turn as prime minister, that the way to handle the queen was that one must, first of all, remember that she is a woman. He had all but forgotten his own advice over the past few years, so he added, "If I had my way, you would rule the world." *Everyone likes flattery, and when you come to royalty you should lay it on with a trowel.* Step two in his plan. He wondered if it was succeeding in planting the seed.

She patted his hand. "Perhaps that would be overreaching, even for you, Mr. Disraeli." But she said it lightly, as if she hadn't dismissed the notion entirely, nor should he. "To the maze then."

"You are, ma'am," he said, "the quickest woman at puzzles I have ever known. I think you will have no trouble at all with my little maze."

He knew he had, indeed, laid it on with a trowel, but evidently he had said the exact right thing, for she was grinning broadly.

"So I have been told, and recently," she said. "Though *you* are the maze, dear sir."

He had no idea what she meant and no reason at all to follow up the conversation.

They walked on, she clinging even more tightly to his arm.

At the top of the rise, she stopped as if to admire the view, which was quite lovely. But really, it was so she could catch her breath. Below, where the hillock smoothed out once again, was the maze. It did not look particularly difficult to her. In fact, she could see immediately straight into the heart of it.

Lightly, as if she were once more the girl she had been when she ascended the throne, she let go of Disraeli's arm and began to run down the hill, a kind of giddiness sending her forward.

She gave no thought to the man behind her. She never gave any thought to the men behind her. Not even dear Albert. Or dear Mr. Brown.

Her delighted laughter trailed behind her like the tail of a kite.

Disraeli was overcome with fear and it almost riveted him to the top of the hill. The queen, corseted and bonneted, was bouncing along like an errant ball let loose by a careless boy. Any moment she might come crashing down and with her, all his dreams.

He *was* the careless boy, letting the ball go. What had he been thinking! This was madness. All his calculations for naught. The maze all by itself was exerting a gravitational pull on the queen and neither he—nor God, he supposed—knew how it was going to end.

He pulled himself loose of his fear and began to run after her.

"Ma'am!" he cried. "Take care. The stones . . . the hill . . . the . . ."

But he needn't have worried. She reached the bottom without misstep, and threaded through the maze as if it were a simple garden walk. Before he was down at the hill's bottom himself, she was already sitting on the stone bench, huffing a bit from the run, her face flushed, a tendril of greying hair having escaped from the bonnet and now caressing her right cheekbone.

"Ma'am," he said when he got to the center, "are you all right?"

"Never better," she said, looking, somehow, years younger, lighter, happier.

She held out her hand and he knelt.

It was then he realized how foolish he had been, playing about with Kabbalistic magic. *She* was the royal here, as high as King David. He knew now that he was only a minor rabbi in this play. *Of course she can command the magic, whether or not she knows it is here.*

"What you will, ma'am," he said.

"I *will* be an empress." She smiled down at him. "But I will *not* ask to be higher, not like the foolish old woman in the story Albert used to tell the children."

"I *can* make you an empress, ma'am," he said. "But will you allow me one question?"

"Of course I will allow it."

Still kneeling, he asked, "What story, ma'am?" He wondered if he would ever understand this woman.

"She wanted to be God," the queen mused.

"Why would anyone want to be God?" he asked. "It's a terrible occupation."

"Ah—that is two questions, dear man. And that I will *not* allow." But she was joking, he could tell. There was a coy smile hesitating at the corners of her mouth.

He felt he was back in familiar territory and grinned at her.

"I will make you empress of India, ma'am," he said. "It will be the jewel in your crown." He dismissed the toad out of mind. It was as if the toad had never happened. *"Forti nihil difficle."*

"Nothing is difficult to the strong. That will be a fine start," she answered. "Now get off your knees, man, we have work to do."

The queen looked at Disraeli, at his sweet curls, his liquid eyes. She thought that she liked him best of any of her prime ministers. And if he *did* somehow manage to make her empress of India, pushing it through a recalcitrant House of Commons, why she was certain that she could find him his just reward.

He has, she thought, *a most original mind. Funny, I have only now noticed. It's just like Albert's, if a tiny bit more . . . more . . .*

She could not think what, until finally it came to her . . . *more Jewish.*

That made her laugh.

And he, standing up at last, laughed, too, though whether he quite understood the joke was another matter altogether.

Author's Note: In 1876, Disraeli did make Victoria empress of India, and India became known as the Jewel in the Crown. She conferred upon him the title of first earl of Beaconsfield that same year, a title he held until his death five years later, though in private she called him "Dizzy." As he lay dying, Victoria asked to come and see him. But he wrote back saying, "No, it is better not." To his secretary he said, "She would only ask me to take a note to Albert." When he died, Victoria sent a wreath "from his grateful and affectionate Sovereign and friend, Victoria R.I.," the "I" standing for India. She lived for twenty more years after Disraeli, and never forgot him. If that odd friendship came out of mutual admiration, mutual interests, or magic, it is not for me to say. I only speculate. —JY

THE GIFT OF THE MAGICIANS,
WITH APOLOGIES TO YOU KNOW WHO

One gold coin with the face of George II on it, whoever *he* was. Three copper pennies. And a crimped tin thing stamped with a fleur-de-lis. That was all.

Beauty stared down at it. The trouble with running a large house this far out in the country, even *with* magical help, was that there was never any real spending money. Except for what might be found in the odd theatrical trunk, in the secret desk drawer, and at the bottom of the pond every spring when it was drained. Three times she had counted: one gold, three coppers, one tin. And the next day would be Christmas.

There was clearly nothing for her to do but flop down on the Victorian sofa, the hard one with the mahogany armrests, and howl. So she did. She howled as she had heard him howl, and wept and pounded the armrests for good measure. It made her feel ever so much better. Except for her hands, which now hurt abominably. But that's the trouble with Victorian sofas. Whatever *they* were.

The whole house was similarly accoutered: Federal, Empire, Art Deco, Louis Quinze. With tags on each explaining the name period. Names about which she knew nothing, but which the house had conjured up out of the past, present, and future. None of it was comfortable, though clearly all of it—according to the tags—was expensive. She longed for the simpler days at home with Papa and her sisters, when even a penniless Christmas after dear Papa had lost all his money meant pleasant afternoons in the kitchen baking presents for the neighbors.

Now, of course, she had no neighbors. And her housemate was used to so much better than her meager kitchen skills could offer. Even if the magical help would let her into the kitchen, which they—it or whatever—would not do.

She finished her cry, left off the howling, and went down the long hallway to her room. There she found her powder and puffs repaired the damage to her complexion speedily. He liked her bright and simple and smelling of herself, and magical cosmetics could do *such* wonders for even the sallowest of skins.

Then she looked into the far-seeing mirror—there were no windows in the house—and saw her old gray cat Miaou walking on a gray fence in her gray backyard. It made her homesick all over again, even though dear Papa was now so poor, and she had only one gold, three coppers, one tin with which to buy Beast a present for Christmas.

She blinked and wished, and the mirror became only a mirror again, and she stared at her reflection. She thought long and hard and pulled down her red hair, letting it fall to its full length, just slightly above her knees.

Now there were two things in that great magical house far out in the country in which both she and the Beast took great pride. One was Beast's gold watch, because it was his link with the real past, not the magical, made-up past. The watch had been his father's and his grandfather's before him, though everything else had been wiped away in the spell. The other thing was Beauty's hair, for, despite her name, it was the only thing beautiful about her. Had Rapunzel lived across the way instead of in the next kingdom, with her handsome but remarkably stupid husband, Beauty would have worn her hair down at every opportunity just to depreciate Her Majesty's gifts.

So now Beauty's hair fell over her shoulders and down past her waist, almost to her knees, rippling and shining like a cascade of red waters. There was a magical hush in the room, and she smiled to herself at it, a little shyly, a little proudly. The house admired her hair almost as much as Beast did. Then she bound it all up again, sighing because she knew what she had to do.

A disguise. She needed a disguise. She would go into town—a two-day walk, a one-day ride; but with magic, only a short, if bumpy, ten minutes away—in disguise. She opened the closet and wished very hard. On went the old brown leather bomber jacket. The leather outback hat. She took a second to tear off the price tags. Tucking the silk bodice into the leather pants, she ran her hands down her legs. Boots! She would need boots. She wished again. The thigh-high leather boots were a fine touch. Checking in the mirror, she saw only her gray cat.

"Pooh!" she said to the mirror. Miaou looked up startled, saw nothing, moved on.

With a brilliant sparkle in her eyes, she went out of the bedroom, down the stairs, across the wide expanse of lawn, toward the gate.

At the gate, she twisted her ring twice. ("Once for home, twice for town, three times for return," Beast had drummed into her when she had first been his guest. Never mind the hair. The ring was her *most* precious possession.)

Ten bumpy minutes later, she landed in the main street of the town.

As her red hair was tucked up into the outback hat, no one recognized her. Or if they did, they only bowed. No one called her by name. This was a town used to disguised gentry. She walked up and down the street for a few minutes, screwing up her courage. Then she stopped by a sign that read MADAME SUZ: HAIR GOODS AND GONE TOMORROW.

Beauty ran up the steep flight of stairs and collected herself.

Madame Suzzane was squatting on a stool behind a large wooden counter. She was a big woman, white and round and graying at the edges, like a particularly dangerous mushroom.

"Will you buy my hair?" Beauty asked.

"Take off that silly hat first. Where'd you get it?" Her voice had a mushroomy sound to it, soft and spongy.

"In a catalog," Beauty said.

"Never heard of it."

The hat came off. Down rippled the red cascade.

"Nah—can't use red. Drug on the market. Besides, if . . . He . . . knew." If anything, Madame Suzzane turned whiter, grayer.

"But I have nothing else to sell." Beauty's eyes grew wider, weepy.

"What about that ring?" Madame Suzzane asked, pointing.

"I can't."

"You can."

"I can't."

"You can."

"How much?"

"Five hundred dollars," said Madame Suzzane, adding a bit for inflation. And for the danger.

Beauty pulled the ring off her finger, forgetting everything in her eagerness to buy a gift for Beast. "Quickly, before I change my mind."

She ran down the stairs, simultaneously binding up her hair again and shoving it back under the hat. The street seemed much longer and much more filled with shops now that she had money in her hands. Real money. Not the gold coin, copper pennies, and crimped tin thing in her pocket.

The next two hours raced by as she ransacked the stores looking for a present for Beast and, not unexpectedly, finding a thing or two for herself: some nail polish in the latest color from the Isles, a faux-pearl necklace with a delicious rhinestone clasp, the most delicate china faun cavorting with three shepherdesses in rosebud-pink gowns, and a painting of a jester so cleverly limned on black velvet that would fit right over her poster bed.

And then she found Beast's present at last, a perfect tortoiseshell comb for his mane, set with little battery-driven (whatever *that* was) lights that winked on and off and on again. She had considered a fob for his grandfather's watch, but the ones she saw were all much too expensive. And besides, the old fob that came with the watch was still in good shape, for something old. And she doubted whether he'd have been willing to part with it anyway. Just like Beast, preferring the old to the new, preferring the rough to the smooth, preferring her to . . . to . . . to someone like Rapunzel.

Then, with all her goodies packed carefully in a string bag purchased with the last of her dollars, she was ready to go.

Only, of course, she hadn't the ring anymore. And no one would take the gold coin or the copper pennies or the crimped tin thing for a carriage and horse and driver to get her back. Not even with her promise made, cross her heart, to fill their pockets with jewels once they got to Beast's house. And the horse she was forced to purchase with the gold and copper and tin crimped thing began coughing at the edge of town, and broke down completely somewhere in the woods to the north. So she had to walk after all, all through the night frightened at every fluttering leaf, at every silent-winged owl, at all the beeps and cheeps and chirps and growls along the way.

Near dawn on Christmas Day, Beast found her wandering alone, smelling of sweat and fear and the leather bomber jacket and leather hat and leather boots and the polished nails. Not smelling like Beauty at all.

So of course he ate her, Christmas being a tough hunting day, since every baby animal and every plump child was tucked up at home waiting for dawn and all their presents.

And when he'd finished, he opened the string bag. The only thing he saved was the comb.

Beauty was right. It *was* perfect.

RABBIT HOLE

The rabbit hole had been there from the first, though everything else had changed.

Especially me, thought Alice, smoothing down her skirt and tucking the shirtwaist back in. She straightened the diamond ring on her left hand, which had a tendency to slip around now that she had lost so much weight. It was certainly going to be more difficult falling down the hole at eighty than it had been at eight. For one thing, the speed would no longer be exhilarating. She knew better now. For another, she feared her legs might not be up to the landing, especially after the operation on her hip.

Still, she wanted a bit of magic back in her life before she died and the doctor, bless him, thought she might go at any time. "Consider that you have had more than your share of years already," he had said. He'd never been a tactful man, though she appreciated his bluntness in this particular instance.

So she had sneaked away from her grandniece, set as a keeper over her, and, still a bit unsteady with the cane, had come back to the meadow where it had all begun.

The tree her sister Edith and she had been reading under

when that first adventure started had long been felled after a lightning strike. Council houses now took up most of the open space: tan-faced two-story buildings alike as cereal boxes. But the rabbit hole was still there, as she had known it would be, in the middle of the little green park set aside for pensioners. She opened the gate and lurked around. No one else was in the park, which pleased her. It would have been difficult explaining just exactly what it was she planned to do.

Closing the gate behind her, she went over to the hole and sat down beside it. It was a smallish hole, ringed round with spikey brown grass. The grass was wet with dew but she didn't mind. If the trip down the hole didn't kill her outright, magic would dry off her skirts. Either way . . . she thought . . . either way . . .

She wondered if she should wait for the rabbit, but he was at least as old as she. If rabbits even lived that long. She should have looked that up before coming. Her late husband, Reggie, had been a biologist manqué and she knew for certain that several volumes on rabbits could be found in his vast library, a great many of them, she was sure, in French. He loved reading French. It was his only odd habit. But the white rabbit might just be late; it had always been late before. As a child she had thought that both an annoying and an endearing quality. Now she simply suspected the rabbit had had a mistress somewhere for, as she recalled, he always had a disheveled and uncomfortable look whenever they met, as if just rumpling out of bed and embarrassed lest anyone know. Especially a child. She'd certainly seen that look on any number of faces at the endless house parties she and Reggie had gone to when they were first married.

She didn't think she had time enough now to waste waiting for the rabbit to show up, though as a child she'd a necessary long patience. Those had been the days of posing endlessly for artists and amateur photographers, which took a great deal of time. She'd learned to play games in her head, cruel games some of them had been. And silly. As often as not the men she posed for were the main characters in the games, but in such odd and often bestial incarnations: griffins, mock turtles, great fuzzy-footed caterpillars. And rabbits. What hadn't she imagined! Mr. Dodgson hadn't been the only one who wanted her for a model, though she never understood why. She'd been quite plain as a child, with a straight-haired simplicity her mother insisted upon. That awful fringe across her forehead; those eyebrows, pronounced and arched. A good characteristic in a woman but awful, she thought consideringly, in a child. In all the photographs she seemed to be staring out insolently, as if daring the photographer to take a good picture. What could Mr. Dodgson have been thinking?

And then there'd been that terrible painter, Sir William Blake Richmond, for whom she'd spent hours kneeling by Lorina's side in the Llandudno sands for a portrait Father never even hung in the house. Though years later, she recalled suddenly, Lorina—who'd really never had very much art sense—displayed it without apology in her sunny apartment. *The Ghastlies*, Father had called that painting, remarking how awful his beautiful girls looked in it. And they had: stiff and uncharming. Like old ladies, really, not young girls. The sand had hurt her knee, the sun had been too hot, and Sir William an utter fool. They'd nicknamed him "Poormond" as a joke. It was her art tutor's idea, actually—Mr. Ruskin. A poor nickname and a poor joke as well, she thought.

Leaning over, she peered down into the hole and thought she saw the beginnings of the shelving that lined the sides, though the first time she'd dropped down the hole it had gone—she seemed to remember dimly—straight like a tunnel for some time. Marmalade, she thought suddenly. That had been on the shelves. The good old-fashioned hand-made orange stuff that her governess, Miss Prickett, had insisted on, not the manufactured kind you get in the stores today. She could almost taste it, the wonderful bits of candied rind that stuck between your teeth. *Of course, that was when I had all my own.*

She sat a bit longer remembering the maps and pictures hung upon pegs that had been scattered between the shelves; and the books—had there been books or was she misremembering? And then, when she was almost afraid of actually doing it, she lowered herself feet first into the suddenly expanding hole.

And fell.

Down, down, down.

As if accommodating to her age, the hole let her fall slowly, majestically, turning over only once or twice on the way. A queen, she thought, would fall this way. Though she had no title, much as Reggie had longed to be on the Honors List. And then she remembered that in Wonderland she was queen. With that thought there was a sudden deliberate heaviness atop her head. It took all the strength she could muster to reach up as she fell, but she just managed. Sure enough, a crown, bulky and solid, was sitting upon her head.

She fell slowly enough that she could adjust her glasses to see onto the shelves, and so that her skirts never ruffled more than a quarter inch above her knees. They were good knees, or at least handsome knees, still. She'd many compliments on them over the years. Reggie, of course, had adored them. She often wondered if that was why she had married him, all those compliments. He'd stopped them once they were safely wed. The crown prince himself—and Dickie Mountbatten, too—had remarked on her knees and her ankles, too. Of course that was when knees and ankles had been in fashion. It was all breast and thigh now. Like, she thought, grocery chickens. She giggled, thinking of herself on a store shelf, in among the poultry. As if responding to her giddy mood, the crown sat more heavily on her head.

"Oh, dear," she said aloud. "We are not to be amused." The giggles stopped.

As she continued falling, she named the things on the shelves to herself: several marmalade jars; a picnic basket from Fortnum & Mason; a tartan lap robe like the one her nanny used to wrap around her on country weekends; a set of ivory fish tile counters; a velvet box with a mourning brooch in which a lock of hair, as pale as that of her own dear dead boys', was twisted under glass; a miniature portrait of the late queen she was sure she'd last seen at a house party at Scone, back in the days before it had become a tourist attraction.

She had not finished with the namings, when she landed, softly, upon a mound of dry leaves and found herself in a lovely garden full of flowers: both a cultivated rose bed and arbor, and an herb garden in the shape of a Celtic knot. It reminded her of her own lovely garden at Cuffnells, the small one that was hers, not the larger-than-life arboretum that Reggie had planted, with its Orientals, redwoods, and Douglas pine. Poor lost Cuffnells. Poor dead Reggie. Poor gone everybody. She shook her head vigorously. She would not let herself get lost in the past, making it somehow better and lovelier than it was. She'd never liked that in old people when she was young, and she wasn't about to countenance it in herself now. The past was a lot like Wonderland: treacherous and marvelous and dull in equal measure. Survival was all that mattered—and she was a survivor. Of course, in the end, she thought, there is no such thing as survival. And just as well. What a clutter the world would be if none of us ever died.

She took a deep breath and looked around the garden. Once, the flowers had spoken to her, but they were silent now. She stood up slowly, the hip giving her trouble again, and waved her cane at them, expecting no answer and receiving none. Then she walked through the garden gate and into Wonderland proper.

"Proper!" she said aloud and gave a small laugh. Proper was one thing Wonderland had never been. Nor was she, though from the outside it must have looked it. But she could still play all those games in her head. Griffins and mock turtles and caterpillars. And rabbits. Men all seemed to fall so easily into those categories. She brushed off her skirt, which was suddenly short and green, like her old school uniform.

"Curioser and curioser," she remarked to no one in particular. She liked the feel of the words in her mouth. They were comfortable, easy.

There was a path that almost seemed to unroll before her. A bit, she thought, like the new path to the Isis from Tom Quad, which Father had had dug. She was not at all surprised when she spied a young man coming toward her in white flannel trousers, striped jacket, a straw hat, and a pair of ghastly black shoes, the kind men had worn before tennis shoes had been invented. She thought tennis shoes were aces. The young man glanced at his pocket watch, then up at her, looking terribly familiar.

"No time," he said. "No time." He stuttered slightly on the n.

"Why, Mr. Dodgson," she said, looking up at him through a fringe of dark hair and holding out a ringless hand. "Why, of course there's plenty of time."

And there was.

OUR LADY OF THE GREENWOOD

In Locksly town, in Nottinghamshire,
In merry sweet Locksly town,
There bold Robin Hood he was born and was bred,
Bold Robin of famous renown.

—from *Robin Hood's Birth,*
Breeding, Valor and Marriage

"**M**y Lord of Locksley, it is a boy."
"And has his mother named him?"

Lady Margaret lay in the great bed, her stomach humped up like leviathan before her. Her face was in a dancing shadow, for the candles on her bedside tables shuddered with each passing breeze.

She called the midwife to her. "I feel the child moving."

"The child has been moving inside thee lo these many months, dearie," the midwife said. She was never one to stand on ceremony with her patrons, not even so fine a lady as Lady

Margaret of Locksley. *What is she but a brood mare?* the midwife thought to herself. *Wed only for the sons she can bear.* She had little patience with the fine folk in the castle, though they were her living. It was the babies who were her chiefest concern.

"This feels quite different," Lady Margaret said. And then she added, "Oh!"

The midwife flipped back the ornately embroidered coverlet and stared at Lady Margaret's legs, nodding. "Oh, indeed. Thy water has broken, dearie. The child will be here before long. Let me call thy women."

"No, Mag, I want only you here," Lady Margaret said. "It will not be a hard birth. He will be born by midnight, christened by noon."

"First children take longer than that, my sweetling," said the midwife.

Lady Margaret sat up and took the midwife's hand, though it was an effort because she was suddenly shaken by a great convulsion. When it was over, she spoke hastily. "Listen, Old Mag, and listen well. This child was promised to the Good Folk ere I came to Locksley's land, that he be a man of the forest, a green man, and their good shepherd."

The midwife sketched a hasty sign of the cross between them. *The Good Folk! The Fey! Whatever was a good Christian woman like Lady Margaret doing mixing with the likes of them?* "What did thee promise them, lady?" she asked, her voice sharp, all pretense of coziness gone. "What did they promise in return?"

"I promised only that they could name the child," Lady Margaret said. "They promised that I might have him," she added.

"And what did thee give up?" asked the midwife Mag, dreading the answer.

"Only my life," said Lady Margaret. She smiled. "Do not look so black, Mag. I have never been hale, girl or woman. Not likely to make old bones, my nurse always said. I have not given up much. And Lord Locksley will have a son. *My* son."

She was shaken by another contraction, much more severe than the first. Squeezing the midwife's hand, she made not a sound till the pain was over. "There," she said, "I feel him creeping from my womb."

"Sliding, more like, dearie," Mag said sweetly, back entire into her old way of speaking. "Just thee work with me and we will have this child born between us as soon as soon."

"By midnight," insisted Lady Margaret, squeezing the midwife's hand again as a third contraction passed through her body, making her belly ripple like an ocean wave. "The Good Folk foresaw it." Mag had never seen the ocean, but she had heard the minstrels sing of it. If it was anything like a woman in labor, she knew she never wanted to be a-sea.

The child—a sturdy boy—was indeed born at midnight. All the candles went out at once from a wind that blew in suddenly through an open window.

Mag held the child, still red with birth blood, overhead. She blessed him silently and consecrated him to the Queen of Heaven, thinking the old words but not saying them aloud:

> *Mary who is o'er us,*
> *Mary who is below us,*
> *Mary who is above us here,*
> *Mary who is above us yonder,*
> *Watch o'er us like a shepherd with sheep*
> *O'er the hills, and valleys,*
> *O'er the steep mountainsides.*

"Promise me, Mag," Lady Margaret whispered. "You will take him at once to the greenwood, foot solid and unstraying upon the path. Go all the way to the great oak at the forest's heart. There you will find a circle. Step in boldly. Do not step out again. You will take the care I bid you and no harm will befall you."

"I promise, my lady," said Mag, not at all sure she would do what Locksley's wife had asked. She had never been into the greenwood. It was not a place for Christian folk.

"Or the hounds will be on your trail. That I *can* promise you."

Mag startled. She knew that Lady Margaret did not mean Lord Locksley's hounds, though that would be bad enough. He had brachets and ratters, several deerhound, and a pair of fierce-looking, stiff-legged mastiffs. But Mag was sure Lady Margaret meant the Gabriel hounds, the hunters belonging to the Fey. She knew of them, of course. Everyone did. There was the old verse:

> *The Devil's dandy dogs course*
> *Hell's skyways hunting.*
> *All wise people seek their beds,*
> *The hours of night counting.*

"I promise," she said again, this time meaning it. The fear of the hounds decided her. Though how she was going to get to the Old Forest with the newborn child and find the very place Lady Margaret spoke of, and all in the black of night, she did not know.

Getting out of the castle with the child was perilously easy. The guards had all turned aside in their watch just as she went past.

Ensorcelled, she thought to herself as she escaped across the moat bridge. Swaddled tight against the midsummer night, the child was still, the dark feathering of his lashes like a bird's wing against the downy cheek. "I will keep thee safe," she whispered to him. "From boggles and nuggles and things that fly in the night." She said it fiercely, but she was sore afraid. For herself as well as the babe.

She slipped down the path that led toward the greenwood. Overhead the moon outlined the Old Forest with a ghostly white light the color of whey. As she went, she kept looking around, right and left, north and south. She did not know what she was looking for, but thought it best to be alert. Once she thought she heard the sound of hounds, but knew it at the last for the soughing of the wind through the trees. All the while the child slept in her arms, that easy, untroubled sleep of the newborn. She hugged him close and moved on.

When she reached the forest edge, where shadows black as raven wings seemed to reach out toward her, she stopped. Hesitated. Changed her mind. Turned to go back home.

This time she heard hounds and it was *not* the wind through trees, for the trees were still.

"Mary who is o'er us," she said aloud to still her galloping heart. Then she turned toward the forest again.

At her voice, the babe opened his eyes. In the moonlight they were not the unfocused milky blue of infant's eyes, but sea green and strangely knowing.

Mag took a step into the shadows, and the dark fully claimed her. She felt herself pulled deep, deeper still into the heart of the woods; the child—his eyes staring up at her—lay heavy in her arms.

She stayed on the path—Lady Margaret had been most specific about that—going past mushrooms that gleamed oddly in the dark; past streams that ran silently, silver against their black banks; past trees that leaned in the night like old men after too many mugs of ale; and over a wide and grassy glade. Little fingers of mist reached out, as if trying to tempt her or pull her off the path, but she kept solidly on.

"Mary who is below us," she whispered.

There was a crying sound, but it was not the child she carried. A white owl, the round circle of its face glowing, flew past her. She felt the wind from its silent wings.

And then—was it a moment? was it an hour?—she was at the great oak that Lady Margaret had spoken of, its branches spread wide and down, making a kind of woody bower within the glade.

"Oh, my lady," Mag said, then caught her breath. The moon was somehow shining through the green interlacings of the oak branches. And there in the very center of the greenwood, under the spreading oak, the moonlight illuminated a circle drawn in the grass.

Lady Margaret had told her to step boldly into the circle with the child and not to stir from there till night was done. "Not a foot out of it," she had warned. "Not a finger. Else you will be lost." *Or somwat as like that*, Mag thought wildly.

So Mag, shivering with more than the cold night air, and feeling every one of her sixty-three years, strode into the circle and, gathering her skirts about her, sat down on the ground within the circle to wait.

She did not have to wait long. Between one blink of the eye and the next, the empty glade was suddenly full of dancing bodies, though one could not rightly call them human. An unseen band piped song after song, and not a one of them was a song she knew.

Among the dancers were creatures scarce a hand's breadth high, the color of fungus. And little mannikins dressed in green with red caps upon their heads. An elf skipped by, holding a lantern made of a campanula out of which streamed a blue-green light. There were fairies no bigger than a singing bird, with darning-needle wings, translucent and veined by moonlight, who flitted about in a complicated reel. But there were larger folk as well, near human size, with long yellow-white hair bound with strips of cloth that glittered like the overhead stars. They were beautiful and terrifying at the same time, and these larger Fey danced in a slow, swaying rhythm that was hypnotic to watch.

And then Mag saw, at the edges of the fairy dancers, ragged human folk, their skirts and trews dirty and torn, their hair tangled in elflocks. They danced, too. And far from seeming sad at their terrible estate, or frightened as Mag was, they kicked up their heels and danced as if they were having a marvelous time. Mag stared at them the longest, for they reminded her of something. And when a couple went capering by, holding hands and spinning wildly, Mag gasped aloud, for the man of the pair was Tom the Swineherd, lost these seven years.

At the sound of her voice, the Good Folk all turned and stared into the circle. One of them, a tall and fiercely handsome Fey, came over and stood at the very edge of the circle. He held out his hand to Mag.

"Come and join us, Mag, and ye shall be young again and beautiful. I shall be thy consort and ye shall live in my hall."

His words were fair and seemingly open, and for a moment she was sorely tempted. *Who would not be, to be young again. And lovely.* But she looked over at Tom and he was neither young nor comely. Nor were any of the human folk there. And besides, there was something dark and hidden in the fairy prince's eyes. Something she did not like or trust.

"Oh, my Lady of the Greenwood," Mag prayed aloud, meaning the Queen of Heaven, "save me and the child." But meaning and magic are held to different tasks under the oak tree. What she meant was, somehow, not what she said.

Suddenly there was before her, shimmering in the moonlight, the most beautiful woman Mag had ever seen. She was as tall as Lord Locksley and slim as a girl, with snow-white hair tied up in a hundred braids. There were bells hanging at her belt and sewn to the bottom of her green skirt, so whenever she moved she made music. "Thee called me, Old Mag, and I am come."

"I called the Queen of Heaven," Mag whispered, clutching the silent child to her breast.

"I am all the queen there is here," said the woman. "But as thee cried out my name, the Lady of the Greenwood, I must give thee what thee wishes."

"You will let me go?" Mag asked.

"Come outside the circle and then thee will surely be free," the dark-eyed prince of the Fey said. But when the queen turned and glared at him, he shook quite visibly and took two steps back.

Then Mag remembered what Lady Margaret had told her and shook her head. "I dare not," she said. "The circle is my protection."

"Thee will not," agreed the queen. "Till the night is done. But let me see the child's face."

As if a geas, a fate, had been laid upon her, Mag obeyed, lifting the blanket away from the baby's head.

The queen clapped her hands. "That is Lady Margaret's child."

Mag was astonished. "How do you know?"

The queen gave her such a look then that Mag was forced to drop her eyes. The fairy woman might not be the Queen of Heaven, but she was the Queen of the *Greenwood*. Of course she would know!

"We have promised to give the child something," the queen said.

"A name," Mag said.

The queen nodded and then, one by one, the trooping fairies came to the circle's edge and gave the boy names.

"Fleet-foot," said one.

"Green kin," said another.

"Straight as an arrow," said a third.

"King's own."

"Child of the wood."

"Giver of riches."

"Merry maker."

"Bow bender."

"Staff breaker."

And on and on and on they went. Such odd things, not a good

Christian name among them. Mag kept shaking her head as if rejecting everyone, till they were all done with their naming.

"A name," the queen said when they were through, "is what one is. It is power and honor and all."

A name, Mag thought, *is but a tag. A man may be born with one name, achieve another. Honor and power come from the heart.* But she did not say that aloud. For just then the first thin red line of dawn shone between the trees.

"Away!" the dark-eyed prince cried. And the rest echoed him, disappearing as suddenly as stars in the morning, one small flicker and they were gone.

Mag waited long into the morning, when sunlight completely lit the little glade, and the Good Folk were gone to their rest. She was just about to stand and step out of the circle, when a little bird flew down out of the tree. It was an undistinguished brown bird with an orange breast. It lit on the outside of the circle, but then hopped in, totally unafraid. Standing still for a moment, it cocked its head to one side and looked at Mag.

"Why, thou art a robin," she said aloud. Suddenly she remembered the story one of the good sisters of Kirklees Abbey had told her: "When Our Lord Jesus was dying, the robin tried to pluck away the thorns on his crown but only managed to tear its own little breast. As its reward, the robin's breast was ever stained to this day in memory of its brave deed."

Why, what better name than this? she thought. *For a child who would be brave and true.* "The Lady of the Greenwood has sent thee thy name, child."

The baby in her arms looked up at her and, though it is said that newborns cannot smile, he smiled.

"My Lord of Locksley, it is a boy."
"And has his mother named him?"

"She did, my lord, before she died, poor sweet lady."
"And what name did she give him?"
"Robin, my lord."

THE CONFESSION OF BROTHER BLAISE

"Many of those who shall read this book or shall hear it read will be the better for it, and will be on their guard against sin."

> —The Infant Merlin to his confessor, Father Blaise,
> in *Vita Merlini* by Geoffrey of Monnouth

Osney Monastery, January 13, 1125

The slap of sandals along the stone floor was the abbot's first warning.

"It is Brother Blaise." The breathless news preceded the monk's entrance as well. When he finally appeared, his beardless cheeks were pink both from the run and the January chill. "Brother Geoffrey says that Brother Blaise's time has come." The novice breathed deeply of the wood scent in the abbot's parlor and then, because of the importance of his message, he added the unthinkable. *"Hurry!"*

It was to the abbot's everlasting glory that he did not scold the novice for issuing an order to the monastery's head as a cruder man might have done. Rather, he nodded and turned to gather up what he would need: the cruse of oil, his stole, the book of prayers. He had kept them near him all through the day, just in case. But he marked the boy's offense in the great register of his mind. It was said at Osney that Abbot Walter never forgot a thing. And that he never smiled.

They walked quickly across the snow-dusted courtyard. In the summer those same whitened borders blossomed with herbs and berry bushes, adding a minor touch of beauty to the ugly stone building squatting in the path before them.

The abbot bit his lower lip. So many of the brothers with whom he had shared the past fifty years were housed there now, in the stark infirmary. Brother Stephen, once his prior, had lain all winter with a terrible wasting cough. Brother Homily, who had been the gentlest master of boys and novices imaginable, sat in a cushioned chair blind and going deaf. And dear simple Brother Peter-Paul, whose natural goodness had often put the abbot to shame, no longer recognized any of them and sometimes ran out into the snow without so much as a light summer cassock between his skin and the winter wind. Three others had died just within the year gone by, each a lasting and horrible death. He missed every one of them dreadfully. The worst, he guessed, was at prime.

The younger monks seemed almost foreign to him, untutored somehow, though by that he did not mean they lacked vocation. And the infant oblates—there were five of them ranging in ages from eight to fourteen, given to the abbey by their parents—he loved them as a father should. He did not stint in his affection. But why did he feel this terrible impatience, this lack of charity toward the young? God may have written that a child would lead, but to Abbot Walter's certain knowledge none had led *him*. The ones he truly loved were the men of his own age with whom he had shared so much, from whom he had learned so much. And it was those men who were all so ill and languishing, as if God wanted to punish him by punishing them. Only how could he believe in a God who would do such a thing?

Until yesterday only he and Brother Blaise of the older monks still held on to any measure of health. He discounted the aching in his bones that presaged any winter storms. And then suddenly, before compline, Blaise had collapsed. Hard work and prayer, whatever the conventional wisdom, broke more good men than it healed.

The abbot suddenly remembered a painting he had seen in a French monastery the one time he had visited the Continent. He had not thought of it in years. It represented a dead woman wrapped in her shroud, her head elaborately dressed. Great white worms gnawed at her bowels. The inscription had shocked him at the time: *Une fois sur toute femme belle* . . . Once I was beautiful above all women. But by death I became like this. My flesh was very beautiful, fresh and soft. Now it is altogether turned to ashes . . . It was not the ashes that had appalled him but the worms, gnawing the private part he had only then come to love. He had not touched a woman since. And that Blaise, the patrician of the abbey, would be gnawed soon by those same worms did not bear thinking about. God was very careless with his few treasures.

With a shudder, Abbot Walter pushed the apostasy from his mind. The Devil had been getting to him more and more of late. Cynicism was Satan's first line of offense. And then despair. *Despair.* He sighed.

"Open the door, my son," Abbot Walter said, putting it in his gentlest voice. "My hands are quite full."

Like the *dortoir*, the infirmary was a series of cells off a long, dark hall. Because it was January, all the buildings were cold, damp, and from late afternoon on, lit by small flickering lamps. The shadows that danced along the wall when they passed seemed mocking. *The dance of death,* the abbot thought, *should be a solemn stately measure, not this obscene capering morris along the stones.*

They turned into the misericorde. There was a roaring fire in the hearth and lamps on each of the bedside tables. The hard bed, the stool beside it, the stark cross on the wall, each cast shadows. Only the man in the bed seemed shadowless. He was the stillest thing in the room.

Abbot Walter walked over to the bed and sat down heavily on the stool. He stared at Blaise and noticed, with a kind of relief crossed with dread, that the man's eyes moved under the lids.

"He is still alive," whispered the abbot.

"Yes, but not, I fear, for long. That is why I sent for you." The infirmarer, Brother Geoffrey, moved suddenly into the center of the room like a dancer on quiet, subtle feet. "My presence seems to disturb him, as if he were a messenger who has not yet delivered his charge. Only when I observe from a far corner is he quiet."

No sooner had Geoffrey spoken than the still body moved and, with a sudden jerk, a clawlike hand reached out for the abbot's sleeve.

"Walter." Brother Blaise's voice was ragged.

"I will get him water," said the novice, eager to be doing something.

"No, my son. He is merely addressing me by name," said the abbot. "But I would have you go into the hall now and wait upon us. Or visit with the others. Your company should cheer them, and a man's final confession and the viaticum is between himself and his priest." The abbot knew this particular boy was prone to homesickness and nightmares and had more than once wakened the monastery hours after midnight with his cries. Better he was absent at the moment of Blaise's death.

The novice left at once, closing the door softly. Geoffrey, too, started out.

"Let Geoffrey stay," Blaise cried out.

Abbot Walter put his hand to Blaise's forehead. "Hush, my dear friend, and husband your strength."

But Blaise shook the hand off. "The babe himself said to me that it should be writ down."

"The babe?" asked the abbot. "The Christ child?"

"He said, 'Many of those who shall read or shall hear of it will be the better for it, and will be on their guard against sin.'" Blaise stopped. Then, as if speaking lent him strength he otherwise did not have, he continued. "I was not sure if it was Satan speaking— or God. But *you* will know, Walter. You have an instinct for the Devil."

The abbot made a clicking sound with his tongue. But Blaise did not seem to notice. "Let Geoffrey stay. He is our finest scribe and it must be written down. His is the best hand and the sharpest ear, for all that you keep him laboring here amongst the infirm of mind and bowels."

The abbot set his mouth into a firm line. He was used to being scolded in private by Blaise. He relied on Blaise's judgments, for Blaise had been a black canon of great learning and a prelate in a noble house before suddenly, mysteriously, dedicating himself to the life of a monk. But it was mortifying that Blaise should scold in front of Geoffrey, who was a literary popinjay with nothing of a monk's quiet habits of thought. Besides, Geoffrey entertained all manner of heresies, and it was all the abbot could do to keep him from infecting the younger brothers. The assignment to the infirmary was to help him curb such apostatical tendencies. But despite his thoughts, the abbot said nothing. One does not argue with a dying man. Instead he turned and instructed Geoffrey quietly.

"Get you a quill and however much vellum you think you might need from the scriptorium. While you are gone, Brother

Blaise and I will start this business of preparing for death." He regretted the cynical tone instantly, though it brought a small chuckle from Blaise.

Geoffrey bowed his head meekly, which was the best answer, and was gone.

"And now," Abbot Walter said, turning back to the man on the narrow bed. But Blaise was stiller than before and the pallor of his face was the green-white of a corpse. "Oh, my dear Blaise, and have you left me before I could bless you?" The abbot knelt down by the bedside and took the cold hand in his.

At the touch, Brother Blaise opened his eyes once again. "I am not so easily got rid of, Walter." His lips scarcely moved.

The abbot crossed himself, then sat back on the stool. But he did not loose Blaise's hand. For a moment the hand seemed to warm in his. *Or was it,* the abbot thought suddenly, *that his own hand was losing its life?*

"If you will start, Father," Blaise said formally. Then, as if he had lost the thread of his thought for a moment, he stopped. He began again. "Start. And I shall be ready for confession by the time Brother Geoffrey is back." He paused and smiled, and so thin had his face become overnight it was as if a skull grinned. "Geoffrey will have a re-trimmed quill and full folio with him, enough for an epic, at least. He has talent, Walter."

"But not for the monastic life," said the abbot as he kissed the stole and put it around his neck. "Or even for the priesthood."

"Perhaps he will surprise you," said Blaise.

"Nothing Geoffrey does surprises me. Everything he does is informed by wit instead of wisdom, by facility instead of faith."

"Then perhaps you will surprise him." Blaise brought his hands together in prayer and, for a moment, looked like one of the stone *gisant* carved on a tomb cover. "I am ready, Father."

The opening words of the ritual were a comfort to them

both, a reminder of all they had shared. The sound of Geoffrey opening the door startled the abbot, but Blaise, without further assurances, began his confession. His voice grew stronger as he talked.

"If this be a sin, I do heartily repent of it. It happened over thirty years ago but not a day goes by that I do not think on it and wonder if what I did then was right or wrong.

"I was confessor to the King of Dayfed and his family, a living given to me as I was a child of that same king, though born on the wrong side of the blanket, my mother being a lesser woman of the queen's.

"I was contented at the king's court, for he was kind to all of his bastards, and we were legion. Of his own legal children, he had but two, a whining whey-faced son who even now sits on the throne no better man than he was a child, and a daughter of surpassing grace."

Blaise began to cough a bit and the abbot slipped a hand under his back to raise him to a more comfortable position. The sick man noticed Geoffrey at the desk in the far corner. "Are you writing all of this down?"

"Yes, Brother."

"Read it to me. The last part of it."

". . . and a daughter of surprising grace."

"*Surpassing.* But never mind, it was surprising, too, given that her mother was such a shrew. No wonder the king, my father, turned to other women. But write it as you will, Geoffrey. The words can change as long as alteration does not alter the sense of it."

"You may trust me, Brother Blaise."

"He may—but I do not," said the abbot. "Bring the desk closer to the bed. You will hear better—and have better light as well—and Blaise will not have to strain."

Geoffrey pushed the oak desk into the center of the room where he might closer attend the sick man's words.

When Geoffrey was ready, Blaise began again.

"She was his favorite, little Ellyne, with a slow smile and a mild disposition. Mild disposition? Yes, that was her outer face to the world. But she was also infernally stubborn about those things she held dear.

"She had been promised before birth to the Convent of St. Peter by her mother, who had longed for a daughter after bearing the king an heir. All his by-blows had been boys, which made the queen's desire for a daughter even greater.

"When Ellyne was born, the queen repented of her promise at once, for the child was bright and fair. Rings and silver candlesticks and seven cups of beaten gold were sent to the church in her stead. The good sisters were well pleased and did not press for the child.

"But when Ellyne was old enough to speak her own mind, she determined that she would honor her mother's promise. Despite the entreaties of her mother and father and the assurances of the abbess that she need not come, she would not be turned aside from her decision.

"I was, at that time, her confessor as well as the king's. At his request I added my pleas to theirs. I loved her as I loved no other, for she was a beautiful little thing, with a quick mind I feared would be dulled behind the convent walls. It was thought that she would listen to me, her 'Bobba' as she called me, sooner than to another. But the child shamed me, saying, 'Can you, who has turned his life entirely toward God, ask me not to do the same?' It was that question that convinced me that she was right for, you see, I was a priest by convenience and not conviction. Yet when she said it, she set me on the path by her side.

"She entered the convent the very next day."

Blaise paused, and the abbot moistened his mouth with a cloth dipped in a bowl of scented water that stood on the table. The *scratch, scratch, scratch* of Geoffrey's pen continued into the silence.

"She was eight when she entered and eighteen when the thing came to pass that led me to Osney—and eventually to this room."

Abbot Walter moved closer to the bed.

"I was in my study when the mother superior herself came bursting into the room. Ordinarily she would have sent a messenger for me, but such was her agitation, she came herself, sailing into my study like a great prowed ship under full sail.

"'Father Blaise,' she said, 'you must come to my parlor at once, and alone. Without asking a single question of me yet.'

"I rose, picked up a breviary, and followed her. We used the back stair that was behind a door hidden by an arras. It was not so much secret as unused. But Mother Agnes knew of it and insisted we go that way. As we raced down the steps, dodging skeins of cobwebs, I tried to puzzle out the need for such secrecy and her agitation and fear. Was there a plague amongst the sisters? Had two been found in the occasion of sin? Or had something happened to little Ellyne, now called Sister Martha? Somehow the last was my greatest fear.

"When we arrived in her spare, sweet-scented parlor, there was a sister kneeling in front of the hearth, her back to us, her face uplifted to the crucifix above.

"'Stand, Sister,' commanded Mother Agnes.

"The nun stood and turned to face us and my greatest fear was realized. It was Sister Martha, her face shining with tears. There was a flush on her cheeks that could not be explained by the hearth for it was summer and there was no fire in the grate."

Blaise's voice was becoming ragged again, and the abbot offered him a sip of barley water, holding the cup to his mouth. Geoffrey's pen finished the last line and he looked up expectantly.

"When she saw me, Sister Martha began to cry again and ran to me, flinging her arms around me the way she had done as a child.

"'Oh, Bobba,' she cried out. 'I swear I have done nothing, unless sleeping is more than nothing.'

"Mother Agnes raised her head and thrust her chin forward. 'Tell Father Blaise what you told me, child.'

"'On my faith, Father, I was asleep in a room several months ago, surrounded by my sisters. Sisters Agatha and Armory were on my right, Sisters Adolfa and Marie on my left. Marie snores. And the door was locked.'

"'From the outside!' said Mother Agnes, nodding her head sharply, like a sword in its downward thrust. 'All the sisters sleep under lock, and I and my prioress hold the only keys.'"

"A barbaric custom," muttered Abbot Walter. "It shows a lack of trust. And, should there be a fire, disastrous."

Blaise coughed violently but after a few more sips of barley water, he was able to go on.

"Ellyne folded her hands before her and continued. 'In my deepest sleep,' she said, looking down as if embarrassed by the memory, 'I dreamed that a young man, clothed in light and as beautiful as the sun, came to my bed and embraced me. His cheeks were rough on mine and he kissed my breasts hard enough to leave marks. Then he pierced me and filled me until I cried out with fear. And delight. But it was only a dream.'

"'Such dreams are disgusting and violate your vows,' spat out Mother Agnes.

"'Now, now, Mother,' I interrupted, 'all girls have such dreams, even when they are nuns. Just as the novice monks, before they are purged of the old Adam, often have similar dreams. But surely you did not call me here to confront Ellyne . . . ah, Sister Martha . . . about a bad dream which is, at worst, a minor venial sin.'

"'A bad dream?' Mother Agnes was trembling. 'Then, Father Blaise, what call you *this*?'

"She stripped away the girl's black robe, and Sister Martha stood there in a white shift in which the mark of her pregnancy was unmistakable."

Geoffrey's quill punctuated the sentence with such vehemence that the ink splattered across the page. It took him several minutes to blot the vellum, and the abbot bathed Blaise's brow with water and smoothed down the brychan around his legs until Geoffrey was ready again.

"'I do not understand, Ellsie,' I said to her, in my anger returning to her childhood name.

"'I do not understand either, Father Blaise,' she answered, her voice not quite breaking. 'When I awoke I was in the room still surrounded by my sisters, all of whom slept as soundly as before. And that was how I knew it had been but a dream. On my faith in God, more than this there was never between a man and myself.' She stopped and then added as if the admission proved her innocence, 'I have dreamed of him every night since but he has not again touched me. He just stands at my bed foot and watches.'

"I put my hands behind me and clasped them to keep them from shaking. 'This sort of thing I have heard of, Mother. The girl is blameless. She has been set upon by an incubus, the devil who comes in dreams to seduce the innocent.'

"'Well, she carries the other marks she spoke of,' said Mother Agnes. 'The burns on her cheeks you can see for yourself. I will vouch for the rest.' She draped the cloak again over the girl's shoulders almost tenderly, then turned to glare at me. 'An incubus—not a human—you are sure?'

"'I am sure,' I said, though I was not sure at all. Ellyne had been headstrong about certain things, though how a young man might have trysted with her with Mother Agnes her abbess, I could not imagine. 'But in her condition she cannot remain in the convent. Leave her here in your parlor, and I will go at once and speak to the king.'"

Blaise's last word faded and he closed his eyes. The abbot leaned over and, dipping his finger into the oil, made the sign of the cross on Blaise's forehead. *"In nomine Patris, et Filii, et Spiritus sancti, exstinguatur in te omnis virtus diaboli per . . ."*

Opening his eyes, Blaise cried out, "I am not done. I swear to you I will not die before I have told it all."

"Then be done with it," said the abbot. He said it quickly but gently.

"Speaking to the king was easy. Speaking to his shrewish wife was not. She screamed and blamed me for letting the girl go into the convent, and her husband for permitting Ellyne to stay. She ranted against men and devils indiscriminately. But when I suggested it would be best for Ellyne to return to the palace, the queen refused, declaring her dead.

"And so it was that I fostered her to a couple in Carmarthen who were known to me as a closemouthed, devoted, and childless pair. They were of yeoman stock, but as Ellyne had spent the last ten years of her life on the bread, cheese, and prayers of a convent, she would not find their simple farm life a burden. And the farm ran on its own canonical hours: cock's crow, feed time, milking.

"So for the last months of her strange pregnancy, she was—if not exactly happy—at least content. Whether she still dreamed of the devil clothed in sunlight, she did not say. She worked alongside the couple and they loved her as their own."

Blaise straggled to sit upright in bed.

"Do not fuss," the abbot said. "Geoffrey and I will help you." He signaled to the infirmarer, who stood, quickly blotting the smudges on his hands along the edges of his robe. Together they helped settle Blaise into a more comfortable position.

"I am fine now," he said. Then, when Geoffrey was once more standing at the desk, Blaise began again. "In the ninth month, for the first time, Ellyne became afraid.

"'Father,' she questioned me day after day, 'will the child be human? Will it have a heart? Will it bear a soul?'

"And to keep her from sorrow before time, I answered as deviously as I could without actually telling a lie. 'What else should it be but human?' I would say. 'You are God's own; should not your child be the same?' But the truth was that I did not know. What I read was not reassuring. The child might be a demon or a barbary ape or anything in between.

"Then on the night before All Hallow's, unpropitious eve, Ellyne's labor began. The water flooded down her legs and the child's passage rippled across her belly. The farmer came to my door and said simply, 'It is her time.'

"I took my stole, the oil, a Testament, candles, a crucifix, and an extra rosary. I vowed I would be prepared for any eventuality.

"She was well into labor when I arrived. The farmwife was firm with her but gentle as well, having survived the birth of every calf and kitten on the place. She allowed Ellyne to yell but not to scream, to call out but not to cry. She kept her busy panting like a beast so that the pains of the birth would pass by. It seemed to work, and I learned that there was a rhythm to this, God's greatest mystery: pain, not-pain, over and over and over again.

"Before long the farmwife said, 'Father Blaise, the child, whatever it be, comes.' She pointed—and I looked.

"From between Ellyne's legs, as if climbing out of a blood-filled cave, crawled a child, part human and part imp. It had the most beautiful face, like an ivory carving of an angel, and eyes the blue of Our Lady's robe. The body was perfectly formed. Up over one shoulder lay a strange cord, the tip nestling into the little hollow at its neck. At first I thought the cord was the umbilicus, but when the farmwife went to touch it, the cord uncoiled from the child's neck and slashed at her hand. Then I knew it was a tail.

"The farmwife screamed. The farmer also. I grabbed the babe firmly with my left hand and, dipping my right finger into the holy oil, made the sign of the cross on its forehead, on its belly, on its genitals, and on its feet. Then I turned it over and pinned it with my left forearm, and with my right hand anointed the tail where it joined the buttocks.

"The imp screamed as if in terrible pain and its tail burst into flames, turning in an instant to ash. All that was left was a scar at the top of the buttocks, above the crack.

"I lifted up my left arm and the child rolled over, reaching up with its hands. It was then I saw that it had claws instead of fingers, and it scratched me on the top of both my hands, from the mid finger straight down to the line of the wrist. I shouted God's name and almost dropped the holy oil, but miraculously held on. And though I was now bleeding profusely from the wounds, I managed somehow to capture both those sharp claws in my left hand and with my right anoint the imp's hands. The child screamed again and, as I watched, the imp aspect disappeared completely, the claws fell off to reveal two perfectly formed hands, and the child was suddenly and wholly human."

Blaise had become so agitated during this recitation that the bed itself began to shake. Geoffrey had to leave off writing and come over to help the abbot calm him. They soothed his head and the abbot whispered, "Where is the sin in all this, Blaise?"

The monk's eyes blinked and with an effort Blaise calmed himself. "The sin?" His voice cracked. Tears began to course down his cheeks. "The sin was not in baptizing the babe. That was godly work. But what came after—was it a sin or not? I do not know, for the child spoke to me. *Spoke.*"

"A newborn cannot speak," said Geoffrey.

"*Jesu!* Do you think I do not know that? But this one did. He said, '*Holy, holy, holy,*' and the words shot from his mouth in gouts of flame. 'You shall write this down, my uncle,' he said, 'Write down that my mother, your half sister, was sinless. That her son shall save a small part of the world. That I shall be prophet and mage, lawgiver and lawbreaker, king of the unseen worlds and counselor to those seen. I shall die and I shall live, in the past and in the future also. Many of those who shall read what you write or who shall hear it read will be the better for it and will be on their guard against sin.' And then the flames died down and the babe put its finger in its mouth to suck on it like any newborn and did not speak again. But the sin of it is that I did *not* write it down, nor even speak of it save to you now in this last hour, for I thought it the Devil tempting me."

Abbot Walter was silent for a moment. *It was so much easier,* he thought, *for a man to believe in the Devil than in God.* Then he reached over and smoothed the covers across Brother Blaise's chest. "Did the farmer or his wife hear the child speak?"

"No," whispered Blaise hoarsely, "for when the tail struck the woman's hand, they both bolted from the room in fear."

"And Ellyne?"

"She was near to death from blood loss and heard nothing." Blaise closed his eyes.

Abbot Walter cleared his throat. "You have done only what you believed right, Blaise. I shall think more on this. But as for you, you may let go of your earthly life knowing that you shall have absolution, that you have done nothing sinful to keep you from God's Heaven." He anointed the paper-thin eyelids. *"Per sitam sanctan Unctionem, et suam piissimam misericordiam, indulgeat tibi Dominus quid quid per visum deliquisti. Amen."*

"Amen," echoed Geoffrey.

The abbot added the signs over the nose and mouth, and Blaise murmured in Latin along with him. Then, as the abbot dipped his fingers once more into the jar of oil, Geoffrey took Blaise's hands in his and lay them with great gentleness side by side on top of the covers, and gasped.

"Look, Father."

Abbot Walter followed Geoffrey's pointing finger. On the back of each of Blaise's hands was a single, long, ridged scar starting at the middle finger and running down to the wrist. The abbot crossed himself hastily, getting oil on the front of his habit. *"Jesu!"* he breathed out. Until that moment he had not quite believed Blaise's story. Over the years he had discovered that old men and dying men sometimes make merry with the truth.

Geoffrey backed away to the safety of his desk and crossed himself twice, just to be sure.

With deliberate slowness, the abbot put his fingers back into the oil and with great care anointed Blaise's hands along the line of the scars, then slashed across, careful to enunciate every syllable of the prayer. When he reached the end, ". . . *quid quid per tactum deliquisiti. Amen,"* the oil on Blaise's skin burst into flames, bright orange with a blue arrow at the heart. As quickly, the flames were gone and a brilliant red wound the shape of a cross opened on each hand. Then, as the abbot and Geoffrey watched, each wound healed to a scab, the scab to a scar, and the scar faded until the skin was clean and whole. With a sigh that seemed a combination of joy and relief, Blaise died.

"In nomine Patris, et Filii, et Spiritus sancti . . ." intoned the abbot. He removed the covers from the corpse and completed the anointing. He felt better than he had all winter, than he had in years, filled with a kind of spiritual buoyancy, like a child's kite that had been suddenly set free into the wind. If there was a Devil, there was also a God. Blaise had died to show him that. He finished the prayers for absolution, but they were only for the form of it. He knew in his inmost heart that the absolution had taken place already and that Blaise's sinless spirit was fast winging its way to Heaven. Now it was time to forgive himself his own sins. He turned to Geoffrey, who was standing at the desk.

"Geoffrey, my dear son, you *shall* write this down in your own way. Then we will all be the better for it. The babe, imp or angel, magician or king, was right about that. Only, perhaps. you should not say just *when* all this happened, for the sake of the Princess Ellyne. Set it in the past, at such a time when miracles happened with *surprising* regularity. It is much easier to accept a miracle that has been approved by time. But you and I shall know when it took place. You and I—*and God*—will remember."

Surprised, Geoffrey nodded. He wondered what it was that had so changed the abbot, for he was actually smiling. And it was said at Osney that Abbot Walter never smiled. That such a thing had happened would be miracle enough for the brothers in the monastery. The other miracle, the one he would write about, *that* one was for the rest of the world.

WONDER LAND

Allison ran down the forest path between her house and Marcie's, ready to tell her the very latest about Billy Jamieson. As she passed by the little clearing, there was a very large yellow butterfly with black spots like microchips on its wings, flying toward her: It had a scrunched-up, old man's brown face, with wrinkles, sort of pruney, she thought. A halo of some kind, cloudy or like smoke, ringed its brown head. Allison ducked, and ran on.

At the path's turning a rabbit hopped in front of her, in a terrible hurry. It was black and white, the black part where pants would be, if rabbits wore pants. Allison thought that kind of funny. Maybe she'd tell Marcie. *After* she told her where Billy Jamieson had tried to put his hand this time.

When she went by the reedy pond, there was a red fox. Just sitting. Only not sitting exactly. It was sort of lying on its back showing its private parts. Which were, Allison had to admit, sort of public parts now, the way it was acting. She had a dog, though, and she knew all about that kind of thing, only seeing it right out in the open air like, that seemed—well—awfully unnatural. The fox grinned as she passed, displaying very white teeth, all terribly close together. Allison turned her head and kept running. Something else to tell Marcie.

By the double tree—the oak that had a second tree growing right out of its center, its *crotch*, her father always said, though her mother usually made a funny face when he said that and gestured at Allison as if she'd never heard the word in school—there were two crows. And they were doing it right there, in the fork place, the crotch of the tree. And the crow on top—it must have been the male because that's how birds did it, she knew from biology class (the kids called it "Birds and Bees, Nuts and Sluts"). And he was squawking away. Allison shook her head because it sounded remarkably as if he were saying "Oooh, baby, ooooh . . ." though of course it couldn't have been, except she remembered that crows *can* be taught to talk. Maybe he had been tame once. The two crows didn't even stop when she got up close, so she actually stood still and watched them for a minute. Maybe longer. She wondered what Marcie would say. Probably "Oh, gross . . ." Maybe not.

When they finished, she took off running again, only more like jogging, thinking about the butterfly and the rabbit and the fox and the crows, and a little, it had to be admitted, about where Billy Jamieson had tried to put his hand. And where she had actually let him. Not the same place of course, but close, only she decided she wouldn't tell Marcie *that*. She could hear the woods now; it seemed as if the entire forest was—well—breathing actually, breathing as hard as Billy did in her ear. And she wished she could sometimes tell him what she was thinking about that, or about anything, but when he was close to her, all she could do was control her own breathing, really. She never actually knew what to say to him. Of course some of the forest's breathing might really be her own breathing, having run so far and so fast. But it was closer now, and in her ear, like Billy's breath.

She stopped dead still and turned and that was when she saw the wolf. It was leaning against a tree, up on its hind legs. She hadn't known they could do that and she guessed she should have been scared, only it wasn't really scary. Only sort of puzzling, even exciting, making her breath, which had been so hard to catch moments before, suddenly seem hot and heavy in her chest.

The wolf stared at her. Its eyes were blue, bluer even than Billy's. Its nose—muzzle she supposed she should call it but didn't want to—was covered with the finest, grayest fur, almost like silk. She knew how it would feel under her hand without even knowing *how* she knew. The wolf licked its mouth—its chops, but that might be insulting so she stopped thinking about it that way—and its tongue was pink and soft looking, like her velveteen dress, only wet. She licked her own mouth in automatic response, then wondered if that might also be insulting or whether it was an acknowledgment, to make them friends now. Or something.

The wolf grinned at her, like the fox, only broader. Then it went down on all fours. And just when she was sure it was going to leap on her, it turned and strolled off into the forest, its hips moving back and forth, back and forth away from her. For a moment—just a moment—she felt something like disappointment. She wondered if she should follow, but the wolf was off the path and into the scraggly underbrush and she had on her good Chinese shoes.

She walked the rest of the way to Marcie's slowly, suddenly and stubbornly determined not to tell her anything at all. There weren't any more strange animals, but she had a feeling she might run into Billy Jamieson on the way home. If she did, she knew exactly what to say to him. "Why, Billy Jamieson," she would whisper, trying it aloud, "what big hands you have."

Somewhere in the forest, the leaves tittered.

EVIAN STEEL

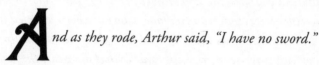

And as they rode, Arthur said, "I have no sword."

"No force," said Merlin, "hereby is a sword that shall be yours, an I may."

So they rode till they came to a lake, the which was a fair water and broad, and in the midst of the lake Arthur was ware of an arm clothed in white samite, that held a fair sword in that hand.

"Lo!" said Merlin, "yonder is that sword that I spake of."

With that they saw a damosel going upon the lake.

"What damosel is that?" said Arthur.

"That is the Lady of the Lake," said Merlin, "and within that lake is a rock, and therein is as fair a place as any on earth, and richly beseen; and this damosel will come to

*you anon, and then speak ye fair to her that she will give
you that sword."*

—*Le Morte D'Arthur*
by Sir Thomas Malory

*Ynis Evelonia, the Isle of Women, lies within the marshy tidal river
Tamor that is itself but a ribbon stretched between the Mendip and
the Quantock hills. The isle is scarcely remarked from the shore. It is
as if Manannan MacLir himself had shaken his cloak between.*

*On most days there is an unsettling mist obscuring the irregular
coast of the isle; and only in the full sun, when the light just rising
illuminates a channel, can any passage across the glass-colored waters
be seen. And so it is that women alone, who have been schooled in the
hidden causeways across the fen, mother to daughter down through
the years, can traverse the river in coracles that slip easily through the
brackish flood.*

*By ones and twos they come and go in their light skin boats to
commerce with the Daughters of Eve who stay in holy sistership on
the isle, living out their chaste lives and making with their magicks
the finest blades mankind has ever known.*

*The isle is dotted with trees, not the great Druidic oaks that line
the roadways into Godney and Meare and tower over the mazed
pathways up to the high tor, but small womanish trees: alder and
apple, willow and ash, leafy havens for the migratory birds. And the
little isle fair rings with birdsong and the clanging of hammer on
anvil and steel.*

*But men who come to buy swords at Ynis Evelonia are never
allowed farther inland than the wattle guesthouse with its oratory
of wicker wands winded and twisted together under a rush roof.
Only one man has ever slept there and is—in fact—sleeping there
still. But that is the end of this story—which shall not be told—and
the beginning of yet another.*

Elaine stared out across the gray waters as the ferret-faced woman rowed them to the isle. Her father sat unmoving next to her in the prow of the little boat, his hands clasped together, his jaw tight. His only admonition so far had been, "Be strong. The daughter of a vavasour does not cry."

She had not cried, though surely life among the magic women on Ynis Evelonia would be far different from life in the drafty but familiar castle at Escalot. At home women were cosseted but no one feared them as they feared the Daughters of Eve, unless one had a sharp tongue like the ostler's wife or Nanny Bess.

Elaine bent over the rim of the hide boat and tried to see her reflection in the water, the fair skin and the black hair plaited with such loving care by Nanny Bess that morning. But all she could make out was a shadow boat skimming across the waves. She popped one of her braids into her mouth, remembering Nanny's repeated warning that someday the braid would grow there: "And what knight would wed a girl with hair agrowin' in 'er mouth, I asks ye?" Elaine could hear Nanny's voice, now sharp as a blade, now quiet as a lullaby, whispering in her ear. She sighed.

At the sound her father looked over at her. His eyes, the faded blue of a late autumn sky, were pained and lines like runes ran across his brow.

Elaine let the braid drop from her mouth and smiled tentatively; she could not bear to disappoint him. At her small attempt at a smile he smiled back and patted her knee.

The wind spit river water into her face, as salty as tears, and Elaine hurriedly wiped her cheeks with the hem of her cape. By the time the boat rocked against the shore her face was dry.

The ferret-faced woman leaped over the side of the coracle and pulled it farther onto the sand so that Elaine and her father could debark without wading in the muddy tide. When they looked up, two women in gray robes had appeared to greet them.

"I am Mother Lisanor," said the tallest one to the vavasour. "You must be Bernard of Escalot."

He bowed his head, quickly removing his hat.

"And this," said the second woman, taking Elaine by the hand, "must be the fair Elaine. Come, child. You shall eat with me and share my bed this night. A warm body shall keep away any bad dreams."

"Madam—" the vavasour began.

"*Mother* Sonda," the woman interrupted him.

"Mother Sonda, may my daughter and I have a moment to say goodbye? She has never been away from home before." There was the slightest suggestion of a break in his voice.

"We have found, Sir Bernard, that it is best to part quickly. I *had* suggested in my letter to you that you leave Elaine on the Shapwick shore. This is an island of women. Men come here for commerce sake alone. Ynis Evelonia is Elaine's home now. But fear you not. We shall train her well." She gave a small tug on Elaine's hand and started up the hill, and Elaine, all unprotesting, went with her.

Only once, at the top of the small rise, did Elaine turn back. Her father was still standing by the coracle, hat in hand, the sun setting behind him. He was haloed against the darkening sky. Elaine made a small noise, almost a whimper. Then she popped the braid in her mouth. Like a cork in a bottle, it stoppered the sound. Without a word more, she followed Mother Sonda toward the great stone house that nestled down in the valley in the very center of the isle.

The room in the smithy was lit only by the flickering of the fire as Mother Hesta pumped the bellows with her foot. A big woman, whose right arm was more muscular than her left, Hesta seemed comfortable with tools rather than with words. The air from the bellows blew up a sudden large flame that had a bright blue heart.

"See, there. *There*. When the flames be as long as an arrow and the heart of the arrowhead be blue, thrust the blade in," she said, speaking to the new apprentice.

Elaine shifted from one foot to another, rubbing the upper part of her right arm where the brand of Eve still itched. Then she twisted one of her braids up and into her mouth, sucking on the end while she watched, but saying nothing.

"You'll see me do this again and again, girl," the forge mistress said. "But it be a year afore I let you try it on your own. For now, you must watch and listen and learn. Fire and water and air make Evian steel, fire and water and air. They be three of the four majorities. And one last thing—though I'll not tell you that yet, for that be our dearest secret. But harken: what be made by the Daughters of Eve strikes true. All men know this and that be why they come here, crost the waters, for our blades. They come, hating it that they must, but knowing only at our forge on this holy isle can they buy this steel. It be the steel that cuts through evil, that strikes the heart of what it seeks."

The girl nodded and her attention blew upon the small fire of words.

"It matters not, child, that we make a short single edge, or what the old Romies called a *glagy-us*. It matters not we make a long blade or a double edge. If it be Evian steel, it strikes true." She brought the side of her hand down in a swift movement which made the girl blink twice, but otherwise she did not move, the braid still in her mouth.

Mother Hesta turned her back on the child and returned to work, the longest lecture done. Her muscles under the short-sleeved tunic bunched and flattened. Sweat ran over her arms like an exotic chain of water beads as she hammered steadily on the sword, flattening, shaping, beating out the swellings and bulges that only *her* eye could see, only her fingers could find. The right arm beat, the left arm, with its fine traceries of scars, held.

After a while, the girl's eyes began to blink with weariness and with the constant probings of the irritating smoke. She dropped the braid and it lay against her linen shirt limply, leaving a slight wet stain. She rubbed both eyes with her hands but she was careful not to complain.

Mother Hesta did not seem to notice, but she let the fire die down a bit and laid the partially finished sword on the stone firewall. Wiping her grimed hands on her leather apron, she turned to the girl.

"I'm fair famished, I am. Let's go out to garden where Mother Sonda's set us a meal."

She did not put her hand out to the girl as she was, herself, uncomfortable with such open displays. It was a timeworn joke on Evelonia that Hesta put all her love into pounding at the forge. But she was pleased when the girl trotted by her side without any noticeable hesitation or delay. *A slow apprentice is no apprentice,* Mother Hesta often remarked.

When they stepped out of the shed, the day burst upon them with noisy celebration. Hesta, who spent almost the entire day every day in her dark forge, was always pleased for a few moments of birds and the colorful assault of the green landscape drifting off into the marshy river beyond. But she was always just as happy to go back into the dark fireroom where the tools slipped comfortably to hand and she could control the *whoosh-whoosh* sigh of the bellows and the loud clangorous song of metal on metal.

A plain cloth was spread upon the grass and a variety of plates covered with napkins awaited them. A jug of watered wine— Hesta hated the feeling heavy wines made in her head when she was working over the hot fire—and two stoneware goblets completed the picture.

"Come," Mother Hesta said.

The word seemed to release the child and she skipped over to the cloth and squatted down, but she touched nothing on the plate until Hesta had lowered herself to the ground and picked up the first napkin. Then the girl took up a slice of apple and jammed it into her mouth.

Only then did Hesta remember that it was mid-afternoon and the child, who had arrived late the evening before and slept comforted in Mother Sonda's bed, had not eaten since rising. Still, it would not do to apologize. That would make discipline harder. This particular girl, she knew, was the daughter of a vavasour, a man of some means in Escalot. She was not used to serving but to being served, so she must not be coddled now. Hesta was gentle in her chiding, but firm.

"The food'll not disappear, child," she said. "Slow and steady in these things. A buyer for the steel comes to the guesthouse table and he be judging us and we he by what goes on there. A greedy man be a man who'll pay twice what a blade be worth. Discipline, discipline in all things."

The girl, trying to eat more slowly, began to choke.

Hesta poured the goblets halfway full and solemnly handed one to her. The child sipped down her wine and the choking fit ended suddenly. Hesta made no reference to the incident.

"When you be done, collect these plates and cups and take them to yon water house. Mother Argente will meet you there and read you the first chapter of the *Book of Brightness*. Listen well. The ears be daughters of the memory."

"I can read, Mother Hesta," the girl said in a quiet little voice. It was not a boast but information.

"Can you? Then on the morrow you can read to me from the chapter on fire." She did not mention that she, herself a daughter of a landless vassal, had never learned to read. However one came to the *Book*—by eye or ear—did not matter a whit. Some were readers and some were read-tos; each valued in the Goddess's sight, as Argente had promised her many years ago when they had been girls. So she comforted herself still.

"Yes, Mother," the girl said. Her voice, though quiet, was unusually low and throaty for one her age. It was a voice that would wear well in the forge room. The last novice had had a whiny voice; she had not remained on the isle for long. But this girl, big eyed, deep voiced, with a face the shape of a heart under a waterfall of dark hair, was such a lovely little thing, she would probably be taken by the mothers of the guesthouse, Sonda, Lisanor, and Katwyn, no matter how fair her forging. Sometimes, Hesta thought, the Goddess be hard.

As she watched the girl eating, then wiping her mouth on the linen square with an easy familiarity, Hesta remembered how mortifying it had been to have to be taught not to use her sleeve for that duty. Then she smiled because that memory recalled another, that of a large, rawboned, parentless ten-year-old girl she had been, plunging into the cold channel of the Tamor just moments ahead of the baron who had claimed her body as his property. He had had to let her go, exploding powerful curses at her back, for he could not himself swim. He had been certain that she would sink. But her body's desperate strength and her crazed determination had brought her safely across the brackish tide to the isle where, even in a boat, that powerful baron had not dared go, so fearful was he of the rumors of magic. And the girl, as much water in as without, had been picked up out of the rushes by the late forge mistress and laughingly called Moses after an old tale. And never gone back across the Tamor, not once these forty years.

In the middle of Hesta's musing, the girl stood up and began to clear away the dishes to the accompaniment of a trilling song sung by a modest little brown bird whose flute-like tunes came daily in spring from the apple bough. It seemed an omen. Hesta decided she would suggest it to Mother Sonda as the bird name for the vavasour's child—Thrush.

There were three other girls in the sleep room when Elaine was left there. Two of the girls were smoothing their beds and one was sitting under a corbeled window, staring out.

Elaine had the braid in her mouth again. Her wide gray eyes took in everything. Five beds stood in a row along the wall with wooden chests for linen and other possessions at each bed foot. A fine Eastern tapestry hung above the beds, its subject the Daughters of Eve. It depicted about thirty women at work on a large island surrounded by troubled waves. Against the opposite wall were five arched windows that looked out across the now placid Tamor. Beneath the windows stood two high-warp looms with rather primitive weavings begun on each.

One of the standing girls, a tall, wraithy lass with hair the insubstantial color of mist, noticed that Elaine's eyes had taken in the looms.

"We have been learning to weave. It is something that Mother A learned from a traveler in Eastern lands. Not just the simple cloths the peasants make but true *tapisseries* such as the one over our beds. *That* was a gift of an admirer, Mother A said."

Elaine had met Mother Argente the night before. She was a small white-haired woman with soft, plump cheeks and hands that disguised the steel beneath. Elaine wondered who could admire such a firm soul. That kind of firmness quite frightened her.

She spun around to set the whole room into a blur of brown wood and blue coverlets and the bright spots of tapestry wool hanging on the wall. She spun until she was dizzy and had to stop or collapse. The braid fell from her mouth and she stood still, hands at her side, silently staring.

"Do you have a name yet?" the mist-haired girl asked.

After a moment came the throaty reply. "Elaine."

"No, no, your bird name, she means." The other standing girl, plump and whey-faced, spoke in a twittering voice.

Mist-hair added, "We all receive bird names, new names, like novices in nunneries, until we decide whether to stay. That's because the Druids have their trees and tree alphabet for *their* magic, but we have our little birds who make their living off the trees. That's what Mother A says. It's all in the *Book*. After that, if we stay, we get to have Mother names and live on Holy Isle forever."

"Forever," whispered Elaine. She could not imagine it.

"Do you want to know *our* bird names?" asked whey-face.

Before Elaine could answer, the tall girl said, "I'm Gale—for nightingale—because I sing so well. And this is Marta for house martin because she is our homebody, coming from Shapwick, across the flood. And over there—that. . . ," she hesitated a moment, as much to draw a breath as to make a point, "that is Veree. That's because she's solitary like the vireo, and a rare visitor to our isle. At least she's rare in her own eyes." She paused. "We used to have Brambling, but she got sick from the dampness and had to go home or die."

"I didn't like Bram," Marta said. "She was too common and she whined all the time. Mother Hesta couldn't bear her, and that's why she had to leave."

"It was her chest and the bloody cough."

"It was her whine."

"Was not."

"Was."

"Was not."

"Was!"

Veree stood and came over to Elaine, who had put the braid back into her mouth during the girls' argument. "Don't let their squabblings fright you," she said gently. "They are chickens scratching over bits of feed. Rumor and gossip excite them."

The braid dropped from Elaine's mouth.

"You think because you're castle born that you're better than we are," scolded Marta. "But all are the same on this holy isle."

Veree smiled. It was not an answer but a confirmation.

"We will see," hissed Gale. "There is still the forging."

"But she's *good* at forging," Marta murmured.

Gale pursed her mouth. "We will see."

Veree ignored them, putting a hand under Elaine's chin and lifting her face until they were staring at one another, gray eyes into violet ones. Elaine could not look away.

"You are quite, quite beautiful," Veree pronounced at last, "and you take in everything with those big eyes. But like the magpie, you give nothing away. I expect they'll call you Maggie, but *I* shall call you Pie."

Beyond the fingers of light cast by the hearth fire was a darkness so thick it seemed palpable. On the edges of the darkness, as if it crowded them together, sat the nine Mothers of Ynis Evelonia. In the middle of the half circle, in a chair with a firm back, sat Mother Argente, smiling toward the flames, her fingers busy with needlework. She did not once look down to check the accuracy of her stitches but trusted her fingers to do their work.

"Young Maggie seems to be settling in quite nicely. No crying at night, no outlandish longings for home, no sighing or sniffles. We needn't have been so worried." Her comment did not name any specific worrier, but the mothers who had voiced such fears to her in the privacy of their morning confessionals were chastised all the same.

Still chafing over the rejection of her suggested name, Hesta sniffed. "She's too much like Veree—high-strung, coddled. And she fair worships the ground Veree treads, which, of course, Veree encourages."

"Now, now, Hesta," Mother Sonda soothed. She made the

same sounds to chickens agitated at laying time and buyers in the guesthouse, a response in tone rather than actual argument. It always worked. Hesta smoothed her skirts much like a preening bird and settled down.

Sonda rose to stack another log onto the embers and to relight a taper on the candlestand. A moth fluttered toward the flame and on reaching it, burst with a sudden bright light. Sonda swept the ashes onto the floor where they disappeared into shadows and rushes. Then, turning, she spoke with a voice as sweetly welcoming as the scent of roses and verbena in the room.

"Mother A has asked me to read the lesson for this evening." She stepped to the lectern where the great leather-bound *Book of Brightness* lay open. Above it, from the sconce on the wall, another, larger taper beamed down to light the page. Sonda ran her finger along the text, careful not to touch either the words or the brightly colored illuminations. Halfway, she stopped, looked up, and judging the stilled expectant audience, glanced down again and began to read.

The lesson was short: a paragraph and a parable about constancy. The longer reading had been done before the full company of women and girls at dinner. Those who could took turns with the readings. All others listened. Young Maggie, with her low, steady voice and ability to read phrases rather than merely piece together words, would someday make a fine reader. She would probably make a fine mother, too. Time— and trial—would tell. That was the true magic on the isle: time and trial.

Sonda looked up from the text for a moment. Mother Argente always chose the evening's lesson. The mealtime reading was done from the *Book*'s beginning straight through to the end. In that way the entire *Book of Brightness* was heard at least once a year by everyone on the isle.

As usual, Sonda was in full agreement with Mother A's choice of the parable on constancy. In the last few months the small community had been beset by inconstancy, as if there were a curse at work, a worm at the heart inching its way to the surface of the body. Four of the novices had left on one pretext or another, a large number in such a short time. One girl with the bloody flux whose parents had desired that she die at home. One girl beset by such lingering homesickness as to render her unteachable. One girl plainly too stupid to learn at all. And one girl summoned home to be married. Married! Merely a piece in her father's game, the game of royalty. Sonda had escaped that game on her own by fasting until her desperate father had given her permission to join the Daughters of Eve. But then, he had had seven other daughters to counter with. And if such losses of novices were not enough—girls were always coming and going— two of the fully vowed women had left as well, one to care for her aged and dying parents and take over the reins of landholding until her brothers might return from war. And one, who had been on the isle for twenty years, had run off with a Cornish miller, a widower only recently bereaved; run off to become his fourth wife. Constancy indeed!

Sonda stood for a moment after the reading was over, her hands lingering on the edges of the *Book*. She loved the feel of it under her fingers, as if the text could impress itself on her by the feel of the parchment alone. She envied Mothers Morgan and Marie, who could write and illumine the pages. They were at work on a new copy of the *Book* to be set permanently in the dining common so that this one, old and fragile and precious, would not have to be shifted daily.

Finally Sonda took her place again on a stool by Mother A's right hand.

Mother A shifted a moment and patted Sonda's knee. Then she looked to the right and left, taking in all eight women with her glance. "My sisters," she began, "tomorrow our beloved daughter Vireo will begin her steel."

215

Elaine awoke because someone was crying. She had been so near crying herself for a fortnight that the sound of the quiet weeping set her off, and before she could stop herself, she was snuffling and gulping, the kind of sobbing that Nanny Bess always called "bear grabbers."

She was making so much noise, she did not hear the other weeper stop and move onto her bed, but she felt the sudden warmth of the girl's body and the sturdy arms encircling her.

"Hush, hush, little Pie," came a voice, and immediately after her hair was smoothed down.

Elaine looked up through tear-blurred eyes. There was no moon to be seen through the windows, no candles lit. The dark figure beside her was faceless, but she knew the voice.

"Oh, Veree," she whispered, "I didn't *mean* to cry."

"Nor I, little one. You have been brave the long weeks here. I have seen that and admired it. And now, I fear that I have been the cause of your weeping."

"No, not you, Veree. Never you. It is just that I miss my father so much. And my brother Lavaine, who is the handsomest man in all the world."

Veree laughed and tousled the girl's hair. "Ah, there can be no *handsomest* man, Pie. All men be the same to the women who love and serve the bright goddess flame here."

"If I cannot still love my Lavaine, then I do not want to *be* here." She wiped at her eyes.

"You will get over such losses. I have." Veree sat back on the bed.

"Then why *were* you crying? It was that which woke me." Elaine would admit that much.

Veree shushed her fiercely and glanced around, but the other two girls slept on.

Elaine whispered, "You *were* weeping. By the window. Admit it."

"Yes, sweet Pie, I was crying. But not for the loss of father or brother. Nor yet for house and land. I cry about tomorrow and tomorrow's morrow, and especially the third day after when I must finish my steel." She rose and went towards the window.

Elaine saw the shadow of her passing betwixt dark and dark and shivered slightly. Then she got out of her bed, and the shock of the cold stone beneath the rushes caused her to take quick, short steps over to Veree, who sat by the open window.

Outside a strange moaning, part wind and part water, sighed from the Tamor. A night owl on the hunt cried, a soft ascending wheeze of sound.

Elaine put her hand out and touched Veree's shoulder, sturdy under the homespun shift. "But what are you afraid of? Do you fear being burned? Do you fear the blade? I had a maidservant once who turned white as hoarfrost when she had to look upon a knife, silly thing."

"I fear the hurting. I fear . . . the blood."

"What blood?"

In the dark Veree turned, and Elaine could suddenly see two tiny points of light flashing out from the shadow eyes. "They have not told you yet about the blood?"

Elaine shook her head. Then realizing the motion might not be read in the blackness, she whispered, "No. Not yet."

Veree sighed, a sound so unlike her that Elaine swallowed with difficulty.

"Tell me. Please."

"I must not."

"But *they* will soon."

"Then let *them*."

"But I must know now so that I might comfort you, who have comforted me these weeks." Elaine took her hand away from Veree's shoulder and reached for a lock of her own hair, unbound from its night plait, and popped it into her mouth, a gesture she had all but forgotten the last days.

"Oh, little Pie, you must not think I am a coward, but if I tell you when I should not . . . I would not have you think me false." Veree's voice was steeped in sadness.

"I never . . ."

"You will when I tell you."

"You are wonderful," Elaine said, proclaiming fealty. "You have been the one to take me in, to talk to me, to listen. The others are all common mouths chattering, empty heads like wooden whistles blowing common tunes." That was one of Nanny Bess's favorite sayings. "Nothing would make me think you false. Not now, not ever."

Veree's head turned back to the window again and the twin points of light were eclipsed. She spoke toward the river and the wind carried her soft words away. Elaine had to strain to hear them.

"Our steel is forged of three of the four elements—fire and water and air."

"I know that."

"But the fourth thing that makes Evian steel, what makes it strike true, is a secret learned by Mother Morgan from a necromancer in the East where magic rides the winds and every breath is full of spirits."

"And what is the fourth thing?" whispered Elaine, though she feared she already knew.

Veree hesitated, then spoke. "Blood. The blood of a virgin girl, an unblemished child, or a childless old maid. Blood drawn from her arm where the vein runs into the heart. The left arm. Here." And the shadow held out its shadowy arm, thrusting it half out of the window.

Elaine shivered with more than the cold.

"And when the steel has been worked and pounded and beaten and shaped and heated, again and again, it is thrust into a silver vat that contains pure water from our well mixed through with the blood."

"Oh." Elaine sighed.

"And the words from the *Book of Brightness* are spoken over it by the mothers in the circle of nine. The sword is pulled from its bloody bath. Then the girl, holding up the sword, with the water flooding down her arm, marches into the Tamar, into the tidal pool that sits in the shadow of the high tor. She must go under the water with the sword, counting to nine times nine. Then thrusting the sword up and out of the water before her, she follows it into the light. Only then is the forging done."

"Perhaps taking the blood will not hurt, Veree. Or only a little. The mothers are gentle. I burned myself the third day here, and Mother Sonda soothed it with a honey balm and not a scar to show for it."

Veree turned back to the window. "It must be done by the girl all alone at the rising of the moon. Out in the glade. Into the silver cup. And how can I, little Pie, how can I prick my own arm with a knife, I who cannot bear to see myself bleed. Not since I was a small child, could I bear it without fainting. Oh, I can kill spiders, and stomp on serpents. I am not afraid of binding up another's wounds. But my own blood . . . if I had known . . . if my father had known . . . I never would have come."

Into the silence that followed her anguished speech came the ascending cry of another owl, which ended in a shriek as the bird found its prey. The cry seemed to agitate the two sleepers in their beds and they stirred noisily. Veree and Elaine stood frozen for the moment, and even after were tentative with their voices.

"Could you . . ." Elaine began.

"Yes?"

"Could you use an animal's blood instead?"

"Then the magic would not work and everyone would know."

Elaine let out a long breath. "Then I shall go out in your place.

We shall use *my* blood and you will not have to watch." She spoke quite assuredly, though her heart beat wildly at her own suggestion.

Veree hugged her fiercely. "What *can* you think of me that you would believe I would let you offer yourself in my place, little one. But I shall love you forever just for making the suggestion."

Elaine did not quite understand why she should feel so relieved, but she smiled into the darkness. Then she yawned loudly.

"What *am* I thinking of?" Veree chastised herself. "You should be sleeping, little one, not staying up with me. But be relieved. You have comforted me. I think. . . ," she hesitated for a little, then finished gaily, "I think I shall manage it all quite nicely now."

"Really?" asked Elaine.

"Really," said Veree. "Trust me."

"I do. Oh, I do," said Elaine and let herself be led back to bed where she fell asleep at once and dreamed of an angel with long dark braids in a white shift who sang, "verily, verily," to her and drew a blood-red crux on her forehead and breast and placed her, ever smiling, in a beautiful silk-lined barge.

If there was further weeping that night, Elaine did not wake to it, nor did she speak of it in the morn.

The morn was the first day of Veree's steel and the little isle buzzed with the news. The nine mothers left the usual chores to the lesser women and the girls, marching in a solemn line to the forge where they made a great circle around the fire.

In due time Veree, dressed in a white robe with the hood obscuring her face, was escorted by two guides, mothers who had been chosen by lot. They walked along the Path of Steel, the winding walkway to the smithy that was lined with water-smoothed stones.

As she walked, Veree was unaware of the cacophony of birds that greeted her from the budding apple boughs. She never noticed a flock of finches that rose up before her in a cloud of yellow wings. Instead her head was full of the chant of the sword.

> *Water to cool it,*
> *Forge to heat it,*
> *Anvil to form it,*
> *Hammer to beat it.*

She thought carefully of the points of the sword: hilt and blade, forte and foible, pommel and edge, quillon and grip. She rehearsed her actions. She thought of everything but the blood.

Then the door in front of her opened, and she disappeared inside. The girls who had watched like little birds behind the trees sighed as one.

"It will be your turn next full moon," whispered Marta to Gale. Gale smiled crookedly. The five girls from the other sleeping room added their silent opinions with fingers working small fantasies into the air. Long after the other girls slipped back to their housely duties, Elaine remained, rooted in place. She watched the forge and could only guess at the smoky signals that emerged from the chimney on the roof.

> *Water to cool it,*
> *Forge to heal it,*
> *Anvil to form it,*
> *Hammer to beat it.*

The mothers chanted in perfect unity, their hands clasped precisely over the aprons of their robes. When the chant was done, Mother Argente stepped forward and gently pushed Veree's hood back.

Released from its binding, Veree's hair sprang forward like tiny black arrows from many bowstrings, the dark points haloing her face.

She really is a magnificent child, Argente thought to herself, but aloud spoke coldly. "My daughter," she said, "the metal thanks us for its beating by becoming stronger. So by our own tempering we become women of steel. Will you become one of us?"

"Mother," came Veree's soft answer, "I will."

"Then you must forge well. You must pour your sweat and your blood into this sword that all who see it and any who use it shall know it is of excellent caliber, that it is of Evian Steel."

"Mother, I will."

The mothers stood back then and only Hesta came forward. She helped Veree remove her robe and the girl stood stiffly in her new forging suit of tunic and trews. Hesta bound her hair back into a single braid, tying it with a golden twine so tightly that it brought tears to the girl's eyes. She blinked them back, making no sound.

"Name your tools," commanded Hesta.

Veree began. Pointing out each where it hung on its hook on the wall, she droned: "Top swage, bottom swage, flatter, cross peen, top fuller, bottom fuller, hot chisel, mandrel . . ." The catalogue went on and only half her mind was occupied with the rota. This first day of the steel was child's play, things she had memorized her first weeks on Ynis Evelonia and never forgot. They were testing the knowledge of her head. The second day they would test her hands. But the third day . . . she hesitated a moment, looked up, saw that Hesta's eyes on her were glittering. For the first time she understood that the old forge mistress was hoping that she would falter, fail. That startled her. It had never occurred to her that someone she had so little considered could wish her ill.

She smiled a false smile at Hesta, took up the list, and finished it flawlessly.

The circle of nine nodded.

"Sing us now the color of the steel," said Sonda.

Veree took a breath and began. "When the steel is red as blood, the surface is at all points good; and when the steel is rosy red, the top will scale, the sword is dead; and when the steel is golden bright, the time for forging is just right; and when the steel is white as snow, the time for welding you will know."

The plainsong accompaniment had helped many young girls remember the colors, but Veree sang it only to please the mothers and pass their test. She had no trouble remembering when to forge and when to weld, and the rest was just for show.

"The first day went splendidly," remarked Sonda at the table.

"No one ever questioned *that* one's head knowledge," groused Hesta, using her own head as a pointer toward the table where the girls sat.

Mother Argente clicked her tongue against the roof of her mouth, a sound she made when annoyed. The others responded to it immediately with silence, except for Mother Morgan, who was so deep in conversation with a server she did not hear.

"We will discuss this later. At the hearth," Argente said.

The conversation turned at once to safer topics: the price of corn, how to raise the milling fee, the prospect of another visitor from the East, the buyer of Veree's sword.

Morgan looked over. "It shall be the arch-mage," she said. "He will come for the sword himself."

Hesta shook her head. "How do you know? How do you *always* know?"

Morgan smiled, the corners of her thin upper lip curling. There was a gap between her two front teeth, carnal, inviting. "I know."

Sonda reached out and stroked the back of Hesta's hand. "You know she would have you think it's magic. But it is the calendar, Hesta. I have explained all that."

Hesta mumbled, pushing the lentils around in her bowl. Her own calendar was internal and had to do with forging, when the steel was ready for the next step. But if Morgan went by any calendar, it was too deep and devious for the forge mistress's understanding. Or for any of them. Morgan always seemed to *know* things. Under the table, Hesta crossed her fingers, holding them against her belly as protection.

"It *shall* be the arch-mage," Morgan said, still smiling her gapped smile. "The stars have said it. The moon has said it. The winds have said it."

"And now you have said it, too." Argente's voice ended the conversation, though she wondered how many of her women were sitting with their fingers crossed surreptitiously under the table. She did not encourage them in their superstitions, but the ones who came from the outer tribes or the lower classes never really rid themselves of such beliefs. "Of course, it shall be a Druid. Someone comes once a year at this time to look over our handiwork. They rarely buy. Druids are as close with their gold as a dragon on its hoard."

"It shall be the arch-mage himself," intoned Morgan. "I know." Hesta shivered.

"Yes." Argente smiled, almost sighing. When Morgan became stubborn it was always safest to cozen her. Her pharmacopeia was not to be trusted entirely. "But gloating over such arcane knowledge does not become you, a daughter of a queen. I am sure you have more important matters to attend to. Come, Mothers, I have decided that tonight's reading shall be about humility. And you, Mother Morgan, will do us all the honor of reading it." Irony,

Argente had found, was her only weapon against Morgan, who seemed entirely oblivious to it. Feeling relieved of her anger by such petty means always made Argente full of nervous energy. She stood. The others stood with her and followed her out the door.

Elaine watched as Veree marched up to the smithy, this time with an escort of four guides. Veree was without the white robe, her forge suit unmarked by fire or smoke, her hair bound back with the golden string but not as tightly as when Hesta plaited it. Elaine had done the service for her soon after rising, gently braiding the hair and twine together so that they held but did not pull. Veree had rewarded her with a kiss on the brow.

"This day I dedicate to thee," Veree had whispered to her in the courtly language they had both grown up with.

Elaine could still feel the glow of that kiss on her brow. She knew that she would love Veree forever, the sister of her heart. She was glad now, as she had never been before, that she had had only brothers and no sisters in Escalot. That way Veree could be the only one.

The carved wooden door of the smithy closed behind Veree. The girls, giggling, went back to their chores. Only Elaine stayed, straining to hear something of the rites that would begin the second day of Veree's Steel.

Veree knew the way of the steel, bending the heated strips, hammering them together, recutting and rebending them repeatedly until the metal patterned. She knew the sound of the hammer on the hot blade, the smell of the glowing charcoal that made the soft metal hard. She enjoyed the hiss of the quenching, when the hot steel plunged into the water and emerged, somehow, harder still. The day's work was always difficult but satisfying in a way that other work was not. Her hands now held a knowledge that she had not had two years before when, as a pampered young daughter of a baron, she had come to Ynis Evelonia to learn "to be a man as well as a woman" as her father had said. He believed that a woman who might someday have to rule a kingdom (oh, he had such high hopes for her) needed to know both principles, male and female. A rare man, her father. She did not love him. He was too cold and distant and cerebral for that. But she admired him. She wanted him to admire her. And—except for the blood—she was not unhappy that she had come.

Except for the blood. If she thought about it, her hand faltered, the hammer slipped, the sparks flew about carelessly and Hesta boomed out in her forge-tending voice about the recklessness of girls. So Veree very carefully did *not* think about the blood. Instead she concentrated on fire and water, on earth and air. Her hands gripped her work. She *became* the steel.

She did not stop until Hesta's hand on her shoulder cautioned her.

"It be done for the day, my daughter," Hesta said, grudging admiration in her voice. "Now you rest. Tonight you must do the last of it alone."

And then the fear really hit her. Veree began to tremble.

Hesta misread the shivering. "You be aweary with work. You be hungry. Take some watered wine for sleep's sake. We mothers will wake you and lead you to the glade at moonrise. Come. The sword be well worked. You have reason to be proud."

Veree's stomach began to ache, a terrible dull pain. She was certain that, for the first time in her life, she would fail and that her father would be hurt and the others would pity her. She expected she could stand the fear, and she would, as always, bear the dislike of her companions, but what could not be borne was their pity. When her mother had died in the bloody aftermath of an unnecessary birth, the entire court had wept and everyone had pitied her, poor little motherless six-year-old

Gwyneth. But she had rejected their pity, turning it to white anger against her mother who had gone without a word. She had not accepted pity from any of those peasants then; she would not accept it now. Not even from little Pie, who fair worshiped her. Especially not from Pie.

The moon's cold fingers stroked Veree's face but she did not wake. Elaine, in her silent vigil, watched from her bed. She strained to listen as well.

The wind in the orchard rustled the blossoms with a soft soughing. Twice an owl had given its ascending hunting cry. The little popping hisses of breath from the sleeping girls punctuated the quiet in the room. And Elaine thought that she could also hear, as a dark counter to the other noises, the slapping of the Tamor against the shore, but perhaps it was only the beating of her own heart. She was not sure.

Then she heard the footsteps coming down the hall, hauled the light covers up to her chin, and slotted her eyes.

The Nine Mothers entered the room, their white robes lending a ghostly air to the proceedings. They wore the hoods up, which obscured their faces. The robes were belted with knotted golden twine; nine knots on each cincture and the golden ornament shaped like a circle with one half filled in, the signet of Ynis Evelonia, hanging from the end.

The Nine surrounded Veree's bed, undid their cinctures, and lay the ropes over the girl's body as if binding her to a bier.

Mother Argente's voice floated into the room. "We bind thee to the isle. We bind thee to the steel. We bind thee to thy task. Blood calls to blood, like to like. Give us thine own for the work."

The Nine picked up their belts and tied up their robes once again. Veree, who had awakened sometime during Argente's chant, was helped to her feet. The mothers took off her shift and slipped a silken gown over her head. It was sleeveless and Elaine, watching, shivered for her.

Then Mother Morgan handed her a silver cup, a little grail with the sign of the halved circle on the side. Mother Sonda handed her a silken bandage. Marie bound an illuminated message to her brow with a golden headband. Mothers Bronwyn and Matilde washed her feet with lilac water, while Katwyn and Lisandor tied her hair atop her head into a plaited crown. Mother Hesta handed her a silver knife, its tip already consecrated with wine from the Goddess Arbor.

Then Argente put her hands on Veree's shoulders. "May She guide your hand. May She guard your blood. May the moon rise and fall on this night of your consecration. Be you steel tonight."

They led her to the door and pushed her out before them. She did not stumble as she left.

Veree walked into the glade as if in a trance. She had drunk none of the wine but had spilled it below her bed knowing that the wine was drugged with one of Mother Morgan's potions. Bram had warned her of it before leaving. Silly, whiny Bram who, nonetheless, had had an instinct for gossip and a passion for Veree. Such knowledge had been useful.

The moon peeped in and out of the trees, casting shadows on the path, but Veree did not fear the dark. This night the dark was her friend.

She heard a noise and turned to face it, thinking it some small night creature on the prowl. There was nothing larger than a stoat or fox on Ynis Evelonia. She feared neither. At home she had kept a reynard, raised up from a kit, and had hunted with two ferrets as companions in her pocket.

Home! What images suddenly rose up to plague her, the same that had caused her no end of sleepless nights when she had first arrived. For she *had* been homesick, whatever nonsense she had told little Pie for comfort's sake. The great hearth at Carmelide, large enough to roast an oxen, where once she had lost the golden ring her mother had given her and her cousin Cadoc had grabbed up a bucket of water, dousing the fire and getting himself all black with coal and grease to recover it for her. And the great apple tree outside her bedroom window up which young Jemmy, the ostler's son, had climbed to sing of his love for her even though he knew he would be soundly beaten for it. And the mews behind the main house where Master Thorn had kept the hawks and let her sneak in to practice holding the little merlin that she had wanted for her own. But it had died tangled in its jesses the day before she'd been sent off to the isle, and one part of her had been glad that no one else would hunt the merlin now.

She heard the noise again, louder this time, too loud for a fox or a squirrel or a stoat. Loud enough for a human. She spoke out, "Who is it?" and held out the knife before her, trembling with the cold. Only the cold, she promised herself.

"It is I," came a small voice.

"Pie!" Her own voice took back its authority. "You are not supposed to be here."

"I saw it all. Veree. The dressing and undressing. The ropes and the knife. And I *did* promise to help." The childish form slipped out from behind the tree, white linen shift reflecting the moon's light.

"I told you all would be well, child. You did not need to come."

"But I *promised*." If that voice held pity, it was self-pity. The child was clearly a worshiper begging not to be dismissed.

Veree smiled and held out the hand with the cup. "Come, then. Thou shalt be my page."

Elaine put her hand to Veree's gown and held on as if she would never let go and, so bound, the two entered into the Goddess Glade.

The arch-mage came in the morning just as Morgan had foretold. He was not at all what Elaine had expected, being short and balding, with a beard as long and as thin as an exclamation mark. But that he was a man of power no one could doubt.

The little coracle, rowed by the same ferret-faced woman who had deposited Elaine on the isle, fair skimmed the surface of the waves and plowed onto the shore, leaving a furrow in which an oak could have been comfortably set.

The arch-mage stood up in the boat and greeted Mother Argente familiarly. *"Salve, Mater. Visne somnia vendere?"*

She answered him back with great dignity. *"Si volvo, Merline, caveat emptor."*

Then they both laughed, as if this exchange were a great and long-standing joke between them. If it was a joke, they were certainly the only ones to understand it.

"Come, Arch-Mage," Mother Argente said, "and take wine with us in the guesthouse. We will talk of the purpose of your visit in comfort there."

He nodded and, with a quick twist of his wrist, produced a coin from behind the boat woman's right ear. With a flourish he presented it to her, then stepped from the coracle. The woman dropped the coin solemnly into the leather bag she wore at her waist.

Elaine gasped and three other girls giggled.

"The girls are, as always, amused by your tricks, Merlin," said Mother Argente, her mouth pursed in a wry smile.

"I like to keep in practice," he said. *"And* to amuse the young ones. Besides, as one gets older the joints stiffen."

"That I know, that I know," Argente agreed. They walked side by side like old friends, moving slowly up the little hill. The rest of the women and girls fell in behind them, and so it was, in a modest processional, that they came to the guesthouse.

At the door of the wattle pavilion which was shaded by a lean of willows, Mother Argente turned. "Sonda, Hesta, Morgan, Lisanor, enter and treat with our guest. Veree, ready yourself for noon. The rest of you, you know your duties." Then she opened the door and let Merlin precede them into the house.

The long table was already set with platters of cheese and fruit. Delicate goblets of Roman glass marked off six places. As soon as they were all seated with Argente at the head and Merlin at the table's foot, Mother A poured her own wine and passed the silver ewer. Morgan, seated at Argente's right hand, was the last to fill her glass. When she set the ewer down, she raised her glass.

"I am Wind on Sea," Morgan chanted.

> "I am Wind on Sea,
> I am Ocean-wave,
> I am Roar of Sea,
> I am Bull of Seven Fights,
> I am Vulture on Cliff,
> I am Dewdrop,
> I am Fairest of Flowers,
> I am Boar for Boldness,
> I am Salmon in Pool,
> I am Lake on Plain,
> I am a Word of Skill,
> I am the Point of a Weapon—"

"*Morgan*," warned Argente.

"Do not stop her," commanded Merlin. "She is *vates*, afire with the word of the gods. My god or your god, they are the same. They speak with tongues of fire and they sometimes pick a warped reed through which to blow a particular tune."

Argente bowed her head once to him but Morgan was already finished. She looked across the table at Hesta, her eyes preternaturally bright. "I know things," she said.

"It is clear that I have come at a moment of great power," said Merlin. "'I am the point of a Weapon' say the gods to us. And my dreams these past months have been of sword point, but swords that are neither *gladius* nor *spatha* nor the far tribes' *ensis*. A new creation. And where does one come for a sword of power, but here. Here to Ynis Evelonia."

Mother Argente smiled. "We have many swords ready, Archmage."

"I need but one." He did not return her smile, staring instead into his cup of wine.

"How will we know this sword of power?" Argente asked, leaning forward.

"I will know," intoned Morgan.

Sonda, taking a sip of her wine, put her head to one side like a little bird considering a tasty worm. "And what payment, Archmage?"

"Ah, Mother Sonda, that is always the question they leave to you. What payment indeed." Merlin picked up his own glass and suddenly drained it. He set the glass down gently, contemplating the rim. Then he stroked his long beard. "If I dream true—and I have never been known to have false dreams— then you shall *give* me this particular sword and its maker."

"*Give* you? What a notion, Merlin." Mother Argente laughed, but there was little amusement in it. "The swords made of Evian Steel are never given away. We have too many buyers vying for them. If you will not pay for it, there will be others who will."

There was a sudden, timid knock upon the door. Sonda rose quietly and went to it, spoke to the mother who had interrupted them, then turned.

"It is nearing noon, Mother. The sun rides high. It is time." Sonda's voice was smooth, giving away no more than necessary.

Mother Argente rose and with her the others rose, too.

"Stay, Arch-Mage, there is food and wine enough. When we have done with our . . . obsequies . . . we shall return to finish our business with you."

The five mothers left and so did not hear the man murmur into his empty cup, "This business will be finished before-times."

The entire company of women gathered at the river's edge to watch. The silver vat, really an overlarge bowl, was held by Mother Morgan. The blood-tinted water reflected only sky.

Veree, in the white silken shift, stood with her toes curling under into the mud. Elaine could see the raised goose bumps along her arms, though it was really quite warm in the spring sun.

Mother Hesta held a sword on the palms of her upturned hands. It was a long-bladed double-edge sword, the quillon cleverly worked. The sword seemed afire with the sun, the shallow hollow down its center aflame.

Veree took the sword from Hesta and held it flat against her breast while Mother Argente anointed her forehead with the basin's water. With her finger she drew three circles and three crosses on Veree's brow.

"Blood to blood, steel to steel, thee to me," said Mother Argente.

Veree repeated the chant. "Blood to blood, steel to steel, I to thee." Then she took the sword and set it into the basin.

As the sword point and then the blade touched the water, the basin erupted in steam. Great gouts of fire burst from the sword and Mother Argente screamed.

Veree grabbed the sword by the handle and ran down into the tidal pool. She plunged in with it and immediately the flames were quenched, but she stayed under the water and Elaine, fearful for her life, began to cry out, running down to the water's edge.

She was pushed aside roughly by a strong hand, and when she caught her breath, she saw it was the arch-mage himself, standing knee deep in water, his hands raised, palms down, speaking words she did not quite understand.

> "I take ye here
> Till Bedevere
> Cast ye back."

Bedevere? Did he mean Veree? Elaine wondered, and then had time to wonder no further for the waters parted before the arch-mage and the sword pierced up into the air before him.

He grasped the pommel in his left hand and with a mighty heave pulled the sword from the pool. Veree's hand, like some dumb, blind thing, felt around in the air, searching.

Elaine waded in, dived under, and wrapping her arms around Veree's waist, pushed her out of the pool. They stood there, trembling, looking like two drowned ferrets, unable to speak or weep or wonder.

"This is the sword I shall have," Merlin said to Mother Argente, his back to the two half-drowned girls.

"I do not understand . . ." began Mother Argente. "But I *will* know."

"I *know* things," said Morgan triumphantly.

Mother Argente turned and spoke through clenched teeth, "Will someone shut her up?"

Hesta smiled broadly. "Yes, Mother. Your will is my deed." Her large right hand clamped down on Morgan's neck and she picked her up and shook her like a terrier with a rat, then set her down. Morgan did not speak again but her eyes grew slotted and cold.

Marta began to sob quietly until nudged by Gale, but the other girls were stunned into silence.

"Now, now," murmured Sonda to no one in particular. "Now, now."

Mother Argente walked over to Veree, who straightened up and held her chin high. "Explain this, child."

Veree said nothing.

"What blood was used to quench the sword?"

"Mother, it was my own."

Elaine interrupted. "It was. I saw it."

Mother Argente turned on her. "You *saw* it? Then it was your watching that corrupted the steel."

Merlin moved between them. "*Mater.* Think. Such power does not emanate from this child." He swung his head so that he was staring at Veree. "And where did the blood come from?"

Under his stare Veree lowered her eyes. She spoke to the ground. "It is a woman's secret. I cannot talk of it."

The arch-mage smiled. "I am man and woman, neither and both. The secrets of the body are known to me. Nothing is hidden from me."

"I have nothing to tell you if you know it already."

"Then I will tell it to thee," said Merlin. He shifted the sword to his left hand, turned to her, and put his right hand under her chin. "Look at me, Gwyneth, called here Vireo, and deny this if you can. Last night for the first time you became a woman. The moon called out your blood. And it was this flux that you used, the blood that flows from the untested womb, not the body's blood flowing to the heart. Is it so?"

She whispered, "It is so."

Argente put a hand to her breast. "That is foul. Unclean."

"It is the more powerful thereby," Merlin answered.

"Take the sword, Arch-mage. And the girl. And go."

"*No!*" Elaine dropped to her knees by Veree's side and clasped her legs. "Do not go. Or take me with you. I could not bear to be here without you. I would die for you."

Merlin looked down at the little girl and shook his head. "You shall not die yet, little Elaine. Not so soon. But you shall give your life for her—that I promise you." He tucked the sword in a scabbard he suddenly produced from inside his cloak. "Come, Gwyneth." He held out his hand.

She took his hand and smiled at him. "There is nothing here to pity," she said.

"I shall never give you pity," he said. "Not now or ever. You choose and you are chosen. I see that you know what it is you do."

Mother Argente smoothed her skirts down, a gesture which seemed to return them all to some semblance of normality. "I myself will row you across. The sooner she is gone from here, the better."

"But my clothes, Mother."

"They shall be sent to you."

The arch-mage swung the cape off his shoulders and enfolded the girl in it. The cape touched the ground, sending up little puffs of dirt.

"You shall never be allowed on this isle again," said Mother Argente. "You shall be denied the company of women. Your name shall be crossed off the book of the Goddess."

Veree still smiled.

"You shall be barren," came a voice from behind them. "Your womb's blood was given to cradle a sword. It shall not cradle a child. I *know* things."

"Get into the boat," instructed Merlin. "Do not look back, it only encourages her." He spoke softly to Mother Argente, "I am glad, *Mater*, that *that* one is *your* burden."

"I give you no thanks for her," said Mother Argente as she pushed the boat off into the tide. She settled onto the seat, took up the oars, feathered them once, and began to pull.

The coracle slipped quickly across the river.

Veree stared out across the gray waters that gave scarcely any reflection. Through the mist she could just begin to see the far shore where the tops of thatched cottages and the smoky tracings of cook fires were taking shape.

"Shapwick-Across-the-Flood," mused Merlin. "And from there

236

we shall ride by horse to Camlann. It will be a long and arduous journey, child. Your bones will ache."

"Pitying me already?"

"Pitying *you*? My bones are the older and will ache the more. No, I will not pity you. But we will all be pitied when this story is told years hence, for it will be a tale cunningly wrought of earth, air, fire—and blood."

The boat lodged itself clumsily against the Shapwick shore. The magician stood and climbed over the side. He gathered the girl up and carried her to the sand, huffing mightily. Then he turned and waved to the old woman who huddled in the coracle.

"Ave, Mater."

"Ave, Magister," she called back. "Until we must meet again."

Yes, men who come to buy swords at Ynis Evelonia are never allowed further inland than the wattle guesthouse with its oratory of wicker wands winded and twisted together under a rush roof. Only Merlin, the old enchanter, ever slept there and is—in fact—sleeping there still. But that is not the end of this story. Yet it is the beginning of another, which has often been told.

SISTER EMILY'S LIGHTSHIP

I dwell in Possibility. The pen scratched over the page, making graceful ellipses. She liked the look of the black on white as much as the words themselves. The words sang in her head far sweeter than they sang on the page. Once down, captured like a bird in a cage, the tunes seemed pedestrian, mere common rote. Still, it was as close as she would come to that Eternity, that Paradise that her mind and heart promised. *I dwell in Possibility.*

She stood and stretched, then touched her temples where the poem still throbbed. She could feel it sitting there, beating its wings against her head like that captive bird. Oh, to let the bird out to sing for a moment in the room before she caged it again in the black bars of the page.

Smoothing down the skirt of her white dress, she sat at the writing table once more, took up the pen, dipped it into the ink jar, and added a second line. *A fairer House than . . .* than what? Had she lost the word between standing and sitting? Words were not birds after all, but slippery as fish.

Then suddenly, she felt it beating in her head. *Prose! A fairer*

House than Prose— She let the black ink stretch across the page with the long dash that lent the last word that wonderful fall of tone. She preferred punctuating with the dash to the hard point, as brutal as a bullet. *I dwell in Possibility.*

Cocking her head to one side, she considered the lines. *They will do*, she thought, as much praise as she ever allowed her own work, though she was generous to others. Then, straightening the paper and cleaning the nib of her pen, she tore up the false starts and deposited them in the basket.

She could, of course, write anytime during the day if the lines came to mind. There was little enough that she had to do in the house. But she preferred night for her truest composition and perhaps that was why she was struggling so. *Then those homey tasks will take me on,* she told herself: supervising the gardening, baking Father's daily bread. Her poetry must never be put in the same category.

Standing, she smoothed down the white skirt again and tidied her hair—"like a chestnut burr," she'd once written imprudently to a friend. It was ever so much more faded now.

But pushing that thought aside, Emily went quickly out of the room as if leaving considerations of vanity behind. Besides the hothouse flowers, besides the bread, there was a cake to be made for tea. After Professor Seelye's lecture there would be guests and her tea cakes were expected.

The tea had been orderly, the cake a success, but Emily headed back upstairs soon after for her eyes—always sensitive to the light—had begun to tear up. She felt a sick headache starting. Rather than impose her ailments on her guests, she slipped away. They would understand.

Carlo padded up the stairs behind her, so quiet for such a large dog. But how slow he had become these last months. Emily knew that Death would stop for him soon enough. Newfoundlands were not a long-lived breed usually, and he had been her own shaggy ally for the past fifteen years.

Slowing her pace, despite the stabbing behind her eyes, Emily let the old dog catch up. He shoved his rough head under her hand and the touch salved them both.

He curled beside her bed and slept, as she did, in an afternoon made night and close by the window blinds.

It was night in truth when Emily awoke, her head now wonderfully clear. Even the dreadful sleet in her eyes was gone.

She rose and threw on a dressing gown. She owed Loo a letter, and Samuel and Mary Bowles. But still the night called to her. Others might hate the night, hate the cold of November, huddling around their stoves in overheated houses. But November seemed to her the very Norway of the year.

She threw open first the curtains, then the blinds, almost certain of a sight of actual fjords. But though the Gibraltar lights made the village look almost foreign, it was not—she decided—foreign enough.

"That I had the strength for travel," she said aloud. Carlo answered her with a quick drum roll of tail.

Taking that as the length of his sympathy, she nodded at him, lit the already ensconced candle, and sat once again at the writing table. She read over the morning's lines:

> I dwell in Possibility—
> A fairer House than Prose—

It no longer had the freshness she remembered, and she sighed.

At the sound, Carlo came over to her and laid his rough head in her lap, as if trying to lend comfort.

"No comfort to be had, old man," she said to him. "I can no longer tell if the trouble is my wretched eyes, sometimes easy and sometimes sad. Or the dis-order of my mind. Or the slant of light on the page. Or the words themselves. Or something else altogether. Oh, my dear dog . . ." She leaned over and buried her face in his fur but did not weep for she despised private grief that could not be turned into a poem. Still, the touch had a certain efficaciousness, and she stood and walked over to the window.

The Amherst night seemed to tremble in on itself. The street issued a false invitation, the maples standing sentinel between the house and the promise of road.

"Keeping me in," she asked the dog, "or others out?" It was only her wretched eyes that forced her to stay at home so much and abed. Only her eyes, she was convinced. In fact she planned a trip into town at noon next when the very day would be laconic; if she could get some sleep and if the November light proved not too harsh.

She sat down again at the writing table and made a neat pile of the poems she was working on, then set them aside. Instead she would write a letter. To . . . to Elizabeth. "Dear Sister," she would start as always, even though their relationship was of the heart, not the blood. "I will tell her about the November light," she said to Carlo. "Though it is much the same in Springfield as here, I trust she will find my observations entertaining."

The pen scratched quickly across the page. *So much quicker,* she thought, *than when I am composing a poem.*

She was deep into the fourth paragraph, dashing "November always seemed to me the Norway . . ." when a sharp knock on the wall shattered her peace, and a strange insistent whine seemed to fill the room.

And the light. *Oh—the light!* Brighter even than day.

"Carlo!" she called the dog to her, and he came, crawling, trembling. So large a dog and such a larger fright. She fell on him as a drowning person falls on a life preserver. The light made her eyes weep pitchers. Her head began to ache. The house rocked.

And then—as quickly as it had come—it was gone; noise, light, all, all gone.

Carlo shook her off as easily as bathwater, and she collapsed to the floor, unable to rise.

Lavinia found her there on the floor in the morning, her dressing gown disordered and her hands over her eyes.

"Emily, my dear, my dear . . ." Lavinia cried, lifting her sister entirely by herself back onto the bed. "Is it the terror again?"

It was much worse than the night terrors, those unrational fears which had afflicted her for years. But Emily had not the strength to contradict. She lay on the bed hardly moving the entire day while Mother bathed her face and hands with aromatic spirits and Vinnie read to her. But she could not concentrate on what Vinnie read; neither the poetry of Mrs. Browning nor the prose of George Eliot soothed her. She whimpered and trembled, recalling vividly the fierceness of that midnight light. She feared she was, at last, going mad.

"Do not leave, do not leave," she begged first Vinnie, then Mother, then Austin, who had been called to the house in the early hours. Father alone had been left to his sleep. But they did go, to whisper together in the hall. She could not hear what they said but she could guess that they were discussing places to send her away. For a rest. For a cure. For—Ever—

She slept, waked, slept again. Once she asked for her writing tablet, but all she managed to write on it was the word "light" ten times in a column like some mad ledger. They took the tablet from her and refused to give it back.

The doctor came at nine, tall and saturnine, a new man from Northampton. Vinnie said later he looked more like an undertaker than a physician. He scolded Emily for rising at midnight and she was too exhausted to tell him that for her it was usual. Mother and Vinnie and Austin did not tell him for they did not know. No one knew that midnight was her favorite time of the clock. That often she walked in the garden at midnight and could distinguish, just by the smell, which flowers bloomed and bloomed well. That often she sat in the garden seat and gazed up at the great eight-sided cupola Father had built onto the house. His one moment of monumental playfulness. Or she sat at the solitary hour inside the cupola contemplating night through each of the windows in turn, gazing round at all the world that was hers.

"Stay in bed, Miss Dickinson," warned the doctor, his chapped hands delicately around hers. "Till we have you quite well again. Finish the tonic I am leaving with your mother for you. And then you must eschew the night and its vapors."

Vinnie imitated him quite cruelly after he left. "Oh, the vaypures, the vay-pures!" she cried, hand to her forehead. Unaccountably, Carlo howled along with her recitation.

Mother was—as usual—silently shocked at Vinnie's mimicry but made no remonstrances.

"He looks—and sounds—quite medieval," Austin commented laconically.

At that Emily began to laugh, a robust hilarity that brought tears to her poor eyes. Austin joined with her, a big stirring hurrah of a laugh.

"Oh, dear Emily," Vinnie cried. "Laugh on! It is what is best for you."

Best for what? Emily asked herself, but did not dare say it aloud. But she vowed she would never let the doctor touch her again.

Having slept all day meant that she was awake at midnight, still she did not venture out of the bed. She lay awake fearing to hear once more the horrid knock and feel the house shake and see the piercing white light. A line of poetry ran through her mind: *Me—come! My dazzled face.* But her mind was so befogged that she could not recall if it were her own line or if she had read it somewhere.

At the last nothing more happened and she must have fallen back to sleep sometime after two. When she woke it was midmorning and there was a tray by her bed with tea and toast and some of her own strawberry preserves.

She knew she was well again when she realized Carlo was not in the room. He would never have left her side otherwise.

Getting out of the bed was simple. Standing without swaying was not. But she gathered up her dressing gown, made a swift toilette, then went downstairs carrying the tray. Some illnesses she knew, from her months with the eye doctors in Cambridgeport, are best treated like a bad boy at school. Quickly beaten, quicker trained.

If the family was surprised to see her, they knew better than to show it.

"Shall we have Susie and little Ned for tea?" she asked by way of greeting.

Sue came over promptly at four, as much to check up on Emily's progress as to have tea. Austin must have insisted. Heavily pregnant, she walked slowly while Ned, a rambunctious four-year-old, capered ahead.

"Dear critic," Emily said, answering the door herself. She kissed Sue on both cheeks and led her through into the hall. "And who is slower today, you with your royal front or me with my rambling mind?"

"Nonsense!" Sue said. "You are indulging yourself in fancies. Neddie, stop jumping about. Your Aunt Emily is just out of a sickbed."

The boy stopped for a moment and then flung himself into

Emily's skirts, crying, "Are you hurt? Where does it hurt? Shall I kiss it?"

Emily bent down and said, "Your *Uncle* Emily shall kiss you instead, for I am not hurt at all. We boys never cry at hurts." She kissed the top of his fair head, which sent him into paroxysms of laughter.

Sue made a *tch* sound with her tongue. "And once you said to me that if you saw a bullet hit a bird and he told you he wasn't shot, you might weep at his courtesy, but you would certainly doubt his word."

"Unfair! Unfair to quote me back at me!" Emily said, taking Sue's hands. "Am I not this moment the very pink of health?"

"That is not what Austin said, who saw you earlier today. And there is a white spot between your eyes as if you have lain with a pinched expression all night."

"And all morning, too. Come in here, Sue," Vinnie called from the sitting room. "And do not chastize her any more than I have already. It does no good you know."

They drank their tea and ate the crumbles of the cake from the day before, though it mortified Emily that they had to do so. But she had had no time to prepare more for their small feast. Neddie had three pieces anyway, two of his own and one Emily gave him from her own plate because suddenly the cake was too sweet, the light too bright, the talk too brittle, and Emily tired past bearing it all.

She rose abruptly. Smiling, she said, "I am going back to bed."

"We have overworn you," Sue said quickly.

"And I you," Emily answered.

"I am not tired, Auntie," Ned said.

"You never are," Vinnie said fondly.

"I am in the evening," Ned conceded. "And sometimes in . . ."

But Emily heard no more. The stair effectively muffled the rest of the conversation as she sought the sanctuary of her room.

I dwell in Possibility—

She sat at the desk and read the wavering line again. But what possibilities did she, indeed, dwell in? This house, this room, the garden, the lawn between her house and Austin's stately "Evergreens." They were all the possibilities she had. Even the trips to Cambridgeport for eye treatments had held no great promise. All her traveling—and what small journeys they had proved—lay in the past. She was stuck, like a cork in an old bottle without promise of wine. Stuck here in the little town where she had been born.

She went over to the bed and flung herself down on her stomach and wept quietly into the pillow until the early November dark gathered around her.

It was an uncharacteristic and melodramatic scene, and when she sat up at last, her cheeks reddened and quite swollen, she forgave herself only a little.

"Possibly the doctor's tonic has a bite at the bottom," she whispered to Carlo, who looked up at her with such a long face that she had to laugh, her cheeks tight with the salty tears. "Yes, you are right. I have the vay-pures." She stood and, without lighting a lamp, found the washbasin and bathed her face.

She was not hungry, either for food or company, and so she sat in the gathering gloom thinking about her life. Despite her outburst, she quite liked the tidiness of her cocoon. She doubted she had the capacity for wings or the ability for flight.

When it was totally dark, she went back to her bed and lay down, not to sleep but to wait till the rest of the household slept.

The grandfather clock on the landing struck eleven. She waited another fifteen minutes before rising. Grabbing a woolen shawl from the foot of the bed, she rose ghostlike and slipped from the room.

The house breathed silent sleep around her. Mother, Father, Vinnie, Cook had all gone down the corridors of rest, leaving not a pebble behind for her to follow.

She climbed the stairs up to the cupola for she had not the will nor might to brave November's garden. Still, she had to get away from the close surround of family and the cupola was as far as she could go.

She knew which risers creaked alarmingly and, without thinking, avoided them. But behind her Carlo trod on every one. The passage was not loud enough to waken the sleepers who had heard it all before without stirring, yet Emily still held her breath till they reached the top unremarked.

Putting her hand on the dog's head for a moment, to steady them both, she climbed up into the dome of the house. In the summer there was always a fly or two buzzing about the windows and she quite liked them, her "speck pianos." But in November the house was barren of flies. She would have to make all the buzz herself.

Sitting on the bench, she stared out of the windows at the glittering stars beyond the familiar elms. How could she have abjured this peace for possibilities unknown?

"Oh, Carlo," she whispered to the dog, "we must be careful what we say. No bird resumes its egg."

He grunted a response and settled down at her feet for the long watch.

"Like an old suitor," she said, looking down fondly at him. "We are, you know, too long engaged, too short wed. Or some such." She laughed. "I think the prognosis is that my madness is quite advanced."

When she looked up again, there was a flash of light in the far-off sky, a star falling to earth.

"Make a wish, Carlo," she said gaily. "I know I shall."

And then the top of the cupola burst open, a great gush of sound enveloped them, and she was pulled up into the light.

Am I dead? she thought at first. Then, *Am I rising to Heaven?* Then, *Shall I have to answer to God?* That would be the prime embarrassment, for she had always held out against the blandishments of her redeemed family, saying that she was religious without that great Eclipse, God. She always told them that life was itself mystery and consecration enough. *Oh, do not let it be a jealous God,* she thought. *I would have too much to explain away.*

Peculiarly this light did not hurt her eyes, which only served to convince her that she was, indeed, dead. And then she wondered if there would be actual angels as well, further insult to her heresy. *Perhaps they will have butterfly wings,* she thought. *I would like that.* She was amused, briefly, in her dying by these wild fancies.

And then she was no longer going upward, and there was once more a steady ground beneath her feet where Carlo growled but did not otherwise move. Walls, smooth and anonymous, curved away from her like the walls of a cave. *A hallway,* she thought, *but one without signature.*

A figure came toward her, but if *that* were an angel, all of Amherst's Congregational Church would come over faint! It wore no gown of alabaster satin, had no feathery wings. Rather it was a long, sleek, gray man with enormous adamantine eyes and a bulbed head rather like a leek's.

A leek—I am surely mad! she thought. All poetry fled her mind.

Carlo was now whining and trembling beyond measure. She bent to comfort him; that he should share her madness was past understanding.

"Do not be afraid," the gray man said. *No—the bulbed thing—*

for she now saw it was not a man at all, though like a man it had arms and legs and a head. But the limbs were too long, the body too thin, the head too round, the eyes too large. And though it wore no discernible clothing, it did not seem naked.

"Do not be afraid," it repeated, its English curiously accented. It came down rather heavily on the word *be* for no reason that Emily could tell. Such accentuation did not change the message.

If not an angel, a demon—But this her unchurched mind credited even less.

She mustered her strength; she could when courage was called for. "Who—or what—are you?"

The bulb creature smiled. This did not improve its looks. "I am a traveler," it said.

"And where do you travel?" That she was frightened did not give her leave to forget all manners. And besides, curiosity had now succeeded fear.

"From a far . . ." The creature hesitated. She leaned into its answer. "From a far star."

There was a sudden rip in the fabric of her world.

"Can you show me?" It was not that she did not believe the stranger, but that she did. It was the very possibility that she had, all unknowing, hoped for, wept for.

"Show you?"

"The star."

"No."

The rip was repaired with clumsy hands. She would always see the darn.

"It is too far for sight."

"Oh."

"But I can show you your own star."

"And what do you want from me in exchange?" She knew enough of the world to know this.

For a moment the creature was silent. She feared she had

embarrassed it. Or angered it. Then it gave again the grimace that was its smile. "Tell me what it is you do in this place."

She knew this was not an idle question. She chose her answer with care. "I tell the truth," she said. "But I tell it slant."

"Ah . . ." There was an odd light in the gray creature's eyes. "A poet."

She nodded. "I have some small talent."

"I, myself, make . . . poems. You will not have heard of me, but my name is . . ." And here it spoke a series of short, sharp syllables that to her ear were totally unrepeatable.

"Miss Emily Dickinson," she replied, holding out her hand.

The bulb creature took her hand in its and she did not flinch though its hand was far cooler than she expected. Not like something dead but rather like the back of a snake. There were but three long fingers on the hand.

The creature dropped her hand and gave a small bow, bending at its waist. "Tell me, Miss Emily Dickinson, one of your poems."

She folded her hands together and thought for a minute of the dozens of poems shoved into the drawer of her writing table, of the tens more in her bureau drawer. Which one should she recite—for she remembered them all? Which one would be appropriate payment for this gray starfarer?

And then she had it. Her voice—ever light—took on color as she said the poem:

> *Some things that fly there be—*
> *Birds—Hours—the Bumblebee—*
> *Of these no Elegy.*
>
> *Some things that stay there be—*
> *Grief—Hills—Eternity—*
> *Nor this behooveth me.*
>
> *There are that resting, rise.*

Can I expound the skies?
How still the Riddle lies!

When she was done, she did not drop her head modestly as Miss Lyons had taught, but rather stared straight into the starfarer's jeweled eyes.

It did not smile this time and she was glad of that. But it took forever to respond. Then at last it sighed. "I have no poem its equal. But Miss Emily Dickinson, I can expound the skies."

She did not know exactly what the creature meant.

"Give me your hand again."

And then she saw. "But I cannot leave my dog."

"I cannot vouchsafe the animal."

She misunderstood. "I can. He will not harm you."

"No. I mean more correctly, I do not know what such a trip will do to him."

"I cannot leave him behind."

The gray creature nodded its bulb head, and she unhesitatingly put her hand in its, following down the anonymous corridor and into an inner chamber that was something like a laboratory.

"Sit here," the starfarer said, and when she sat in the chair a webbing grew up out of the arms and bound her with filaments of surprising strength.

"Am I a prisoner?" She was not frightened, just curious.

"The lightship goes many miles quickly. The web is to keep you safe."

She thought how a horse starting too quickly to pull a carriage often knocks its passenger back against the seat, and understood. "And my dog?"

"Ah—now you see the problem."

"Can he sit here in the chair beside me?"

"The chair is not built for so much weight."

"Then he may be badly hurt. I cannot go."

The creature raised one of its long fingers. "I will put your dog in my sleeping chamber for as long as we travel." It took Carlo by the collar and led the unprotesting dog off to a side wall, which opened with the touch of a button, letting down a short bed that was tidily made. "Here," the creature commanded the dog and surprisingly Carlo—who ordinarily obeyed no one but Emily—leaped onto the bed. The starfarer pushed another button and the bed slid back into the wall, imprisoning the now-howling Carlo inside.

"I apologize for my shaggy ally," Emily said.

"There is no need." The gray creature bent over a panel of flashing lights, its six fingers flying between them. When it had finished, it landed back into its own chair and the webbing held it fast.

"Now I will show you what your own planet looks like from the vantage of space. Do not be afraid, Miss Emily Dickinson."

She smiled. "I am not afraid."

"I did not think *so*," the starfarer said in its peculiar English.

And then, with a great shaking, the lightship rose above Amherst, above Massachusetts, above the great masses of land and water and clouds and air and into the stars.

She lay on her bed remembering. Carlo, still moaning, had not seemed to recover quickly from the trip. But she had. All she should think about was the light, the dark, the stars. And the great green-blue globe—like one of Ned's marbles—that was her home.

What could she tell her family? That she had flown high above them all and seen how small they were within the universe? They would say she had had a dream. *If only I could have returned, like Mother from her ramblings, a burdock on her shawl to show where she had been,* she thought.

And then she laughed at herself. Her poems would be her burdocks, clinging stubbornly to the minds of her readers. She sat up in the dark.

The light. The marble of earth. She would never be able to capture it whole. Only in pieces. But it was always best to make a start of it. *Begin,* as Cook often said, *as you mean to go on.*

She lit a small candle which was but a memento of that other light. And then she went over to the writing table. Her mind was a jumble of words, images.

I do not need to travel further than across this room ever again, she thought. *Or further than the confines of my house.* She had already dwelt in the greatest of possibilities for an hour in a ship made of light. The universe was hers, no matter that she lived only in one tiny world. She would write letters to that world in the form of her poems, even if the world did not fully understand or ever write back. Dipping the pen into the ink jar, she began the first lines of a lifetime of poems:

> *I lost a World—the other day.*
> *Has Anybody found?*
> *You'll know it by the Row of Stars*
> *Around its forehead bound.*

STORY NOTES AND POEMS

Andersen's Witch

When editor Jonathan Strahan asked me for a story for his witch anthology, *Under My Hat: Tales from the Cauldron*), I'd just finished a picture book for children about the life of Hans Christian Andersen: *The Perfect Wizard*. So the idea of doing a story about Andersen wasn't much of a stretch. Andersen (1805-1875), the great Danish storyteller and *dichter* (poet-writer), was known for his fairy tales.

He was a sad, strange, skinny little boy who became a sad, strange, gangly man who—with little schooling or training—became the most famous storyteller in all of Europe and the world. The only thing that made sense was that he'd had a bargain with a witch or wizard or the devil—take your pick. And as I was thinking that, I thought of the story he wrote about the Snow Queen. Maybe *she* had been a witch . . . and the story began.

It didn't hurt that I have been called the Hans Christian Andersen of America (though I insist I am really the Hans

Jewish Andersen of America). However, I'd had a much easier childhood than he, and am much better socialized! It didn't hurt that I owned dozens of books about him from my research for the picture book. It didn't hurt that I could write the story as a quasi–fairy tale after years of practice. And it certainly didn't hurt that Jonathan loved the story enough to take it for the anthology.

The poem below references the Snow Queen story, for Kai (the hero of Andersen's tale) has had a shard of glass placed in his heart by the Queen so he cannot love. And my story is about the boy Hans wrestling with his own ice shard until he finds at the end how to melt it. (Though in Andersen's story, and my poem, it is Gerda, Kai's childhood friend, who looks for a way to melt that ice.) The poem, though, is really about my husband's death and my long widowhood.

Note on a Dried Cod

I would write on anything,
even the unyielding skin
of a preserved fish,
to find my lost love.
That's the easy part.

I'd use my knucklebone
as a stylus, blood for ink.
The stink of it
would keep me awake
for the cold journey.

How long does it take
to remove a shard of ice
from a cankered heart?

I would melt it
with my tears.

But the cod, the message
On the skin,
writing things down,
that's always easy.
It's the long hope,
the death between us,

that's the hard part,
the only hard part.

Lost Girls

The Scottish writer J. M. Barrie (1860–1937) was a novelist, essayist, and playwright of some note, but he is by far best remembered as the creator of Peter Pan. *Peter Pan* was first a London play and afterwards a book (or rather two books— *Peter and Wendy* and then *Peter Pan in Kensington Gardens*). Barrie was born in Kerriemuir, Scotland, his father a weaver. A family tragedy—one of the Barrie brothers was killed in a skating accident two days before his fourteenth birthday—tore the family apart. Eventually, with the help of another (older) brother who was a schoolmaster, J. M. Barrie received a good education and then moved to London to work as a journalist and essayist, before becoming a short story writer. Novels and plays soon followed.

After meeting and befriending a young mother with four boisterous boys, and becoming the patron to the boys when their father died of cancer, Barrie unofficially adopted them three years later, when the boys' mother died of cancer as well.

Before he died, Barrie gave the rights to the Peter Pan stories to Great Ormond Street Hospital for Children in London, which continues to receive royalties for the books and plays and movies to this day.

I wrote *Lost Girls* because I couldn't forget the uneasy scene in which Peter Pan is weeping because he can't re-attach his shadow. When Wendy sews it on for him, he crows and cries out, "Oh the cleverness of me!" As if Wendy had done nothing and he had done it all.

And then, I had an original thought—Peter might be eternally young in his looks, but his eyes betray his real age. He has seen so much, he would have an old and narcissistic soul. Alison Lurie wrote this quick study of Peter in a 2012 essay in the *New York Review of Books*, but I had figured it out when I wrote my story in 1997: She notes that "Like a small child, he is easily distracted and lives almost entirely in the present. He forgets the past rapidly and has little understanding of the future. For him, real life and make-believe are almost the same thing. He also lacks empathy, and is only rarely aware of other people's feelings. Today, this view of a child's psychology is fairly common, but in Barrie's time it was almost shocking when he declared in the famous last words of *Peter and Wendy* that children are 'gay and innocent and heartless.' Peter is gay and innocent, but he is also deeply self-centered and without remorse; at one point he declares that he cannot even remember the names of the pirates he has killed."

The story I wrote is about the above, though my story was published before Lurie had written her essay. Great minds etc. "Lost Girls" is novelette length and won the 1999 Nebula. It was first published in my collection *Twelve Impossible Things Before Breakfast*. Afterwards, I wrote a picture book biography of Barrie, called *Lost Boy*, which was published in 2010. Sometimes I actually sneak in right before a trend happens. Usually I am either ten years ahead of the curve or ten years behind.

From: Five Meditations On Us

I owe you something.
From the past you are in,
from the past I was in,
there is a debt to be paid.
Call it a thimble of love.
We travel first star to the right
and straight on until morning,
hand in hand, where the air is thin.
I do not want to leave those children behind.

Tough Alice

I was teaching a class in writing fantasy, and I gave the students twenty minutes to write the beginning of an alternate *Alice in Wonderland* story. I told them I would be working on one myself and got as far as the pork loin sentence when our twenty minutes were up. It went into my Must Finish Some Day file. And there it sulked for several years.

At that time, I was putting together a collection of my fantasy short stories that were readable and appropriate for middle schoolers—you know the ones who still loved picture books and at the same were galloping through Jane Austen and Stephen King. I was calling the collection *Twelve Impossible Things Before Breakfast* (1997). The title was a tweak of something the White Queen in *Alice in Wonderland* says: "Why, sometimes I've believed as many as six impossible things before breakfast." Of course six was far too few stories for such a collection, so I simply doubled it. The majority of the stories I'd written and published at that time were for adults. And since I'd quoted *Alice in Wonderland* for the title, it behooved me to write a new story set in Wonderland. Appropriate for middle graders.

Since I'm an ex-tough girl myself (captain of the high school girls' basketball team and a top fencer in college), it wasn't a stretch to make Alice tough. In her own inimitable way, of course.

Managing Your Flamingo

So there she is, Alice underground,
life more complex than imagined.
A game, she's told, though without
rules or white lines or a sense of finality.
They hand her a bird, the pink of longing,
beak as sharp as an executioner's sword,
its gangle of legs tangling her skirt.
The queen growls: *Manage your flamingo,*
and the others shout: *Play on, play through.*
As if it were life.
As perhaps it is.

Blown Away

I always try to write a short story for an anthology when asked. Usually the deadline is so far away, it seems a likelihood that I'll finish in time. But sometimes it doesn't work that way. Often I've forgotten I said yes, until the last minute when the editor asks plaintively if I've finished, and then I have to admit I got stuck. Usually that means I'm not in the book.

Not from want of wanting. Not from want of trying. Just because I find it hard to deliver magic on demand.

When I was asked about writing for *Oz Reimagined*, I remembered a poem I'd written and sold that had a line about wanting to read a story about a dog on wheels. That became the beginning of the story, but as with many of my stories (and poems) things veered left or south after that. Of all the possible stories I mention in the poem, "Blown Away" is the only one I've actually written. Maybe I should try more.

So "Blown Away" began with that image. And for the first half dozen or so revisions, the story was called "The Dog on Wheels." Being in Oz, of course the dog had to be Toto. But what a strange ride this tale was. None of it planned and yet suddenly in the end all of it seemed of a piece. I'm not sure how that happened. Magic? Hard work? A brilliant muse? All of the above? Plus a visual cue: I found an old photograph in an antique store and thought, "That's Dorothy before Oz." A poem came from it . . . and it became how I envisioned the young Dorothy in my story.

The editor asked for the title change. Actually he came up with it. It makes better sense for the story as a whole. But I still think of the piece as "The Dog on Wheels."

Dorothy Before Oz

There's a flatness in her eyes and smile
from the prairie years, a shyness, too,
as if she prefers animals to people.

She knows twisters, they're part of her life,
but fear doesn't show in her eyes.
Neither does humor.

She's been cleaned up for the photograph,
the dust of home, the grayness scrubbed,
but it's still in her stare.

Oz is ahead, the colored lands,
talking animals, men of metal, scarecrows,
leading a troop against a witch.

I see her returning home changed,
becoming a missionary in Africa,
as odd in her mind as Oz, but reachable.

Bones in her ears, pet monkeys,
wearing dashikis. "Gone native,"
Aunt Em writes, a bit of Kansas

stuck between her teeth.
Dorothy sends but two words back.
"Finding home."

A Knot of Toads

I live three to four months a year in Scotland, and so I write a
lot of Scottish-based poetry. Various editors in Scotland ask me
to submit stories and poems to anthologies and I try to comply
whenever I can. Glasgow Worldcon was coming up, and I was
Guest of Honor. It was a tough time, as my husband had cancer
and was starting into chemo, so I ended up going for only two
days. I'd been asked for a Scottish short story for a fantasy
anthology that was going to be debuting at the convention—
Nova Scotia: New Scottish Speculative Fiction compiled by Neil
Williamson and Andrew J. Wilson. The book was among the
finalists for the 2006 World Fantasy Award for Best Anthology
and my story got picked up by a Best of the Year anthology.

However, it almost didn't get written. The opening was based on a fragment of a story written by Montague Rhodes James (1862–1936) about a toad. James, who published under the name M. R. James, was an English author, medievalist scholar, and provost of King's College, Cambridge, and of Eton College. I was a big fan of his stories.

Though James's work as a medievalist is still highly regarded, he is best remembered for his ghost tales. James redefined the ghost story, abandoning many of the formal Gothic clichés of his predecessors.

So there I was with about a page's worth of toad story going nowhere, sitting in my short story folder for a year or two. And only when I got the request from the Scottish publisher and remembered the fragment did I finally know what to do with that first couple of paragraphs. The story is set in the small Fife town of St. Monans about twenty minutes from my Scottish home, so research was pretty easy. I spent time at the church, a lovely building on the headlands. The church had some pamphlets that proved helpful. And I had a couple of books about Scottish witches that proved useful as well, for witches play a part in the story. In fact, this story went together so easily once I got started on it again—just as my life was falling apart—that I was thankful to have it to work on.

I Am the Apple

I am the apple
dappled by sun,
polished by rain,
garnished by galls,
cut by the witch,
stitched by her hand,
injected with poison,
suspected by none.

The Quiet Monk

The story of the hidden grave reported in a book by the Tudor Antiquary Bale had always fascinated me. Between two pyramids in Glastonbury Abbey was a buried casket of hollowed oak reputedly engraved (in Latin) The Once and Future King. When it was unearthed and opened, it was seen that the casket contained two bodies, one a woman's bones crowned with golden hair that when exposed to the air, turned to dust.

Our modern take on the story of the two bodies in the hollowed oak is that they were not—as legend has it—Arthur and Guenivere. The monks simply made up a story to help fund the rebuilding of the abbey which had been mostly destroyed by a fire in 1184. It was a publicity trick to bring in more pilgrim visitors.

For years I had that stored in a file folder waiting to be used. After *Merlin's Booke* came out—my fantasy short stories about Merlin—I wanted to do Guinevere's Booke, and after that Arthur's Booke. This was the second Guinevere story I'd written for it.

Alas, the publisher was not interested in a trilogy of linked Arthurian stories and poems. So I sent the story to *Asimov's* magazine, where it was first published in 1988, and then had several reprintings thereafter.

The trilogy is still laying dormant, dead in its own oak tree, should anyone want to talk to me about writing it.

<u>Oak Casket</u>

It's a Druid thing,
casking in an oak,

human bones being
finer than wine.
They lie together here,
man and woman
closer than when
they ruled a kingdom
and lies drove them apart.
The heart is a puzzle
not easily solved.
But pieced together
in the tomb
a part becomes two
partners one,
the druid's work
done for eternity
or history, whichever
finds them first.

The Bird

Early morning December 20, 2016, about four days before I
was to turn in the final pieces of this book, I wrote a new short
story—two drafts early, and later in the day two drafts more.

I had been thinking about writing a new story ever since
Tachyon bought the collection, even had several ideas that
didn't pan out. (The white whale in *Moby Dick* as an alien
spaceship was one. Tam O'Shanter finding his own wife at
the witches' dance another. A Pre-Raphaelite–based tale using
Christina Rossetti's "Goblin Market" poem a third.) They may
get written a month or a year or a decade from now but not in
time for this book.

I've long been a fan of Edgar Allan Poe, though his personal life was messy even for a writer. Hard to live, but great stuff for a story. The idea for *this* story arrived pretty much whole cloth not because of Poe or his poem or his difficult love life, but because the bird reminded me of the damned budgie my son Jason owned when he was about seven. He let it fly free in his bedroom. I hated that bird because of the mess it made when sitting on the bookcases or perching on picture frames. But being a good—no, a *great*—mom, when the bird died, I gave it mouth-to-beak resuscitation and it lived for another six months before I let it die the True Death. Also, the few weeks before I wrote this story, I'd been mired in bird research for a different book that was due right after this one was to be turned in. So I had corvid material already in hand.

Donna Plays Fiddle at Her Mother's Wake

There is a note much higher than an angel's wing,
and pure.
If I believed in anything, then this
would make me sure.

I see that holy moment, a monument
so clear,
as if God's apron hem was solid, lucent,
and quite near.

There's nothing that's more sacred than this music
sounds to me,
except a tiny line or two of perfect
poetry.

When Donna plays her fiddle, I can hear the birds
all sing:

eternity like wind through feathers
on a raven's wing.

Belle Bloody Merciless Dame

I was getting my master's in Education at the University of
Massachusetts, Amherst, but was able to take a course in The
Ballad at my old alma mater, Smith College. One of the poems
we read—and I wrote a paper on—was "La Belle Dame sans
Merci," by John Keats, who wrote the poem in 1819 using
the phrase he'd found in a courtly French ballad of 1424. My
paper was a bit snarky about the Dame, seeing her as a kind of
Bohemian free love girl based on someone from the sixties I'd
known. And I looked back to that old friend, but forward to my
house in Scotland, where I knew I could write about those pubs,
those hillsides, those stupid young men.

Maiden v. Unicorn

Not much of a battle, the ending
known in advance, a glance
from that simpering girl, a lap
unfolding like a net, and the unicorn
caught in the amber of legend.

I would have watched from under a tree,
as he grazed on acorns, walnuts,
the exact crunch of them like a heartbeat.
I'd measure his beauty with my eyes,
not lead him, like a Vichy collaborator,
into the brownshirts' trap.

But love, or its partner in crime, desire,
makes maidens foolish. Men
do not favor us for our cooperation
but hang our skins next to the golden horns,
on their trophy walls.

The Jewel in the Toad Queen's Crown

This began as part of a different short story called "The Barbarian and the Queen: Thirteen Views," which was published in 2001 in Patrick Nielsen Hayden's *Starlight 3* and of which *Publishers Weekly* said, "Jane Yolen's series of set pieces, 'The Barbarian and the Queen: Thirteen Views,' offers surprising insights into the nature of, well, barbarians and queens (how about sword-toting exotic dancers and drag queens?)."

I liked the small premise in "The Barbarian and the Queen" of Disraeli and Queen Victoria's conversation so much that I'd long wanted to write it in an entire story on its own. But I hadn't gotten around to it. So when I was invited into Ellen Datlow and Terri Windling's *Queen Victoria's Book of Spells*, I got the push I needed. Along the way I learned some fascinating stuff about Disraeli's life. A Jew (but Christian convert) who lived from 1804 to 1881, he served two times as prime minister, was first earl of Beaconsfield, and wrote ten published novels as well as some slim volumes of poetry. I learned as well about anti-Semitism in Victorian England, and cabbalistic magic. One of the true pleasures in being a writer is having the leisure to learn new stuff all the time.

Mission

Her mother sometimes brings home scraps
from the sewing she does for the queen.
One day she makes a hood the color
of a rich woman's fingernails,
bright as sun going down
behind the mountain,
deep as trillium by the river,
warm as blood.

When the girl puts the hood on
to walk through the woods,
no one can touch her.
The hood is a sign.
The basket carries her heart.
The trees point sharp fingers.
But only the wolf knows the way.

The Gift of the Magicians

This satire is a response to the very famous short, powerful, and moralistic story by O. Henry, "The Gift of the Magi." O. Henry was the pen name for William Sydney Porter, and his story was allegedly written in Pete's Tavern on Irving Place in New York City. O. Henry was famous for his twist endings. The story's original publication was in the *New York Sunday World* on December 10, 1905, and has remained a sentimental Christmas favorite ever since. It has been adapted for movies, theater, pop songs, and television. Somewhere in America every holiday season it's read over the air.

On my thirteenth birthday—as was our family's observance—I

woke early to find my birthday presents at the foot of my bed. By early, I mean I woke at midnight. I tore into the package that was clearly books and found two volumes: *The Complete O. Henry Short Stories* and *The Complete Sherlock Holmes*. I sat up the rest of the night reading the O. Henry stories (they were individually a lot shorter than the Holmes tales). Luckily it was a weekend, and so I got to read them all from start to finish in one sitting. The story that I remembered the most from the collection was "The Gift of the Magi." Forty-one years later, casting around for an idea for a story for a Marty Greenberg Christmas anthology starring mythical animals, *Christmas Bestiary*, my mind went quickly to Beast of "Beauty and the Beast." And from there bounced to my childhood favorite, the O. Henry piece.

The following poem was written to my husband on one of our later anniversaries. He died before our forty-fifth.

Beauty and the Beast: An Anniversary

It is winter now,
and the roses are blooming again,
their petals bright against the snow.
My father died last April;
my sisters no longer write
except at the turnings of the year,
content with their fine houses
and their grandchildren.
Beast and I
putter in the gardens
and walk slowly on the forest paths.
He is graying
around the muzzle
and I have silver combs
to match my hair.

I have no regrets.
None.
Though sometimes I do wonder
what sounds children
might have made
running across the marble halls,
swinging from the birches
over the roses
in the snow.

Rabbit Hole

How prescient I was back in 1996–1997 when I wrote "Rabbit Hole." It was for a friend of mine, Melissa Mia Hall (alas, now long gone), who was putting together a book of feminist fantasy short stories both new and reprinted.

I was only in my late fifties, but what I said then about old age (I am now seventy-eight) is spot on. And I tell you, I would definitely go down that rabbit hole if I had a chance. In fact, *Alice in Wonderland* and *Alice Through the Looking Glass* were both key books in my childhood. (As were the Oz books, which, alas, have not held up well as literature.) I was probably about five when I read them. My parents had given me a boxed edition of the two Alice books, which I still own.

I saw myself as Alice. I even had the bangs (or *fringe*, as the Brits call it), though the rest of my hair was in pigtails. What I wouldn't have given then—and now—to meet up with a Gryphon or a Cheshire Cat or any of the wonders in Wonderland. Well, in a way I have—they are part of a vast array of invisible friends I still chat with on a regular basis. And aren't I lucky! Not a crazy old lady, but a lucid and varied writer of tales.

Dorothy and Alice Take Tea

Two Victorian girls,
long hair caught up
in bunches, in bows,
staring down into
the brown landscapes
of their tea
as if finding a road there
to get back home.

So ordinary.
So extraordinary.
Their little lives
boundaried
by the every day,
now blown away,
fallen down
into new lives, liberties.

Much to talk about.
Little to say.
It is a calculus
beyond their counting.
Witch, rabbit,
shifting their priorities,
moving through wonder,
following the weird.

And the oddest of all?
They are safe home,
still longing for the wildness
where neither gender nor age

bound them, and friends came
in many shapes,
many colors,
many sexes,
many tribes.

Our Lady of the Greenwood

My first encounter with Robin Hood was as an eight-year-old reading *The Merry Adventures of Robin Hood* by Howard Pyle. Nobody told me it was a "boy's book." So I was forsoothly hooked.

So after putting together an anthology of Arthurian stories by a diverse bunch of writers (*Camelot*), I proposed doing the same for Robin Hood stories—called *Sherwood*. I wrote my story last, thinking I would fill in for anything missing.

It turned out, the only thing missing was a story about Robin Hood's birth. That rarely features in any of the Robin Hood canon, so it gave me a lot of room to simply go for it. And that's the true story about why I wrote "Our Lady of the Greenwood."

Green Man

Go, Green Man,
with your leafy incantations,
your mask showing your intentions,
your feet dancing the patterns
of the world's heart.

Go, Green Man,
reminding us we are all green,
root and rootling,

our skin but a fragile shield
against the cold.

Go, Green Man,
burn in winter, rise again
in the curls of spring,
masked and unmasked,
birth and rebirth—you do it all,

even as you walk the maze.

The Confession of Brother Blaise

I wrote several stories about Merlin, Arthur, the whole Camelot
scene, and after publishing some of them in magazines such as
Fantasy & Science Fiction, and anthologies, I realized that I had
the start of a book. As most of them featured Merlin, I called it
Merlin's Booke. (Some of my friends insisted on calling it *Merlin's
Bookie,* as if Merlin's job was as a tout at major races.)

But I didn't have enough stories for an entire book, so I sat
down to write what was missing. When I reread *Vita Merlini* by
Geoffrey of Monmouth, one of the earliest tellings of Merlin's
beginnings, one part of it was about a priest named Father Blaise,
who was the priest of the nunnery where Merlin's mother gave
birth. And that's how this story began.

Merlin: A Haiku

An imp at his birth,
Tattooed with the devil's marks,
Always turning towards the Light.

Wonder Land

I had already sold my old friend Susan Shwartz a long (for me) story for her first *Sisters in Fantasy* anthology, and there she was back again wanting a story for *Sisters in Fantasy 2*. I wasn't sure I had another one in me, for I was working on a novel and didn't want to stop. But Susan is good at Jewish guilt. I relented and told her I would do one, then promptly forgot. She got back to me when the due date was really tight. And as I was working on a fairy tale novel and was in the mode, I thought about "Little Red Riding Hood" as told by Charles Perrault in his groundbreaking book of French fairy tales.

LRRH was a tale I'd lectured about at Smith College and elsewhere. It's a short, strange story that has three major variants: One where Red gets eaten along with Grandma, end of story! One where the woodcutter kills the wolf. And one really strange variant where the woodsman knocks the wolf out and cuts open its belly for a bizarre C-section, birthing both Little Red and her grandmother. Then the three of them sew the wolf back up with stones in his belly and haul him outside. When he wakes up, he is dreadfully thirsty and heads to the river. There, overbalanced by the stones, he falls in and drowns. No blood on Little Red's hands.

But mostly what fascinated me was the kind of knowingness that surrounds the girl in the French version of the story. I don't think she's fooled for a moment by the wolf in the nightgown. The story at its heart is about seduction, only who is the seducer?

I believe that's where my take on "Wonder Land" comes from, out of the Charles Perrault tradition of courtly French stories for young women as warning into our own modern times.

As to the poem below, another courtly French tradition was that of the *Compère Le Loup*, Grandfather Wolf—an older (elderly?) courtier chosen to both instruct the young woman in his charge and keep her safe about sexual matters until she has made a fine marriage. Yea, I believe that, don't you? What big and yellowed teeth that old wolf has.

Compère Le Loup

Consider him no stranger, no danger,
but godfather to the child in the red cape.
Instruction is his duty, his joy.
He has long been a best friend
of the duke whose seed sowed this child.
Why then should he not God father her,
that seedless, sexless connection
that has been prized throughout the West.

He and her Père agree—she is to remain
a prize, fit for a prince, a pawn
in the game of kingdom come.
Not for her the gropings with the gardener
by the lilies, dog boy in the kennels,
woodcutter under a bending oak.
Le Loup has his instructions.
Follow the girl. Keep her safe.

And oh he does his duty, using his big eyes,
big shoulders, big ears, big teeth.
All of him.

Evian Steel

One of the first stories I put in *Merlin's Booke* was a novella that appeared first in Robin McKinley's anthology *Imaginary Lands*, called "Evian Steel." I'd begun the story right before my husband and I were at conferences in England and we had a week in-between the two conventions. So in that week, we went on a two-day trip through the English fen country. We got to walk on the ancient boards that created paths there, saw the place called the Isle of Glass, smelled the smells, felt the wind, breathed in the essence of that still, small, strange, perfect world. Then we went up to the Scottish Highlands, where we fell in love with the entire country, eventually—a few years later—buying a house there.

I'd always envisioned "Evian Steel" as the middle part of a novel. The first part would be about the two main women who began the sword-making women's community, the second would be when Guinevere gets there, the third when she marries Arthur and is the one who actually brings the sword Excalibur to him as part of her bride price. I wanted the three linked novellas to be part of a trilogy of Arthurian stories including *Merlin's Booke*, which was published. I had *Guinevere's Booke* and *Arthur's Booke* in mind, and then I hoped to have the entire novel brought out on its own. But that never happened. Doesn't mean it can't still. . . .

A Different Kind of Bone: A Compressed Sonnet

Where is it written that a girl
Cannot go on a major quest;
Is it her cheek the sheen of pearl,
Or that she has to bind her breasts?
Cut her hair, lower her voice,

Ride astride a heavy steed?
Really, isn't her own choice,
Her vocation, passion, need?

I see her enter the magic woods,
The trees a-tremble at her advance.
You would stop her if you could,
Before she raises her sword, her lance.
The bones she leaves inside the hedge,
Are light, and fine. Gives you your edge.

Sister Emily's Lightship

I live twenty minutes from the Emily Dickinson Homestead in Amherst.

My husband was a professor at the University of Massachusetts in Amherst.

I've been a huge fan of Emily Dickinson's poetry for as long as I can remember. And I've lived for over fifty years in the Connecticut River Valley near The Homestead (now a museum). Yet I didn't go to visit that house and her brother's house next door until about fifteen years ago.

Now I am a constant visitor. I have published three children's picture books about her (*My Uncle Emily*, *The Emily Sonnets*, and the upcoming *Emily Writes*). I read every new biography about her that comes out. I reference her poems in almost every speech I give. You might say I am obsessed, and I've written many poems about her, though this short story is the only one I've committed to.

I thought of this story as "Emily Dickinson Meets a Martian" while I was writing it, but I think the story is really about inspiration, how poetry can make souls meet across a universe. It also makes as much sense as any other explanation about why she became so reclusive in her later years. Though I only thought that after the story was published.

It almost wasn't.

I had the first several pages done, promised ahead of time to editor Patrick Neilsen Hayden for an anthology he was doing. But I got royally stuck after setting down Emily's lines: *I dwell in Possibility—A fairer House than Prose.* And the deadline for the story was well and truly passed.

At that point, my husband and I were in Scotland for the summer. I had my daughter send on five Emily biographies to me at enormous expense because St Andrews University (five blocks from my house) and the local bookstores had none. Patrick and his wife Theresa were coming for a visit, and the books beat them to our door by mere days. I was frantic, often a good way to get a story moving again.

I finished it in a white heat a couple of hours before the visitors arrived, printed it out, and put it on the bedside table in their room.

We went on great trips through the Highlands, into Edinburgh for the day, through Sir Walter Scott's bizarrely wonderful house, and for the whole trip nothing was said about the story. I figured Patrick hated the story and didn't want to say so as he was a guest, and so was being quiet.

After breakfast on the day they were to leave, I said plaintively (something I *never* do!), "Did you get a chance to read the story?"

He looked at me, deer in the headlights. I thought it the end of what was—till then—a great editor/author friendship. He turned without word and ran back up the stairs. He came down with the manuscript in hand, thrust it at me, said, "I'm taking it for *Starlight*. It needs editing in three places," then ran back upstairs to finish his packing.

The anthology won a World Fantasy Award. The story won

the Nebula. Patrick and Theresa and I are still dear friends. And Emily—well, she got to ride around the universe with a Martian (or some kind of alien). So I guess everything worked out just fine.

Emily D and Bird Play St. Pete's

It is eternal dusk on the stage
But her white dress illumines.
Holding one of several fascicles,
those small hand-sewn packets
of torn paper on which she's scribbled,
Uncle Emily—as she calls herself
in these performances—steps up,
grabs the microphone with her left hand,
and commences to speak.

The room is electric. Behind her, Bird
spit-casts a run on the sax. A paradiddle
soft as a drum lullaby accompanies them.
Emily does not read the words exactly as written,
but improvises each poem. Syllables
flutter out, pop percussively, invent
and reinvent themselves; they take flight
while Bird decorates, illustrates,
illuminates each line.

Emily is volcanic; the lava of each poem
touches all corners of the room
till her eyes roll back and she falls
onto the wooden floor in an ecstasy
of poetics and seizure. One angel arranges
her dress so that her ankles don't show.

Another puts a harp tuning fork
between Emily's teeth and tongue.
But otherwise they let her lie.

God knows, they know, the difference
between epilepsy and being seized
by the sacred, though it's a secret
they have yet to share.

ABOUT THE AUTHOR

Jane Yolen has been called the Hans Christian Andersen of America and the Aesop of the twentieth century. In 2018, her 365th and 366th books will come out. Her books include children's fiction, poetry, short stories, graphic novels, nonfiction, fantasy, and science fiction. Her adult books include poetry, short-story collections and anthologies, novels, novellas, and books about writing. Her best-known books are *Owl Moon*, the How Do Dinosaurs series, *The Devil's Arithmetic, Briar Rose, Sister Emily's Lightship and Other Stories*, and *Sister Light, Sister Dark*. Among her many honors are the Caldecott and Christopher medals, two Nebulas, the World Fantasy Award, three Mythopoeic awards, the Golden Kite Award, the Jewish Book Award, the World Fantasy Association's Lifetime Achievement Award, the Science Fiction/Fantasy Writers of America Grand Master Award, and the Science Fiction Poetry Grand Master Award. Yolen is also a teacher of writing and a book reviewer. Six colleges and universities have given her honorary doctorates. She lives in Western Massachusetts and St. Andrews, Scotland.

Extended Copyright